Pearls

Lisa Mills

Vicki,
Store up treasures
in things that are
eternal

Lisa

Faith Press

Pearls

April 2012

Published by Faith Press

© 2012 by Lisa Mills

Printed in the United States of America
ISBN-13: 978-1470165932
ISBN-10: 1470165937

Publisher's Note: This novel is a work of fiction. Names, characters, places, and incidents are either products of the author's imagination or used fictitiously. All characters are fictional, and any similarity to people, living or dead, is purely coincidental.

One

Awe bloomed in Isabel Palmer's chest as she traced a line of the ancient script. The parchment, yellowed with age, felt soft like old linen beneath her fingers. "*Abuela*, this is a national treasure. It belongs in a museum," she breathed.

"*Sí*," Magdalena Montez answered, speaking her native Spanish. "But the descendants of Rodrigo Velasquez have not wanted to part with it."

Isabel understood why. *Imagine! A five-hundred-year-old journal. Rodrigo must have been one of the first Europeans to see Venezuela.* "Mama spoke of this journal, but I never imagined something so extraordinary. To be honest, I thought she made it up because she always rambled on about some legend of stolen treasure." Isabel chuckled at the absurd notion.

"The tales she spoke of are true, Isabel. Your ancestor, Rodrigo Velasquez, stole a case of pearls from the Spanish Navy."

"Not you too, *Abuela*." Isabel shook her head and smiled at her aging grandmother.

"Read it for yourself. You will see."

Intrigued, Isabel looked more closely at the family heirloom. "My Spanish is good, but I'm afraid I'd need several reference books from the university library to translate these sixteenth century words. The phrasing reminds me of Shakespeare, only in another language. Too much to tackle in one afternoon, but I'm thrilled you let me see it."

"Isabel, I am not *showing* you the journal. I am *giving* it to you."

Isabel's eyes widened in surprise. "Giving it to me?"

"I do not intend to live forever, *Nieta*. The Velasquez journal is a priceless piece of family history. I refuse to leave its fate to the greedy lawyers who will handle my estate. As my heir, you will see

1

to its safekeeping."

Isabel saw the determined glint in her grandmother's eyes and knew further arguing would prove useless. Doña Montez was a woman who knew her mind, and here in the living room of her beautiful estate home, she commanded respect. "As you wish, *Abuela*."

Her grandmother's face softened, and she reached out to touch Isabel's cheek. "Having you here in Caracas these last few months has brought such joy to my heart. I am proud of the woman you have become, beautiful inside and out. Your decision to study at Central University and pursue an education relating to your Venezuelan heritage pleases me. My daughter cared little about such things and brought me great sadness when she chose to move so far away."

"*Abuela*, she loves Venezuela more than you could know. She never failed to tell me about the land of her birth."

"But she loved your father more."

Isabel laid a hand over her grandmother's thin, wrinkled fingers. "Is that so terrible? They have a good life in America."

"Venezuelan families stay together. We do not abandon one another as you Americans do."

Isabel smiled. "If I'd followed the Venezuelan tradition and stayed close to my parents, I wouldn't be here with you."

Magdelena's lips twisted in a wry grin. "You are a clever one, my Isabel. You trapped me with my own complaint."

"You were not complaining. Just voicing your love for your family. No one can fault you for that. And I love the Venezuelan tradition of staying close together. It's wonderful to have so many cousins and relatives living within walking distance on the lands of your hacienda."

"Fourteen Montez families have houses on my land. I am responsible for them, and they for me. We take care of each other. This is our way."

A servant entered, interrupting their talk. "Doña Montez, Alejandro is at the kitchen door. He wishes to speak with you and says his business is urgent."

Magdelena gave a queenly nod and rose. "I must attend to Alejandro now. My foreman knows you are here and would not disturb me unless he truly needed my help."

"Of course, *Abuela*. Go and see to him. I believe I'll take a siesta in my room."

Isabel watched her grandmother depart, admiring her ability to oversee the hacienda at seventy-one years of age. When her husband died eight years earlier, she'd taken over his responsibilities, directing and organizing her small kingdom with the grace and style of a true family matriarch.

Isabel placed the journal in the special airtight case which kept it safe from light, humidity, and other elements that would decay its delicate pages. Taking it with her, she strolled through the tiled hallways, enjoying the feel of the smooth stone floors beneath her bare feet. She loved Casa Grande, the main house on the hacienda and came to stay here whenever she could get away from the university for a few days.

Surrounded by acres of avocado groves and peaceful farmland, the whitewashed stucco walls and red tiled roof stood majestic in the green terrain. The rich soil of the land nurtured exquisite tropical plant life, serving up a feast for her eyes after long weeks in a concrete jungle. Inside its walls, the arched doorways and breezy halls of her grandmother's estate offered her a peaceful retreat from her tiny apartment in the bustling, crowded city of Caracas.

Arriving at her doorway, Isabel entered her room and tucked the journal into her suitcase. She would take a closer look at it when she returned to Caracas. Now, in the heat of the day with her stomach full of a hearty lunch, she only wanted to rest. Crossing the tiled floor to her bed, she slipped between the cool sheets and drifted off to sleep.

~ * ~ * ~ * ~ * ~

During breakfast the next morning, the sound of an approaching car caught Isabel's attention. Hurrying, she polished off the last few bites of her *arepa*. The cook served the flat disks of bread with every meal, but at breakfast, she filled them with eggs, fried meats, onion, and tomato, Isabel's favorite morning meal.

"I think Raúl is here, *Abuela*." She dabbed her napkin to her lips and smiled in anticipation of seeing the man who'd become very special to her since her relocation to Venezuela four months ago.

Her grandmother continued to eat, showing no enthusiasm about the arrival of Isabel's *novio*.

"*Abuela*, must you show such disdain for him? I've never seen you treat anyone this way. I would think you'd be grateful to Raúl. I don't know how I would have survived my first weeks in Caracas without his help."

Magdalena wiped her fingers on her napkin and lifted stern brown eyes to meet Isabel's gaze. "We shall have a talk about Venezuelan men soon."

The thought of getting dating tips or a "birds-and-bees" lecture from her aging grandmother turned up the corners of Isabel's lips. "Maybe during my next visit," she suggested, barely suppressing the laugh that bubbled up inside.

At her grandmother's scowl, Isabel made an effort to be serious. "If his behavior concerns you, I assure you, he treats me better than most of the men I dated in the United States."

"He is different," her grandmother assured, pronouncing the words like a prophecy of doom.

"We'll talk next weekend." Isabel leaned to kiss her grandmother's cheek. "I love you, *Abuela*."

Isabel hurried to the door and met Raúl on the porch. Deep dimples appeared on either side of his smile, sending her heart into a staccato rhythm. His pale linen shirt and tan pants offset his dark curling hair and dreamy brown eyes.

"Hello, Raúl." She lowered her eyes, feeling suddenly shy.

He pulled her into his embrace and planted a kiss on her brow. "You look rested. Did you enjoy your weekend here, *mi amor*?"

My love. Her heart thrilled at the endearments that rolled off his tongue, made more beautiful by the fluid grace of his speech. "You know I did. The hacienda is peaceful."

He nodded and looked to the door. "Is your grandmother going to greet me today?" His smile reflected the amusement he felt at Magdalena's continual rebuffs.

"She's finishing her breakfast. Did you eat?"

"I did. I am ready to return to the city. May I carry your bags to the car?"

When they reached the luxurious Mercedes Benz, Raúl loaded her luggage in the trunk and came to open the car door for her.

"Did your business dealings go well?" she asked.

"Yes, I purchased several older pottery pieces and a striking painting by a newer artist. I think they will sell quickly in my gallery."

"I'm glad to hear it." Isabel turned and slid into the soft leather passenger seat. A moment later, Raúl took his place behind the wheel. He held a beautiful cluster of tropical flowers, which he deposited on her lap..

"They're wonderful, Raúl. You spoil me." She raised them to her nose and breathed in their delicious scent. From the moment of her arrival, she'd fallen in love with the sweet fragrance of the tropical blooms. Often the wind at Casa Grande carried the perfumes of the tropical plants that grew profusely in her grandmother's gardens. Raúl had discovered her love of flowers, and he indulged her often.

"The man who sold me the pottery had a green finger," he explained.

Isabel laughed. "I think you mean a green thumb."

Raúl smiled at his mistake. "He was a fine gardener. When I told him how much my beautiful *señorita* would like his flowers, he cut some from his garden."

"Thank you." She reached for his hand and wove her fingers through his.

"I missed you, *mi amor*. We have not spent much time together lately."

She turned to him, puzzled. "We meet at the coffee house for lunch almost every day."

"*Sí*, but it is such a public place. Perhaps next Sunday we could go out on my yacht and spend the day sailing. It sounds romantic, no?"

Disappointment wafted through her like a cool, damp breeze. "I promised my grandmother I'd attend church with her. Remember, we talked about it. I had hoped you would join me, Raúl."

The look he gave her made Isabel feel as if she'd suggested something outrageous. She pulled her hand from his and turned to stare out the window.

Raúl reached over and placed his warm hand on her knee, dragging his thumb in lazy circles over her skin. Currents of electricity surged along her nerves, and her irritation waned with every stroke. When she glanced at him, his charming, confident smile went straight to her heart and melted away her remaining displeasure.

"*Mi amor*, I have told you, God and I have an understanding. Though I do not attend services regularly, I am a devoted follower. As for Sunday, I've already committed to taking some of my friends out on the yacht. We can meet later Sunday evening. I will take you to dinner."

"Good. I'll look forward to it." She smiled his way.

Raúl nodded and changed the subject, launching into a description of the art pieces he'd purchased.

Isabel closed her eyes and focused on the timbre of Raúl's voice. His velvety baritone and smooth, cultured Spanish lent a poetic quality to his words. Just being near him filled her with a sense of well-being.

Handsome, charming, and affluent—she couldn't believe he'd been attracted to her. They'd first met at a coffee shop in Sabana Grande, a popular business and shopping district near the university. He sat at the table beside her, looking utterly appealing in his business attire, and she couldn't help but steal glances at him. To her embarrassment and thrill, he caught her eye and smiled. Outgoing and gregarious, he struck up a conversation. Soon he sat at her table, suggesting plans to spend the evening together.

After only one date she was addicted to the playful, romantic way he treated her. He made her feel like a beautiful princess with his compliments, gifts, and solicitous behavior. She'd never been so pampered and adored. *Abuela is right. He is different from American men. He's better by far.*

~ * ~ * ~ * ~ * ~

Laden with books, Isabel spied an empty study carrel in a quiet corner of the library and hurried to deposit her heavy burden on the desk.

"Why are reference books always so heavy?" she muttered as she settled into the chair and dug through her backpack in search of her tablet and pen. After finding them, she took out the journal's case. With slow, careful movements, she snapped open the clasps and removed the precious book from its protective shell. Opening to the first entry, she began the arduous task of translating the five-hundred-year-old script.

The reference books smelled of dust, and the light bulb overhead flickered and danced as she bent over her work. Once the first few paragraphs took shape on her notepad, excitement swept through her, and she forgot all else.

June 5th, 1505

We have become the vilest of animals. With our lips we proclaim we are from the civilized world, but our actions betray the truth of our dark nature. We call them savages, and in the same breath, we order atrocities committed against them. Our cruelty is unparalleled. We sentence the natives we enslave to death without cause, and to their misfortune, death at the hands of the Spanish Navy is despairingly slow and painful.

The men are pressed into service as pearl divers, forced to make repeated trips to the bottom of the ocean from morning to night without rest. We brutally whip them if they delay for even a moment between dives. Without time to adequately rest and regain their breath, drowning and exhaustion claim many. The sharks lurking in the coastal waters take others. Thousands have submerged into watery graves never to walk in the light of the sun again.

Those men who endure the torture we inflict on them develop sores on their skin from hours in the salty water. We feed them rotting oysters and perhaps a bit of bread. Their bodies grow skeletal from lack of proper food. For their hard labor and suffering we reward them with a block of wood to sleep on and chains to ensure they do not escape the fate to which we have sentenced them in the name of greed and power.

But while the physical suffering of the men is great, it is by far preferable to that which the women endure. When the

*slave ships arrive to unload their fleshly cargo, the men
stationed here at Cubagua crouch on the docks like hungry
jackals, eager to satiate their foul lusts on the female
captives. The officers callously give the women and girls
over to the soldiers and ignore the chilling screams that fill
the air when the carnage begins. Every female over the age
of eight is subjected to this inhumane treatment. Those who
survive their initial trial are kept under lock and key, forced
to endure the violence day after day, subject to the whim of
any sailor who will part with a few coins in exchange for
female company.*

*At 24 years of age, I am not immune to or unaffected by
the sight of the naked women unloaded from the cargo
holds. Though looking on the beauty of their exposed flesh
causes my blood to stir and awakens my carnal needs, as of
yet I have not participated in the evil. I cannot feel satisfied
in my abstinence, for I have done nothing to stop their
torture either. In my eyes I am as guilty as those who
partake in the flesh trade.*

*My complacency condemns me. The dark, round eyes
and smooth, fresh faces of the young native women remind
me of my younger sister. If circumstances were different, the
soldiers might feast their lusts upon her. Such thoughts
torture me daily. For this reason I cannot participate, and
for this cause I have been moved to commit a rebellious act
of treason for which I could be hanged.*

*An unusually high number of women arrived on the
slave ship that entered Cubagua's harbor today. Fewer
soldiers lurked on the docks, as two fully-manned
battleships were sent to deal with rogue pirates attempting
to poach the pearl beds off the western coast of the island.
Usually the soldiers outnumber the women five to one, and
they are forced to "share" the bounty. Today, there would
be enough women for each man to have his own companion.*

*My feet carried me into the midst of the rowdy sailors,
and I soon laid claim to one of the maidens. I rushed her
into a grove of banana palms unnoticed and pressed further*

*into the undergrowth until we were hidden from sight. I
removed my shirt and gave it to her. As she was small of
stature, the shirt hung to her knees, covering her modestly.*

*I led her further away from the port, following the
shore but careful to stay hidden in the trees and vegetation.
She shrank away from my touch and refused my help, but
she did not offer undue resistance. After a two-hour walk,
we arrived at the abandoned hut once occupied by an
Indian fisherman now captured and enslaved.*

*The small, crude hut would serve as a refuge for the
maiden, at least for a time. Set a distance away from the
beach, trees and brush surrounded the structure. Vines and
mosses grew over its walls, providing effective camouflage.
I entered the hut alone, checking for snakes or scorpions
lying in wait for a victim.*

*When I emerged and gestured for her to enter, she
recoiled in terror, as if certain I intended her harm. The
fearful way she looked at me made me ashamed to be a
man. Rather than force her in, I decided to coax her with
food and drink. I removed my canteen and set it inside the
doorway. Nearby trees offered a variety of foods including
bananas, guavas, and avocados. I gathered a selection and
placed them inside with the water, then strolled away,
giving her time to make her choice.*

*When I returned, she sat inside, eating and drinking the
meal I had provided. Upon seeing me, she scrambled into
the corner, bearing the look of a frightened animal. I left
her crouching in the hut, unsure whether I'd see her again.*

~ * ~ * ~ * ~ * ~

Isabel leaned back and quietly expelled the breath she'd been
holding, feeling as if she could breathe for the first time in an hour.
The words had swept her into another time and place, full of
danger and intrigue and life-or-death struggles the likes of which
she had never experienced. The journal was more spectacular than
she could have imagined, the entries full of raw emotions and the
setting vivid with harsh realities and cruel fates.

She ran her finger along a line of script. This man, Rodrigo

Pearls

Velasquez, was her ancestor. She'd come to Caracas seeking information about the Venezuelan side of her heritage, who she was, where she'd come from. The answers lay before her, written in the careful handwriting of the man who'd begun it all, the story of how her people came to live in this part of the world. The entries offered her a poignant glimpse into his life ... and his heart.

She looked at the clock with a woeful eye. Suddenly she wanted to translate all night, but her classes would start early the next morning and she had yet to tackle her homework assignments. Reluctantly, she returned the journal to its case and packed her bag. "Tomorrow, Rodrigo Velasquez, we will meet again."

Two

I have to focus. Taking university-level classes in Spanish is hard enough without distractions. Isabel glanced at the clock and willed the last five minutes of class to pass quickly.

Since translating the first journal entry, she'd been able to think about little else. This was why she'd come to Venezuela, to learn about her heritage and maybe discover herself in the process. Who she was. Where she belonged.

The moment the professor dismissed them, she started the long trek to the library. Central University accommodated nearly 70,000 students on its expansive campus. As she hiked across the substantial grounds, she felt like a pack animal weighted down by all the books in her backpack. She ignored her aching shoulders and continued on, beckoned by the mysteries waiting to be uncovered in the journal.

In contrast to the tropical heat outside, the interior of the library felt cool and comfortable. Isabel shuffled into the elevator that would carry her to the floor bearing the reference books she needed. When the doors opened, the librarian on that level greeted her with a smile.

"Isabel, *cómo estás?*"

"*Muy bien,*" Isabel answered. "May I have my books?"

When Isabel had explained she would be using the reference books on a daily basis, the woman had graciously agreed to keep them near the reference desk for the duration of her project. Isabel retrieved the heavy tomes and hurried to a quiet corner of the room, unable to contain her curiosity. Now familiar with some of the older phrasing, she translated more quickly than she had the night before.

June 6th, 1505

I returned to the hut today, unsure if I would find her there. Nevertheless, I carried with me a blanket, rations of dried meat, and a small loaf of bread—items intended to make her more comfortable if she chose to remain in my care. I felt both surprise and relief to find her sitting in the center of the hut when I stepped into the doorway. My sudden presence startled her, and she moved warily toward the corner, eyeing me with fear.

I smiled and said hello, but my good humor did not alleviate her apprehension. Her dark, watchful eyes remained fixed on me, her body tensed as if preparing to flee at the first sign of danger. I knelt in the doorway, hoping to appear less threatening by lowering myself to her level. Moving slowly, I extended my arms, offering her the gifts I'd brought. She glanced at the package but refused to move toward me to accept it. Sighing, I set it on the floor and went to forage for more fruit in the surrounding trees. I could not be sure when I would return, and I wanted to ensure an ample food supply for her. Though I knew she could retrieve the fruit herself—perhaps with more skill than I—doing it for her gave me pleasure.

When I returned, she sat with the blanket in her lap, examining the meat and bread I'd brought. As my shadow fell across the doorway, she glanced up, her eyes focusing for a moment on the fruit I held in my hands. Her gaze rose to meet mine, and I saw the questions in her eyes. Why? Why was I doing all of this for her? Why had I not abused her as the other men surely had?

I offered her no answers. I could not put into words the forces that drove me to act as I did. Even if I could, she would not understand me, for only a few Indians have learned enough Spanish to communicate.

I set the fruit near the door and bade her farewell with a smile.

June 7th, 1505

I worked long and hard today, and if I had adhered to my logical nature, I would not have made the arduous trek to the hut. Yet my feet had a will of their own, and I found I could not resist the urge to see her.

My arrival was met with less apprehension than before. She must have heard my approach, because as I neared the hut, she appeared in the doorway. Her expression did not hold fear as before, nor did she welcome me. Her steady, probing gaze suggested I was a curiosity to her, a puzzling specimen she struggled to understand.

Moving slowly, I drew near, stopping only a few feet away from her. When she did not startle or protest, I felt a sense of accomplishment, though I don't know why it mattered so much. I offered her the gifts I'd brought: a small knife for cutting fruit or fish, and a basket, woven from the branches of the palms growing in abundance on the island. On a whim, I'd stopped to pick a few tropical flowers from the trees and vines along the path to her hut, so the basket spilled over with fragrant and colorful blossoms.

The gift seemed to please her, though I cannot say how I knew this. She does not smile or show emotion in the way of other women I've known. But I do not expect her to react to me as to an old friend. We are strangers, brought together by nightmarish circumstances.

Tired from the long day, I decided to rest a spell before I returned to the navy's base. I walked to a fallen palm a few yards away and sat upon its trunk, enjoying the moment of respite at the end of a busy day. She watched me for several minutes before disappearing into the hut with her basket. I read the action as a dismissal, but soon she emerged and came to stand before me. I smiled and patted the log, inviting her to sit. Her gaze followed my hand then returned to my face. She made no move to join me.

Her silent refusal to take orders amused me, and I laughed. The sober look in her doe-like eyes softened, and the corners of her full lips turned up ever so slightly. Deciding the time had come for introductions, I placed my hand against my breast and pronounced my name with deliberation. "Rodrigo," I told her. I repeated my name several times, but she did not acknowledge my attempt to communicate. She stared for a long moment then turned toward the hut. My disappointment at her rebuff quickly fled when she stopped at the doorway and offered me one word.

"Karwa," she said, her graceful fingers brushing over her collarbone before she disappeared inside.

~ * ~ * ~ * ~ * ~

"... he rescued her from the Spaniards who'd enslaved her, and he hid her away. I don't know how it ends yet, because I've only translated three entries, but already I think it's the most romantic story I've ever heard. I hope they fall in love...."

Raúl sat across the table from Isabel, admiring the way enthusiasm enhanced her appearance. She looked lovely in the mellow lighting of the jazz club, her blue eyes sparkling with excitement. The candlelight danced over her chestnut hair, capturing the silky texture and firing her golden highlights. Realizing his thoughts had strayed from her words, he pulled his attention back to the conversation.

"So what do you think? Have you ever heard anything so intriguing, Raúl?"

"Your tale is captivating. I should like to see this journal. I am certain it has value as an artifact."

"You aren't suggesting I sell it, are you? It's a piece of family history."

"No, but you should be certain to carry adequate insurance on such a unique piece. A journal written by one of the first Europeans to see Venezuela would be of great value to a museum or historian."

"You're right. I'll ask *Abuela* if she carries a policy on it. If not, will you help me get it insured?"

"Of course, *mi amor.*" He reached across the table and took her hand in his. "I've missed you this week. You didn't come to the café for lunch even once."

"Were you there every day?"

"*Sí.*"

"If I had known you wanted to see me, I'd have come."

"I always want to see you, Isabel. You are the most important part of my life." He watched a blush spread across her creamy cheeks. She had no idea how beautiful or special she was, and he found her modesty appealing.

Smoothing a strand of hair behind her ear, she regained her voice. "I'm sorry if you felt neglected. You're important to me, too, but school dominated my schedule this week. Aside from translating the journal, semester finals are just weeks away. I've been finishing up a few papers and studying for my tests."

"During Christmas break you will set aside some time for me, no?"

"Of course. *Abuela* invited me to the hacienda for the holidays. Would you like to come?"

The face he made brought a smile to her lips. "Doña Montez does not approve of me, Isabel."

"I know, but she doesn't know you like I do. Maybe if the two of you spent some time together...." Her voice trailed off.

"But not over the holidays. I don't want your celebrations overshadowed by tension because of my presence. Besides, I must visit my mother. I am all the family she has."

"How is she?"

The emptiness that pervaded his family interactions echoed hollowly in his his chest. "The same. Bitter. Angry. I don't expect to enjoy myself, but I must go."

"Why shouldn't you enjoy yourself?"

"I will have to listen to her endless tirades about my father. She despises him for never leaving his wife, despite his many promises through the years. Her life as his mistress seemed exciting in the beginning, but in the end, she regrets her decision. I believe she regrets having given birth to me, as well, but she would not say so. I pay her rent and give her spending money."

A worry line formed between Isabel's eyebrows. "I can't imagine any mother feeling that way."

"She does, I assure you. She has told me again and again that I look and act just like him."

"That's not a crime."

15

"To my mother it is."

Isabel fidgeted with the silverware on the table, and Raúl realized he'd upset the mood with talk of his mother's problems. Isabel had descended from people who valued family and honor. When she spoke of her parents, he sensed the love and commitment between them. She could not comprehend life in the run-down, crime-infested *barrios*, or a woman like his mother who would devote herself to a man who didn't really love her. She did not know the shame of a father's rejection or the difficulties Raúl had faced to rise to his current position of respect and prestige. *But I didn't need family and support. I made something of myself without them.* As if she could hear his thoughts, Isabel met his gaze, compassion and pity in her eyes.

He did not want her pity and quickly changed the subject. "I apologize. We've strayed from our earlier conversation. May I have the honor of your company over Christmas break?"

The tense line of her shoulders eased. "I intend to stay at the hacienda for a few days. After I return, I'm all yours."

Raúl raised his eyebrows, a smile teasing his lips. "All yours? Is this another of the delightful sayings from your English language?"

She gave him a playful grin. "Hmmm, let's see. It's English and it's a saying, but I couldn't vouch for the delightful part. I think that's a matter of personal preference."

He leaned closer to her, breathing in the scent of her and admiring the smooth texture of her skin. "If you were all mine, my personal preference would be to never let you go, *mi amor*. You captured my heart the moment I first saw you. Have you given any more thought to staying here in Caracas after graduation next summer? Perhaps I am selfish, but I want to keep you close to me always."

She gazed at him, her face alight with tenderness. "Have I told you how wonderful you are?"

~ * ~ * ~ * ~ * ~

June 10th, 1505

My inability to visit Karwa these last few days has distressed me. Feverish with desire to prepare a shipment of pearls for Spain, the admiral insisted we work extra hours. The Spanish royal court grows impatient to receive a return on their investment, and admirals have lost their commissions and their heads for lesser offences. Working from dawn to dusk for a week straight, we filled the cargo holds of two sturdy ships with pearls and prepared them to sail. The ships left harbor at dawn, and in celebration of our accomplishments, we were allowed a day of rest.

I rose early and journeyed to the hut to see Karwa. I feared she might have interpreted my long absence as abandonment, but when I arrived she stood before the hut. Relieved to see her, I greeted her with enthusiasm, speaking in a rush of language she did not understand. When she cocked her head to study me, I felt foolish for my outburst. I dropped the supplies I carried and knelt to sort through them, lowering my head so she could not see my embarrassment.

To my surprise, she came to kneel before me and softly spoke my name. Unaccustomed to speaking my language, her tongue confused the vowels and changed the inflections of the Spanish pronunciation, yet I thought it the most beautiful word ever spoken. Her soft voice swept over me like a caress. When I looked up and met her gaze, her smile grew and so did the boundaries of my heart.

We spent the day together, fishing, gathering fruit, weaving palm leaves into mats, and repairing the hut. Sometimes we worked in amiable silence, while other moments prompted a sharing of language. I learned several words in her tongue, and she learned some in mine. Soon we will be able to talk and share our thoughts. I find myself eager for that day to arrive.

Late in the evening as the sun hovered over the ocean, I dug a pit and built a fire inside. With Karwa's help, I wrapped the fish we'd caught in banana leaves and laid them on the glowing coals. We covered the pit with sand and allowed the fish to cook. Karwa brought out cups made from the halved shells of coconuts and poured me some water from her canteen. We scraped the soft fleshy pulp from a coconut and laid our feast of fish and fruit out on banana leaf plates. Though crude in its simplicity, I do not remember a meal more delightful.

By the time we finished, the sky had grown dark, and I felt reluctant to trek back to my camp. I watched Karwa disappear into the hut to settle in for the night. Though she had accepted my presence all day, I did not think she would feel comfortable letting me bed down in her hut. I had to bank the fire in order to avoid attracting attention, but without it, the snakes, scorpions, and wildlife inhabiting the area made it dangerous to sleep out in the open.

I decided to make my bed just outside the doorway of the hut, leaning my back against the frame for support. Just as I settled into a comfortable position and closed my eyes, Karwa poked her head out the door and tugged at my sleeve. By the light of the moon, I could see the confusion in her face. She found my choice of a resting place unreasonable. Waving her hands, she beckoned me inside and pointed to a corner of the hut.

I followed her instructions and lay on a mat of woven palm leaves. She returned to her place on the other side, curled beneath her blanket, and soon her breathing took on the peaceful rhythms of sleep. I lay awake, staring at the roof of the hut and listening to her breathe. The magical sounds of the night beyond the crude walls of our shelter seemed to intensify the unfamiliar feelings inside me. The song of the cicadas accompanied the whisper of waves, lapping at the shore nearby. The leaves of the palms fluttered in the gentle ocean breeze. The night grew cool, and I wrapped my arms tight around myself for warmth as I drifted off to sleep.

When I awoke some hours later, the cold no longer afflicted me. I moved my arm and felt the blanket covering me. Curious, I turned my head and found her lying at my side, her head resting on her arm, her face angelic in repose. My heart swelled as I considered her concern for my comfort and her willingness to share her blanket. It would seem I have passed her scrutiny and earned her trust.

~ * ~ * ~ * ~ * ~

Isabel flipped through the pages of the dictionary to no avail. She tried another reference book, and still another, not finding the answers she needed. Pushing the books away, she rubbed her tired eyes. *Why can't I find definitions for these words?*

She stared at the list of indecipherable words and wondered if she'd missed some important clue. The translating had gone well for nearly two weeks, but suddenly she'd come to a standstill. *Maybe a fresh pair of eyes will help.*

Isabel rose and carried her list to the reference librarian who'd been aiding her quest to translate the journal.

"Adelina, will you look at this list and tell me if you recognize any of these words?" Isabel placed the paper on the desk in front of her friend.

Adelina adjusted her glasses and bent to study Isabel's neat handwriting. After several minutes she looked up with a puzzled frown. "These are not Spanish."

"Are you sure?"

"They do not follow the Spanish patterns of spelling and pronunciation. I would guess they are from an Indian language."

"Of course!" Isabel hands flew up, and she gestured emphatically as she spoke. "Why didn't I think of this sooner? He spent all his free time with Karwa, so it would not be unusual for him to learn and use words from her language. Thank you, Adelina! You're a genius."

Smiling, the woman handed the list back to Isabel.

"One more thing." Isabel folded the paper and put it in her pocket. "I'm going to need some reference books on old Indian languages."

Adelina's smile faded, and she shook her head. "I would love to help you, but I do not think I can. Hundreds of tribes inhabited Venezuela before the Spaniards arrived, and they all spoke their own language or dialect. None of them used a formal written language, Isabel. You should know that from your studies."

A nervous flutter started in her stomach and reverberated up into her chest. For the first time, Isabel feared she might not be able to finish the translation. "Yes, but surely there were explorers or missionaries who recorded information on the native languages.

You must have something."

"I do, but without knowing which tribe or language to search for, we could spend years looking and not find the answers you need."

Defeat hovered over her, threatening to swallow the enthusiasm she had enjoyed the last few weeks. The journal had given her a sense of purpose and a heritage more wonderful than any she could have imagined. The thought of never completing the translation disheartened her. "Please, will you at least try?" she begged.

"I don't know how, Isabel, but I think I know someone who can." Adelina opened her desk drawer and pulled out a directory of university faculty. "Here," she said, tapping her manicured fingernail against a name on the second page. "Manuel Santiago is teaching an archaeology class this semester. He is knowledgeable about the ancient populations that inhabited this region. If anyone can help you, he can." Adelina scribbled his office address and phone number on a scrap of paper.

"Thank you!" Isabel accepted the note with a grateful smile. "Now, if you'll excuse me, I think I'll drop by his office before I head home."

Three

Manuel stared at the full-page picture accompanying the feature article in the archaeology journal. Julio, his old college classmate, had made the find of a lifetime in Egypt, and his success had received worldwide acclaim. Manuel knew he should feel proud of his friend, but his own sense of failure overpowered any goodwill.

"Figures! I spent three lousy years as a dig *assistant*, and now I'm stuck in a classroom. Julio probably has sponsors lined up, begging to fund his digs, and I can't get anyone to even listen to my requests." Manuel thumped the magazine down on his desk and stared at the stack of reports that needed grading. While he appreciated the rigors of academia, he had no desire to spend his career in archaeology behind a podium or a desk. He wanted to work in the field—exploring, digging, and discovering.

With a sigh he opened his drawer and pulled out a red pen. *I may as well get to it.* He had just lifted the first paper from the stack when a knock sounded at his office door.

"Come in!"

The door swung open, revealing a striking young woman. She was tall by Venezuelan standards, probably in her early twenties. Her appearance and coloring denoted a Spanish bloodline, but her clothes and her body language suggested she was a foreigner. "Manuel Santiago?" She eased into the room, glancing around at the floor-to-ceiling bookcases lining every wall, shelves bowing under the weight of their load.

A wave of self-consciousness swept over Manuel as she eyed his less than tidy desk. He quickly shuffled a stack of student reports and dropped the journal he'd been reading into a drawer. "Can I help you?" He gestured to a chair in front of his desk. She slid her backpack from her shoulders and set it beside the chair, then took a seat.

"Professor Santiago, my name is Isabel Palmer. I'm working on a project and could use your assistance. If I could have a moment of your time to show you this...." She bent to rummage through her backpack.

Though she spoke his language fluently, he noted her slight accent did not sound Venezuelan and guessed that Spanish was not her native language. "Where are you from?"

She paused and lifted her face to look at him. "Why is that important?"

"I'm just curious. It's obvious you aren't Venezuelan."

"It is?" Her shoulders slumped at his declaration, making him wonder if he'd somehow hurt her feelings.

"Yes. Where are you from?"

"The United States. What gave me away?"

"Your accent."

Her brow furrowed. "I don't have an accent."

"You're right about that. You don't have a Venezuelan accent."

She frowned at him a moment then shook her head. Returning her attention to the backpack, she pulled out a smooth metal case and laid it across her lap. "Can we get back to the reason I came?"

He nodded, enjoying the irritation that sparked through her eyes.

"I've recently inherited a piece of family history—a journal—and I've been trying to translate the old Spanish phrasing. I was doing a decent job of it until I started coming across words that aren't Spanish in origin. The librarian suggested they might be an Indian language, and I believe she's correct. The man who wrote the journal spent a good deal of time with an Indian woman."

Great. Some random request that had nothing to do with him or his class. Where did these people find him? "And you've brought it to me because...."

"I was wondering if you would take a look at the Indian words and tell me if you recognize the language."

"I'll take a look, but I can't make any promises. Do you know how many tribes lived in this region?"

"I know it's a long shot, but please?"

Something about the undisguised hope on her face made him feel obligated to at least take a look. With a huff, he conceded. "Let me see it." He'd take a quick glance at whatever she'd brought then send her on her way so he could get back to brooding over his current dismal situation and grading boring papers.

She lifted the leather-bound journal from its case and laid it before him with reverent care.

As he examined the cover, his interest was piqued. "How old is this?"

"Five-hundred years."

He swallowed hard. "Are you sure?"

"The entries are dated. See for yourself."

He pulled open his desk drawer and took out a pair of cotton gloves.

"Why are you doing that—putting on gloves, I mean?"

He stared at her. Was this *gringa* a little *loca*? "You don't mean to tell me you've been handling these pages with your bare hands, do you?"

"Yes."

"Never—and I mean never—do that again! Do you understand?"

She shrank away from him, as if the tone and volume of his voice made her uncomfortable. "Why not?"

"The oils in your skin will increase the rate of decomposition. I'll give you a pair of gloves to take with you."

Manuel opened to the first entry and began to read. His practiced eye made a rough translation without the aid of a dictionary. The story would interest a historian, but he saw no immediate value to an archaeologist. *Maybe I can send her to someone else. I don't have time to bother with this sort of thing.* He pretended to give the first entry a careful examination then flipped to a page further into the journal. A line of script caught his eye, sending a chill down his spine.

"Where did you get this?" he asked, his voice sharp with interest.

"I told you, it's a piece of family history. My grandmother recently placed it in my care. Why?"

Manuel's voice rose to match his excitement. "Do you know what this is? Do you know the value of this journal?" When she backed away from him, he realized he was shouting at her. He paused and drew a deep breath. "Sorry. I'm having something of a bad day, and you happened to walk into the middle of it. I don't mean to take out my frustration on you."

She watched him with impassioned eyes. "Can you help me translate the journal?"

"Yes. And maybe I can do something better."

"Better?"

"Did you know there's a legend connected to the man who wrote this journal?"

Isabel smirked. "Are you going to talk about stolen treasure now?"

"So, you know?"

"I've heard the fairy tales, yes."

"You don't believe them?"

She waved her hand dismissively. "Stolen treasure? Are you serious? Maybe in the movies, but…."

"*Señorita* Palmer, if you'd read some of the later entries, you'd understand."

"I tried, but I kept running into Indian words that I couldn't translate."

Manuel nodded. "I see them. I think they're a Pachacamac dialect because I remember seeing this name, Karwa, associated with this tribe before. I'd need to pull some resources to confirm it. Translation would be tricky because there isn't much from that tribe. They were largely extinct before anything could be recorded about them."

"The slavers killed them."

"Yes, slavery took a heavy toll on the native population." Manuel leaned back in his chair and took a moment to assess her. A plan began forming in his mind, and he wondered how she would react to it. He needed an opportunity to get his career off the ground. This could be just the ticket.

"I'll make you a deal," he blurted. "I'd like to translate this journal, and I'll do it for free on one condition."

"Yes?" A look of apprehension accompanied her smile.

"I'd like your permission to use the information we uncover."

"Use it? How?"

"Several years ago, one of my European colleagues did a study of sixteenth century captains' logs. He specializes in locating and exploring sunken ships, preferably ones containing treasure. The logbooks often give valuable clues about the location of sunken treasure."

"Wouldn't the logbooks sink with the ships?" Isabel asked.

"Yes. But ships often traveled in groups, so a fellow captain might record the sinking of a sister ship in his log. Or a captain who sunk an enemy ship would write down the incident. Anyway, my friend found the log of a Spanish captain stationed off the coast of Cubagua during the time the Spaniards harvested the pearls. The pearl beds at that time were rich and ripe for harvest. Having never been touched, the oysters had enough time to multiply and mature, offering an incredible bounty. The pearls the navy transported to Spain eventually totaled forty percent of the world's wealth."

Her eyebrows lifted and he could see that his brief history lesson was answering questions she hadn't even known to ask.

"As my friend read, he found an entry about a chest of pearls stolen from the Spanish Navy. These weren't just any pearls. They were the best and largest pearls harvested off the coast of Cubagua. Some were said to have been the size of a man's eyeball. The admiral overseeing the fleet insisted the most valuable pearls be set aside in order to make a special and impressive gift to the royal court upon his return. To his dismay, the chest containing the queen's gift disappeared one night without a trace."

Manuel pointed to an entry in the journal. "I see similarities in the story outlined here. I believe your ancestor may have stolen the pearls, and this journal could hold the key to their location."

She fixed him with a blue-eyed stare, her eyebrows drawing together in a frown. For a moment he thought she would turn down his offer, but when she broke the silence, she sounded interested. "Will you look for the pearls if the journal gives you enough information?"

The change in her voice made him uneasy, but he knew he couldn't lie to her. "I would if I could find a sponsor to fund the expedition."

"Then I'll agree to your condition if you agree to mine."

"And that is...?"

"If you go looking for the pearls, I'm going with you."

He slammed his palm against the desktop. "Absolutely not! You are not qualified or prepared for fieldwork."

She shrugged her shoulders and reached for the journal. "Then I'll be leaving, Professor Santiago. I'm sorry we couldn't come to an agreement, but I thank you for your time."

He watched in disbelief as Isabel returned the journal to its case and tucked it into her backpack, her face and posture confirming her resolve. Desperation mounted inside him. His teaching contract with the university ended after this semester, and he had no job lined up after the holidays. Work in the archaeology field could be scarce at times, and he had suffered his share of unemployment over the last few years. Aside from his desire to make a name for himself, he also needed to repay the debts he'd accumulated during his jobless stints. *This could be the break I've been waiting for, and this stubborn female is not going to blow it for me.*

Manuel swallowed hard. "Please, I'm sure we can work something out." He rose from his chair and stood in the doorway, blocking her escape. "I could send you daily updates or arrange for you to visit me on site once a month to look over my work."

She rose from the chair and faced him, her chin tilted at a determined angle. "He's *my* ancestor. This is *my* journal. Either you agree to work with me from start to finish, or there's no deal."

They glared at one another, locked in a contest of wills.

It didn't take long for Manuel to realize, she wasn't going to concede defeat, and then he had to admit that she had the upper hand. *Dang.* If he wanted access to the journal, he'd have to be accommodating to the owner. The prospect was already promising to be a huge pain. If he had any sense, he'd let her walk, pursue a less troublesome lead. Problem was, he didn't have any other leads and desperation could force a man to do idiotic things.

"Very well." He sighed, running his fingers through his hair.

"I want the deal in writing so you can't finagle your way out of it."

He nodded. "Okay, but don't say I didn't warn you. Fieldwork isn't going to be a picnic for someone like you."

"Someone like me?" she asked, challenge in her voice.

"You don't look like the outdoorsy type."

Despite his mildly insulting tone, she flashed him a brilliant smile. "I might surprise you."

He resisted the urge to roll his eyes. The only surprise he wanted was the kind he experienced when he pulled some amazing treasure out of the ground. It seemed for the moment that going through her was the only way to achieve that goal.

~ * ~ * ~ * ~ * ~

Two days after Christmas, Isabel entered the coffee shop and spotted Raúl in the corner booth. He waved when he saw her, his expression grim.

"Isabel, how good to see you," he said as she slid into the bench across from him. "I was beginning to wonder if you'd moved back to the United States. I could not reach you by telephone. Have you been avoiding me?"

Isabel felt a pang of guilt at his last question. Right after her final exams, she'd tossed her suitcase in a rental car and drove to the hacienda. She treasured the warm, homey days with her *abuela*, yet she couldn't get her mind off the journal. After their Christmas celebration, she returned to the city and delved into research at the university library. In her enthusiasm, time and the world beyond the journal had ceased to exist.

"I'm sorry, honey. I've been translating the journal I told you about. Manuel seems incredibly capable, and I'm looking forward to his help."

Raúl's dark eyes narrowed. "Who is Manuel? Are you seeing another man, *mi amor*?"

Isabel laughed. Of course he would think that. Why else would she neglect him? She reached across the table and laced her fingers through his. "No, silly. Manuel Santiago is a professor at Central University. He's going to help me translate the more difficult parts of the journal after he returns from his holiday."

Raúl seemed to relax at her explanation. "This professor, he is an old man with gray hair and a sagging belly, no?"

Isabel shook her head. *He's jealous. How sweet.* "Actually, he's around our age. Middle to late twenties I'd guess. But you don't have anything to worry about, Raúl. He's as grumpy as an old troll and not nearly as handsome as you."

Raúl smiled, revealing straight white teeth and deep dimples. Her heart fluttered as he leaned across the table to kiss her. "Mmm, I missed you, Isabel."

After four months of dating, his kiss hadn't lost its effect. She decided to sit beside him rather than across the table. When she moved to his bench, he draped his arm around her as she knew he would. Snuggled against him, a wonderful sense of acceptance and belonging pervaded her soul.

"This is nice." He caressed her cheek with his free hand. "Tell me what has kept you from me, *mi amor*."

Isabel sighed contentedly. "So much has happened since we last spoke. I'm not sure where to begin."

"My entire afternoon is free, Isabel. I had hoped to spend it with you."

She smiled. "That sounds promising."

"Good. Now, tell me about this translating."

"Okay. You're never going to believe the story I've discovered in the journal. I told you it was written in the early 1500s, right?"

He nodded.

"Well, it turns out that my ancestor, Rodrigo Velasquez, stole a chest of pearls right out from under the admiral's nose and hid them somewhere. Manuel thinks the journal will tell us where to find them, and I made him promise to take me with him when he goes to search for them."

Raúl stared at her, his face void of expression.

"Sorry. Did I tell you too much too fast? I know it's a lot to absorb. I didn't fully comprehend the importance of this information for a week after I found out."

Raúl pulled her hand to his lips and brushed a feather-light kiss across her fingers. "You certainly know how to get a man's attention, Isabel. I'd like to hear more about this project. Start at the beginning, and tell me everything."

~ * ~ * ~ * ~ * ~

Isabel dropped her purse on her dining table and hurried to answer the phone. "Hello?"

"Isabel?"

The voice was familiar, one she'd been expecting to hear. "Oh hi, Professor Santiago. Did you have a nice holiday?"

"Yes, but I'm back and ready to work. I'd like to arrange to pick up the journal and begin working on the project."

Isabel stiffened. "I thought I made it clear this would be a joint venture. We work together or not at all."

"Yes, yes. I understood that, but I thought the translating might progress faster if I had the journal at my disposal. I'm a single man, and I often work sixteen to eighteen hours a day. Now that the semester has ended, I can devote all my time to your interests."

Right, buddy! Try and make it sound like you're doing me a favor. I'm still not going to trust you.

"I think I'd prefer to stick with the original agreement."

His disgusted sigh seemed to confirm her suspicions. "Very well. Can we set up a work schedule? I have no further obligations during the holiday break. I can commit as much time as you're able to give me."

"My plans are minimal." Raúl's handsome face flashed through her mind, and she remembered her promise to spend some time on his yacht. *Maybe we won't be able to go sailing, but I'm sure we can find a few hours together here and there.* He'd been fascinated when she'd recounted what she'd learned from the journal and Manuel thus far and had encouraged her pursuit. He'd understand. "All right. I have my day planner in front of me. How does tomorrow look to you?"

~ * ~ * ~ * ~ * ~

The man walked toward the front door of his apartment building, his thoughts far away from the darkened street. As he stood in the dim light fumbling with his keys, two men seized his arms from behind.

"Hey!" He thrashed against their iron grip.

The larger man pinned him against the wall, while the other addressed business. "You missed your last payment, *mi amigo*. The boss is short of cash because of you."

He tried not to let fear show on his face or in his voice. "Look, I ran into some problems, but I swear I'll have the money for you soon."

29

Pearls

"How soon?"

"I ... I'm not sure." He swallowed hard, knowing what would come next.

Wearing a sadistic smile, the smaller man delivered a crushing blow to his abdomen. "I suggest you make your payment very soon."

The two thugs disappeared into the shadows of the night, leaving him sagging against the wall, gasping for air.

Four

Isabel paused outside the office door and prepared to deal with Manuel's surly disposition. He'd acted grouchy as a bear awakened from hibernation during each of their work sessions. After three weeks of enduring his temperament, she wondered if she should consider looking for another archaeologist to partner with in the venture. Her conscience pricked her. *I gave my word, and as a Christian, I need to keep my promise. But, Lord, please give me the opportunity to tell Manuel about You so suffering through his moods won't be in vain.* She thought it amusing that his last name, Santiago, translated into English meant Saint James. Him, a saint? Talk about irony.

After a quick rap on the door, she let herself in. When Manuel glanced up from his work, a giant smile spread across his face.

"Hey, Isabel, good to see you!"

"Professor Santiago?" Shock caused her greeting to sound more like a question. He looked like Manuel, but he didn't sound or act like him.

He laughed, a deep, pleasant sound, and pulled a chair up to the table next to him. "Have a seat, Isabel. I want to show you what I've found."

Recovering from her stupor, she sat beside him. "Sure, Professor, let's see it."

"You're always so formal toward me. We're partners now. Don't you think it's time you called me Manuel?"

"You don't like 'Professor'?"

"It's just that I'm not *your* professor. We're really more like colleagues. And, besides, every time you call me Professor I have the urge to look over my shoulder to see if there's a gray-haired geezer in the room. Something about the title makes me feel like an old man, when in reality I'm only a few years older than you."

"How do you know how old I am?"

"Just a guess. You're studying for your master's, right?"

She nodded.

"Judging by that information and your looks, I assume you're twenty-three or twenty-four."

"Twenty-four," she conceded.

"And I'm twenty-eight. Only four years difference, so call me Manuel."

Isabel didn't know whether to feel glad or suspicious about his total change in behavior. *Is this a plot to get me to let down my guard?* She hadn't forgotten his attempt to wheedle the journal away from her.

"Are you feeling all right, Professor?"

"Manuel," he corrected. "And I'm feeling great. I finally got that tooth fixed, and I feel like a new man."

"Tooth?"

"Oh, didn't I mention it? I've had a molar that needed some work, but the dentist couldn't see me until yesterday. It hurt pretty bad, but it's better now."

Toothache. Could that be why he's been so unbearable?

"Look what I received in today's mail." He pushed a book toward her. "This was written by an early missionary to the Pachacamac tribe."

Isabel picked up the book and turned to the first page. "It's written in English."

"Yes. He was an Englishman, commissioned by the Catholic church to set up a mission in the New World."

"So how will this help us?"

He reached for the book and laid it on the table between them. Opening to the middle, he pointed out neat rows of handwriting. "Look here. He's learned some of the native words, and he's written them down with their definitions."

She studied the crude list Manuel pointed out. "Do any of the words match the ones on our Indian word list?"

"Not exactly." The corners of Manuel's lips quirked upward.

"Then I don't understand. How will this help us?"

"The words don't match because the priest was an

Englishman. He used a system of English phonetics to spell out the words he learned from the Indians."

"And Rodrigo, my ancestor, used Spanish phonetics."

Manuel smiled. "Now you're thinking like an archaeologist. The vowels and some of the consonants are pronounced differently in the two languages."

Isabel felt a surge of excitement. "So if we can take the words the priest recorded and convert them to a Spanish system of phonetics, we may be able to find some matches?"

"Exactly."

Isabel flipped through the priest's recordings and doubt crept in. "What are our chances? This list he made isn't more than a few hundred words long. It couldn't contain all the definitions we need."

"No, but your ancestor gave us something almost as valuable as a dictionary. We can ascertain the meaning of some of Rodrigo's Pachacamac words by the context of his sentences. And I haven't given up hope that we'll find some other resources. I've sent out inquiries to any number of libraries, museums, and historians, asking for Pachacamac information, but the holidays have slowed their response time."

"Of course. People haven't worked much this last week. Did you contact any of the potential sponsors?"

Discouragement descended over Manuel's features. "I did."

"Not good news, I guess?"

"No. They all turned me down. Some stated I need more experience before they'll fund me. The rest claimed to have recently committed to other projects. I think it'll be easier to secure a sponsor if we find evidence in the journal about where he hid the pearls."

"And if we don't find evidence?"

He remained silent for a moment. "Don't worry about it, Isabel. I'll think of something. I want this as much as you do." His attention returned to the missionary's book, and he scribbled notes on a blank notepad. Frown lines creased his brow.

His smile was gone, suppressed by the sobering weight of the problems they faced. He took the project so seriously, a fact that Isabel was grateful for. She felt compelled to try to cheer him, bring back some of the good humor she'd seen earlier. She rather liked the smiling, amiable Manuel. "Don't you worry either, Manuel. I'll pray about it, and something will turn up."

"Good, you do that."

Because of the way he spoke the phrase, Isabel couldn't be certain whether he'd said it to be polite, or if he sincerely wanted her to pray. *Lord, if You want us to work together during the next few months, please provide a sponsor. And more importantly, give me the opportunity to talk to him about You.*

~ * ~ * ~ * ~ * ~

June 24, 1505
I spent the entire day with Karwa, enjoying the sweet sound of her voice, the curve of her full lips, the peacefulness that emanates from deep within her. This afternoon, as we walked hand in hand along the shore, we encountered an old boat hidden by the sea oats and tall grasses. After a quick examination I realized, with a little work, I could make the boat seaworthy again. Karwa and I dragged it back to her hut and began repairing it. A day may come when we will wish to leave Cubagua, and we will need a vessel to carry us over the sea.

~ * ~ * ~ * ~ * ~

June 30, 1505
Karwa has become my addiction. The smile she reserves for me alone lends purpose to my days and brings sweet dreams to my nights. My chest is heavy with the need to see her daily, though my visits to her hut grow more perilous, bringing danger to us both.

My departures from the naval camp have aroused suspicions. The men ask what activity draws me from their midst and causes me to spend hours in solitude. I have thus far concealed my activities with tales of a fishing hole that I visit, but they grow insistent in their requests to accompany me on my treks. I must exercise caution when I journey to see her now. At times, the men follow me, and I am forced to abandon my plans in order to lead them astray.

*When I am able to visit her, I do not walk the same path
twice for fear my daily treks will wear a path into the
ground and lead the enemy to my love. Strange, I have come
to think of my own people as the enemy. I feel less and less a
part of their ranks as I see the torture inflicted upon
Karwa's people. I no longer desire to harvest the treasure
from the coastal waters. I have found a treasure infinitely
more valuable.*

~ * ~ * ~ * ~ * ~

Manuel rubbed his sweaty palms on his pant legs as he
followed Isabel into the classy restaurant. After three weeks of
translating the journal, the location of the pearls remained a
mystery. His final paycheck from the university had been spent,
and he'd moved out of his campus office and set up work in his
apartment. Bill collectors called daily, and he'd not made a payment
on his larger debt, the one he didn't like to think about, in months.

He knew he needed to find a sponsor immediately, but all his
contacts had turned him away. He'd resigned himself to taking
work as a dishwasher or menial laborer when Isabel surprised him
with the invitation to lunch. "I think I found a sponsor, but he
wants to talk with you," she'd told him. "Wear something nice.
The restaurant is fancy."

His stomach knotted as he followed Isabel and the maitre d' to
a table in a private room. She looked stunning in a vivid blue dress
that matched her eyes. The cut was flattering without being
revealing. Classy and conservative—like her. The more time he
spent with her, the more he realized she was a quality woman, the
kind with some depth and integrity. When their professional
relationship came to an end, he would consider extending it into
something more personal if she gave any indication she'd be
interested in him.

As they entered the private dining area, a well-dressed man
rose to greet them, his tailored suit and snakeskin shoes
announcing his wealth as assuredly as a statement from his bank.
The man smiled at Isabel and bent to kiss her cheek. "*Mi amor*,
how lovely you look today."

Isabel blushed under his praise.

A boyfriend? The intimate glances passing between them caught

Pearls

Manuel off guard. *In all the hours we've worked together, she never mentioned another man.*

"Manuel, I'd like you to meet Raúl Guerrero. Raúl, this is Professor of Archaeology, Manuel Santiago."

Manuel accepted Raúl's hand and gave it a perfunctory shake. "Mr. Guerrero, good to meet you."

He endured Raúl's scrutiny for a moment, willing himself not to shrink from the man's intimidating gaze. He couldn't decide whether he'd passed or failed the examination when Raúl turned his back to him and fawned over Isabel.

"Let me seat you, *mi amor*." With a hand on her back, Raúl guided her to the circular table and pulled out a chair. He then took the seat next to her, making no invitation to Manuel.

So that's how this is going to work. I'll play el peón *to his* rey. *Servant and king. Well, I'll let him feel important if it gives me access to his bank account.* Manuel easily recognized the type of man he was dealing with. Raúl needed to feel in control, to make the decisions, to be superior. If he couldn't coerce a person with his charm and wit, he'd resort to using money and power for leverage. Manuel took the chair on the other side of Isabel and asked for a menu.

"I have already ordered for you both," Raúl informed.

Of course you have, Your Majesty. Manuel forced himself to smile and nod.

Raúl's penetrating stare drilled into Manuel. "Isabel has told me of this journal and the translating you two have done. I am interested in this project and would be willing to fund a search for the pearls if you can find evidence of their location. Has the journal provided you with this information?"

"Not yet. But we're less than half done with the translation."

"Do you expect to find proof of the pearls' whereabouts?"

Manuel paused to choose his words carefully. He could not afford to damage his chances of securing Raúl's sponsorship with a dismal report, but he didn't want to lie either. "If not the exact location, then definitely some solid clues about where to look."

Isabel cleared her throat. "As Manuel mentioned, we're only half done with the translating. We're just coming to the part where he steals the pearls and leaves the island. If he's written the pearls' hiding place in the journal, it would be in the second half."

"How long will it take you to finish the translating?" Raúl asked, glancing between Manuel and Isabel.

"A couple of weeks," Isabel answered.

"Longer than that," Manuel disagreed. "The new semester is starting. With classes you won't be able to spend as much time."

Isabel shook her head. "I've already canceled my classes for the semester. I'm not going to miss out on this opportunity. Besides, we're entering the dry season. If we find the information we need, we'll want to launch the expedition while the weather is good."

Manuel stared at the tablecloth and tried to decide how to explain his lack of funds without sounding desperate. "Then you will have to work on the translation alone during the days, Isabel. I'll be taking a job."

Isabel's eyes narrowed, and a crease appeared on her brow. "Why, Manuel? You promised to help me through this, and now you're abandoning me?"

He felt his face warm as he tried to make her understand. The elegant setting of the restaurant and the arrogance of the rich man sitting across from him made his admission of poverty seem even more embarrassing. "I'm not wealthy. I need income to pay my bills. Without a teaching job or work supervising a dig, I'll have to take whatever work I can get."

Isabel pursed her lips. "That won't do. I need your help." She glanced at Raúl as if to ask for assistance, but he offered no suggestions. He wore a look of indifference, as if he found the financial struggles of the common man tedious and boring.

Shrugging her shoulders, she sighed. "Do what you have to, Manuel, and maybe we'll think of something along the way."

The waiter arrived and set plates of steaming lobster in front of them.

Manuel placed his napkin over his lap and plucked a succulent piece of white meat from the shell. *If nothing else, I've gained a decent meal from this meeting.* As they ate, a heavy silence surrounded them, and Manuel felt certain his chances were sinking by the moment.

The waiter refilled Raúl's wineglass. Holding the stem of the glass, he swirled the pale golden liquid in hypnotic circles. "Though your evidence is sketchy and the project is obviously a risk, I can afford the gamble. I will fund your project."

Isabel squealed and smiled ear-to-ear. "Wonderful!" She leaned to offer Raúl a kiss.

"Yes, wonderful," Manuel echoed with less enthusiasm. *I need the job and the money, but do I need it this badly? An American woman and a self-important stuffed shirt for partners. This just keeps getting more ridiculous.*

~ * ~ * ~ * ~ * ~

He dialed the number with apprehension, hoping his gamble would pay off. A click on the other end of the line interrupted his reverie.

"Yes?"

"It's me."

"You have my money?"

He willed his heartbeat to slow down. "Not yet. I'm calling to make you a deal."

"I don't deal. You know that."

"Please, hear me out. This could work in your favor."

Silence. He gripped the telephone, cold sweat trickling down the side of his face. "I just made a business connection that could bring in millions. If you'll extend my loan for a few more months, I'll pay you double what I owe."

"Triple."

"That's criminal!" he shouted, then reined in his temper. They would not hesitate to take his life for his failure to pay the debt he owed them now. He needed to buy some time. "Fine. Triple."

"Good. You know where to find me."

The click in his ear signaled the close of a deal with *el Diablo*.

Five

Weary from a long day, Isabel climbed the stairs leading from the subway to the street. Though *el metro* was well maintained and convenient, she missed the luxury of owning a car. But the streets of Caracas suffered overcrowding, and driving meant long and frustrating delays in traffic. Riding the subway allowed her time to study or daydream. Her favorite fantasy involved a flowing white dress and a dimpled groom waiting at the end of the aisle. She smiled. Raúl would look so handsome in a black tuxedo.

The wail of a fire engine interrupted her pleasant musings. She turned and watched a large truck scream past, sending up a gust of wind that lifted her hair from her shoulders and sent it whirling in disarray. *I wonder what that's all about?* Following the path of the truck, she rounded the next corner and headed toward her apartment building. Police barricades and flashing lights filled the street. Squinting, she peered through the haze and saw the flames and smoke pouring from the windows of her building.

"No!" Adrenaline coursing through her, she broke into a run.

A policeman stepped into her path and grabbed her by the arms. "You can't go down there," he stated firmly in Spanish. "*Es peligroso.*"

"I know it's dangerous, but that's my apartment building." She spoke English in her frustration, bringing a frown to the officer's face. Forcing herself to calm down, she repeated her reply in his language.

"The fire has been burning for an hour. The firemen have given up trying to save the building. Now they are attempting to keep the fire from spreading to the surrounding structures."

"So all my stuff is gone?" Tears pooled in her eyes.

"I'm sorry, *señorita.*" The policeman returned to his duties, restraining the crowd and maintaining a safe perimeter.

Swiping at a tear, Isabel clutched the bag she carried with her. *Thank goodness I had the journal with me.* She walked a block to a payphone and dialed. *"Abuela,* can I come stay with you?"

~ * ~ * ~ * ~ * ~

Isabel hurried to the ringing telephone, hoping to answer before the noise awakened her grandmother. Doña Montez had stayed up long into the night to comfort Isabel and help her settle into her room at the hacienda. Getting on in years, the old woman needed her rest, and Isabel didn't want to disturb her.

Grasping the receiver, Isabel lifted it to her ear. *"Hola."*

"Isabel, is that you?"

"Yes, Raúl."

"Gracias, Dios. I have been worried sick since I heard of the fire in your building. Several died in the blaze, and I was devastated to think you might have been one of the casualties."

"I was out doing a little shopping and taking care of some errands. When I came home at dusk, the fire had already destroyed my building. I'm safe, but everything I owned is gone."

"Everything, Isabel? Even the journal?"

His concern touched her. He realized how much this project meant to her. "No, not that. I had been working on the translation at Manuel's apartment most of the day. I had errands to run before I went home, so I had it in my bag while I was shopping."

"A stroke of good fortune."

"A blessing of God," she countered.

"I am relieved to hear of your safety, *mi amor.* Now that I know you are well, my next concern is when I will see you again. You have kept busy with your journal project, and I feel neglected. Your sweet kisses inspire me to be a better man."

Giddiness welled up inside her. "You're perfect already, Raúl."

"At times I feel I am not worthy of you. You are so exquisite."

Isabel's laugh carried through the phone lines. "I'd like to hear more of this. How about I borrow *Abuela's* car and drive into Caracas for dinner tomorrow night?"

~ * ~ * ~ * ~ * ~

Isabel met Manuel at the door and took one of the boxes he carried in his arms. "Follow me," she said, smiling. *"Abuela* and I set up one of the guest rooms for you to sleep in, and an office for our work. Where do these boxes go?"

"To the office, if you don't mind." He followed her through the elegantly appointed hallways and into a study furnished with a desk, a large table, a couch and several comfortable-looking chairs. "Wow, this is great, Isabel. I really appreciate your invitation to stay here at the hacienda. Are you sure your grandmother doesn't mind storing my possessions for a while? If we decide to go hunt for the pearls, we may be gone a few months."

"She doesn't mind. She lives in this big old house by herself, so there's plenty of room." They set their boxes in a corner and returned to the car for another load.

Manuel handed her a box, but he didn't let go immediately. She looked up at him, wondering why he hadn't released her.

"Isabel, thank you for inviting me here. You probably don't know this, but I was about to lose my apartment. Your invitation was an answer to prayer."

The reference to prayer snagged Isabel's attention. He'd never hinted he believed in God or practiced any sort of religion. She wondered if he actually prayed, or if he'd said it for her benefit. "I'm glad to help out, Manuel, but you should know my reasons for inviting you were purely selfish. I don't have a car. *Abuela* probably could have loaned me hers, but I had no desire to make the hour's drive into Caracas every day to work with you. Bringing you here seemed more convenient."

Manuel glanced out over the groves of avocado trees and fields that would yield a bountiful harvest. "This is beautiful land. I think I'll enjoy my stay."

Isabel laughed and turned toward the house with her box. "Wait until you taste Maria's cooking. You will never want to leave."

~ * ~ * ~ * ~ * ~

An hour later, Isabel and Manuel settled into the study to continue their translating efforts. The fire had disrupted their work for nearly a week, and Manuel felt eager to resume. They worked side-by-side at the large table, the journal open between them. Isabel studied the Spanish text and wrote a rough translation on her notepad. Occasionally, she would point out an Indian word or phrase to Manuel, and he would jot them on his tablet. He'd volunteered for the more difficult job of translating the Pachacamac words. They fell into a rhythm, working silently for over an hour before combining their work and reading the next journal entry.

~ * ~ * ~ * ~ * ~

July 10, 1505

Today, I killed a man. I suspect he followed me to the hut and spied on Karwa and me for a time before showing himself. His face registered disgust and hatred as he stepped into the open and confronted me for hiding a savage. Assessing her with a leering gaze, he offered to keep my secret if I would agree to share her with him. His attitude and vile suggestion rankled, and my fear turned to anger.

She whimpered when he stepped forward and grabbed hold of her, and though he did not harm her, I beat him soundly for touching her at all. With his body and pride wounded, he staggered away from the hut, threatening to bring back reinforcements. I watched him retreat into the vegetation, knowing he would make good on his threat. My superiors would not hesitate to hang me for my treason, and Karwa would suffer a fate worse than death. I could not bear to imagine her subject to the Spaniards' cruelty.

Since the moment I'd whisked her away to safety, I'd known this dreaded day might come. I stared into her eyes as I struggled with the most difficult choice of my life. From my youth I dreamed of a career with the Spanish navy, rising to a position of power and authority, as had my father and his father before him. Yet my earlier dreams seemed empty and meaningless without her at my side.

Karwa seemed to understand my predicament. She stepped forward and placed her hand on my arm, fixing me with a look of trust. Knowing I could not allow her to fall into the hands of the enemy, I pursued my shipmate and took his life in order to save hers. Dios, have mercy on my soul, for I do not feel guilty about the sin I have committed.

~ * ~ * ~ * ~ * ~

Isabel released a long, low whistle as she finished reading the journal entry. "I wasn't expecting to read about murder, but I guess something had to motivate him to get off the island."

Manuel nodded. "And this entry explains why the captain's log I told you about stated two crewmen were missing. The captain assumed they were in cahoots, but really, Rodrigo Velasquez acted alone. The other missing man was the one he killed."

Isabel wrinkled her nose. "Puts a bit of a damper on the romantic story he had going. I think I've lost my enthusiasm for translating today."

"I don't mind stopping either."

Isabel stood and lifted her arms over her head, stretching with the grace of a dancer. "Let's go ask Maria for some fruit juice and sit on the porch for a while. It's stuffy in here."

Ten minutes later, they'd settled into the wicker furniture on the screened porch, and sat sipping their drinks and talking aimlessly. During the last few weeks of working together, Isabel had grown comfortable with his company, so that hanging out with him now gave her the same feeling she got when she slipped into her favorite pair of old blue jeans. Soon the topic of the fire came up.

"Hard to believe the stuff they're saying about that fire at your building."

Isabel sat up straight. "What do you mean? Who are 'they' and what are they saying?"

"You mean you haven't heard?" Manuel cocked his head and gave her a puzzled stare.

"Manuel, I've been here for a week. We don't listen to the radio much, and we don't receive a newspaper. Here at the hacienda we're isolated from the rest of the world. It's not like city life."

"That's for sure." He sighed, looking as if he did not miss modern society in the least.

"Manuel, the fire?"

He shifted in his chair. "The investigators are saying it's a case of arson."

"Who would deliberately set a fire like that?" Isabel wondered

43

aloud. "They killed four people, and they could have burnt down half the city and injured dozens more. The buildings are so close in my part of town, and the people so tightly packed together."

Silent, Isabel pondered the cruelty behind the unnecessary disaster. "Have they released the names of the victims yet?" She had become acquainted with many of the people in her building and dreaded finding out one of her friends had perished in the fire.

Manuel shook his head. "No. They're holding back most of the information while they investigate and put together a list of suspects. I'm surprised they haven't contacted you, Isabel."

"Me? I never even considered they might want to talk to me. They might presume I died in the fire. I don't suppose anyone would know where I'm staying. Maybe I should call them."

"Wouldn't hurt," Manuel agreed. "The newspaper said they're interviewing the former residents, looking for information."

"I'd like to take care of this as soon as possible. Excuse me, Manuel."

Isabel went inside the house and called the police from the phone in the living room. After explaining her situation and awaiting a transfer to the correct extension, Isabel talked with one of the detectives on the case.

"Miss Palmer, we've been hoping to speak to you. Are you available to meet with us?"

"I don't know what I could possibly tell you that you don't already know, but of course, I'd be willing to answer any questions." She gave them her grandmother's address.

"Would tomorrow after lunch work with your schedule?"

"Tomorrow would be fine. Yes, I'll be watching for you."

She set the phone back on the cradle and tried to dismiss the uncomfortable feeling in her gut.

~ * ~ * ~ * ~ * ~

Isabel and Manuel rose early and began work right after breakfast, hoping to translate a fair amount of entries before the police arrived to question Isabel. Excited at having reached the entry about the stolen pearls, Isabel forgot the unpleasantness related to the fire and delved into her work.

July 11, 1505

While I awaited the cover of darkness last night, a terrible and compelling plan filled my mind. As my feelings for Karwa increase, so does my compassion for her people. Simply fleeing the atrocities no longer seems sufficient. I desire to strike at the heart of the greed that drives these men to their evil.

I found the admiral's cabin unoccupied and unguarded, and it seemed to me that Dios had sanctioned my treachery. I stepped inside and laid hold of that which the admiral finds most dear: his treasure. He has set aside a small chest of pearls, the finest and largest harvested off the coast, to make an impressive gift to the royal court upon his return. He hopes to buy favor and promotion with this gift. Many Indians have been sacrificed to fuel the admiral's ambition. From the luxury of his well-appointed quarters, he orders the cruelty and carnage around him. He does not deserve to profit from his sins.

The chest is heavy, and the pearls, stained with the blood of thousands of Karwa's people, hold no value for me. Yet I will take the admiral's hoarded treasure and steal away with Karwa. May the admiral's heart fail him when he discovers my treason.

~ * ~ * ~ * ~ * ~

Isabel was helping clear the lunch dishes from the table when she heard the rumble of an approaching vehicle. Her stomach quivered as she went to the door and admitted the two uniformed men. Maria followed them into the living room and set a tray of refreshments on the coffee table. Nerves making her breathless, Isabel offered the men a seat.

While Maria poured glasses of iced tea and urged little dessert cakes on the officers, Isabel used the opportunity to study her visitors. They were an odd pair if ever she'd seen one. The older of the two carried a thick paunch around his middle. Streaks of silver and gray lined his dark hair. The younger officer appeared around thirty years of age. A wide gap separated his two front teeth, and numerous cowlicks turned his hair in disorderly swirls.

Pearls

As soon as Maria left the room, the older man set his refreshments aside and initiated business. "Miss Palmer, my name is Office Ramirez and this is my partner, Officer Galván. We appreciate your willingness to meet with us. As I'm sure you realize, we are eager to find the person or people who committed the crimes in your apartment building."

Isabel rested her glass of tea on her blue-jean clad leg. "I'm happy to meet with you, though I'm not sure if I'll be of any help."

The men exchanged a glance that sent a jolt of fear through her. *They're hiding something from me.*

Officer Galván spoke next. "Where were you the night of the fire, Miss Palmer?"

"Let's see," she murmured as she collected her thoughts. "I was working at a colleague's apartment until 4:30 or so. Then I ran errands, did a little shopping, and got some dinner too. I believe it was just after seven when I got off *el metro* and found my apartment burning."

"Can you prove you were out of the apartment around six o'clock?" asked Officer Galván.

Isabel's stomach tightened at the suspicion evident in his voice. "I think so," she stammered. "I bought a shirt that night. The bag is still in my room and the receipt is probably inside. Most cash registers record the time of purchase."

"We'll need to see that." The older officer leaned back in his chair and crossed his arms over his ample belly. He gave Officer Galván a nod. "Go with her and find it."

"Now?" she croaked.

"If you don't mind, it's important." His tone stifled any argument.

Isabel led the young officer to her room and dumped her purchase on the bed. A white slip of paper fluttered out, and the officer snatched it up in his hand. As he stared at the receipt, Isabel thought he looked disappointed. "We'll have to confirm this, of course. We'll check with the store's employees and look over their security film to be sure you were the one who made this purchase."

They had to verify it? Did they suspect her of the crime? Unease turning her stomach, she led Officer Galván back to the living room.

"Looks like she was shopping, Ramirez."

Isabel stared hard at the men as she returned to her seat. "What exactly is this about?" she asked, her tone sharp.

"We apologize if we've offended you, Miss Palmer, but you've been a key suspect since the fire."

Isabel's heart lurched hard enough to bruise her ribs. "Me? Why on earth would you suspect me?"

"You lived in apartment 3C, right?"

"Yes."

"The investigation showed the fire started in your apartment, and an accelerant was used. Was anyone in your apartment when you left?"

"No! I live alone and seldom have friends over."

"Did you store any lighter fluid in the apartment, like for a grill or a fireplace?"

"No. I don't have any use for it."

Officer Ramirez scratched his jaw. "Do you know of any reason why someone would target your apartment? Have you made any enemies recently?"

"Not that I can think of, Officer." She heard the tremor in her own voice.

"Though it's impossible to be certain because of the destruction, the investigators found evidence that your apartment had been ransacked. Did you own anything of value?"

"I was a college student until just a few weeks ago. I live simply." Isabel swallowed hard, trying to absorb the shocking news the men had revealed. Had someone targeted her? But what could they possibly want? She didn't have anything of value ... except maybe the journal, but only a handful of people knew about that.

She heard footsteps in the foyer and turned to see Manuel crossing to the door. Had he been lurking out of sight, listening as the police questioned her? Did he know something?

Isabel pulled in a deep, slow breath and tried to calm the panic that threatened to claim her. What had she gotten herself into? Until now, translating the entries and dreaming of chasing after lost treasure had seemed like a grand adventure. She'd never considered it might put her in danger. That was naive of her. Whenever there was something of great value involved, greed had a way of rearing its ugly head. She'd simply have to be more cautious about whom she trusted.

Six

July 13, 1505

Today, Karwa and I reached the mainland. We stood on a hilltop in the light of the setting sun, and there I vowed to share my life and love with her for eternity. In the absence of a priest, Dios himself officiated our wedding ceremony. I believe His blessing will cover our union. The sky burned with shades of fiery color matching the intensity of my passion as I bent to claim Karwa's lips for the first time. Encouraged by the wild sweetness of her response, I carried her to our shelter and made her my wife.

How incredibly romantic! Isabel stared at the translation she held in her hands, but her mind saw the scene he'd vividly painted with his words. "Oh, Manuel, this is my favorite entry so far. Can't you just imagine it? Two people standing alone on a hilltop silhouetted against a fiery sunset, vowing to love one another, not because anyone is watching, but because they've found something wonderful and unexpected."

She glanced up from her notes and found Manuel staring at her, wearing a look she'd not seen before. Her chest clenched, and she gave a nervous laugh to hide her embarrassment. "We females like to indulge in these silly romantic notions from time to time."

He stared at her a moment longer before dropping his gaze to the table. "They're not silly if that's what you want in life."

"Romance?"

"I was referring to love and marriage."

Isabel studied him for a moment, realizing he'd never mentioned any romantic entanglements or even shown interest in the subject. Though he didn't have Raúl's striking good looks,

Pearls

Manuel was clean-cut and attractive, certainly an eligible bachelor the ladies would notice. Figuring they knew one another well enough now, she dared to ask him a personal question. "What about you, Manuel? Are you interested in love and marriage?"

"No."

She thought he answered too quickly. "Why not?"

"I want a career. I want to travel the world and work on archaeology digs."

"Can't you have both?" To Isabel the answer seemed obvious.

"No woman would want to live in a tent half her life, traveling from one dusty, dirty location to the next. At least no woman I've ever met would."

She sensed he'd rather change the topic, but she couldn't resist pushing just a little more. "Maybe you just need to find the right one."

"Maybe I'm too realistic to believe that will ever happen."

His voice had taken on a sharp edge that told her he wanted to drop the topic. But she couldn't resist on last comment on the subject. "Well, I believe a person can have love and a career. I intend to pursue my career, and Raúl can continue his."

Manuel raised his dark eyebrows in question. "He's asked you to marry him, then? You didn't mention that before."

Isabel lifted her chin and stared him in the eye. "Nothing is official yet, but he loves me and I love him. Marriage is the natural course of things so it's just a matter of time."

"Quite sure of yourself, aren't you? You have a lot to learn, little girl. Little *American* girl."

As if he'd aimed his arrow straight at her weakness, his barb pierced the most tender spot in her heart. Isabel bristled at the undeserved insult. *Why must he always remind me that I don't quite fit in? As if I didn't suffer enough of that growing up.* Scenes from her childhood flashed through her mind. Standing in line for the bus alone while the white children huddled and whispered a short distance away. Playing hopscotch by herself on the playground. Sitting at home every Friday and Saturday night because no one wanted to date the girl who was different.

At times she hated her father for making them live in the white, conservative neighborhood where she'd spent her miserable childhood. He never seemed to understand the pain his decision caused her. Though people respected her father too much to behave in an openly cruel manner, they didn't offer her the same respect. Her skin was darker than everyone else's. She could speak two languages, and her mother sent unusual food in her lunchbox. She felt like the oddball, the misfit of the neighborhood, a leper at school.

Though her escape to college had placed her in a multi-cultural atmosphere and eased some of her suffering, Isabel never healed from the wounds of her early childhood. Nor did she outgrow the feelings of inadequacy brought on by her uniqueness. By moving to Venezuela, she had hoped to find a place of acceptance, assuming she could blend into the country of her mother's birth.

But cultural prejudice lived and thrived on other continents too, and he seemed to relish educating her on the subject—that first day in his office when he'd informed her she did not speak with the accent of a Venezuelan, and now by insinuating that she did not understand the culture because of her American background. *Too Venezuelan for America, and too American for Venezuela.*

Furious and wounded, she pushed away from the table and started to leave.

"Isabel, wait!" He stood and grabbed her sleeve before she could escape. "I'm sorry. Look, I don't even know why I said that. I didn't mean anything by it."

Her eyes stinging with tears, she lifted her gaze to meet his. "It's okay. I guess deep down I know I don't really fit in here. You're just stating facts, right?" Jerking away from his touch, she retreated to her room.

~ * ~ * ~ * ~ * ~

Isabel hurried to the pier, hoping she'd not missed Raúl. *He'll be so surprised to see me. How many times has he invited me to go on the yacht with him?* She'd risen early, intending to escort her grandmother to church. But when Magdalena begged off due to a severe headache, Isabel had rushed to the sunrise service and left the church in time to meet Raúl for a day of yachting.

Marina business was conducted in a stately clubhouse, and she stopped to inquire where she would find his yacht.

Pearls

"Slip 79," the attendant told her.

Isabel walked down the weathered planks of the pier, enjoying the briny scent of the ocean breeze and the warm sunshine. "73, 75, 77, here it is." Her gaze roamed over the impressive craft. Raúl obviously took good care of the yacht because every inch of its forty-five foot length sparkled, reflecting the pristine maintenance.

Grasping the railing, she pulled herself up the high step to the deck. The boat rolled and shifted beneath her feet, causing her to grip the rail for support until she grew accustomed to the movement of the vessel. When she found her sea legs, she removed her sandals and strolled the warm planks. The upper deck was empty, and her calls below went unanswered.

Finding a seating niche near the stern, she sat to enjoy the sun while she waited for Raúl to arrive. Seagulls flew radical patterns above the turquoise water, and the waves lapped at the sandy coastline in a steady rhythm that soothed and comforted. It felt good to be out of the house and doing something fun for a change. As much as she loved the research and translation, she was feeling cooped up from all the hours spent hunched over the books. And besides, a weird tension had developed between her and Manuel since their spat. Hopefully a day off would remedy the situation.

After a time, she heard voices and moved toward the bow. Just as she prepared to step out from behind the helm cabin, she caught a glimpse of the new arrivals. Ducking down behind a storage bench, she watched with morbid fascination as Raúl boarded the yacht with a stunning *señorita* in a tiny bikini and a flimsy cover-up that didn't actually cover anything. The woman clung to his arm and pressed herself against his side in an unmistakable invitation. Hot jealousy flared in Isabel's breast.

A gust of wind carried pieces of their conversation to Isabel's ears.

"Yachting is a sport?" the woman asked, staring up at Raúl, her eyes framed by thick, black eyeliner.

"To some it is. Depends on the sportsman."

"What kind of sportsman are you?" she purred, tipping her chin up and presenting her full lips in invitation.

"Let me show you."

Horror swept through Isabel as Raúl turned to the woman and

wrapped his arms around her. Their lips met in a hungry kiss, and his hands roamed along the woman's body, leaving Isabel fiery red with shame and anger. Sickened, she turned away from the scene.

"Come to my cabin, *mi amor*. Let us make some sport of our own before the other guests arrive."

"Let the games begin," the woman answered in a seductive tone.

She heard their footsteps and their intimate whispers fade away as they retreated below deck.

Fool! Stupid, naive fool! She raged as she hastily climbed off the boat and ran back to the car she had borrowed to make the trip into the city. *Abuela* had tried to tell her, but she wouldn't listen. Hurt and humiliated, she shut herself in the car and drove to a quiet stretch of beach where no one would observe her tears.

~ * ~ * ~ * ~ * ~

From his bedroom window, Manuel saw Isabel return just before noon and wondered why she'd come home so early. She'd left him a note that morning, telling him where she intended to spend her day. He hadn't expected to see her until nightfall. Curious, he walked toward the front entrance to greet her. When she entered, she tried to avoid his gaze, but he couldn't help noticing her reddened eyes and pale, distraught face.

"Isabel?"

She rushed past him and fled down the hallway to her room, shutting the door with a resounding thud. He followed and stood outside her room for a few minutes, trying to decide what to do. Ideally, he would find Doña Montez and explain the situation to her. She would be the best choice to aid Isabel with her problems. But the older woman remained in bed with a headache, and Maria, the cook, had given Manuel stern orders not to disturb the matriarch. Concerned, he couldn't just ignore her obvious distress. Drawing a breath for courage, he knocked on Isabel's door.

She answered with a tremulous, "Who is it?"

"Isabel, are you all right?"

"Not really." He heard her sniffle and blow her nose.

"I feel silly talking to your door. Can you come and tell me what's wrong?"

"No."

"Why not?"

"Because it's humiliating."

"Isabel, please don't make me stand out here all night pleading. Just open up and talk to me. We're friends, right? Friends are there for each other. I promise you'll feel better if you talk about it."

He heard her soft footfalls crossing her room and the door swung open. Her face was red and blotchy and she held a wad of tissue in one hand. "If you must know, that … that *horrible* man I've been dating, he…." A sob choked off her words.

"He what, Isabel? Did he hurt you?" Manuel felt a surge of protectiveness as he studied Isabel's sorrowful face, teary eyes, and drooping shoulders. She looked more vulnerable than he'd ever seen her, and he couldn't help but lay a protective hand her shoulder.

To his surprise, she moved into his arms and buried her face against his shoulder. "Raúl was with another woman on the yacht," she sobbed, wetting his shirt with her tears. "They were kissing and touching, and—" She stopped suddenly and looked up into his face. "How could he do that to me? He's been hinting about marriage, then I find him…." Her teeth clenched, and she pounded her fists against his chest in frustration before tears caused her to melt against him again.

He wrapped his arms around her and held her, stroking her hair and back as she struggled with her hurt and pain. The gentle fragrance of her perfume wafted up to his nose and filled him with a heady sensation. He'd noticed how beautiful she was, but he never realized how good she'd feel in his arms. He longed to pull her tighter against him and rest his cheek against her silky hair. *No you don't, Santiago. This is not the time for that.* To suppress the feelings she stirred in him, he tried to focus on a less dangerous subject. *Work. Think of work. The journal project.*

Oh no, the journal project! With dismay, he realized that if Isabel and Raúl broke off their relationship, he would probably lose their only sponsor for the project. And then where would he be? He needed the money to pay his debts, and he needed the recognition he could gain from this discovery to further his career.

He knew he was selfish to worry about money and prestige in the midst of her suffering, but there it was. Reality crashing in hard, he felt like crying right along with Isabel. Raúl's betrayal would likely destroy both of their dreams.

~ * ~ * ~ * ~ * ~

Isabel cringed when she saw Raúl's Mercedes coming down the lane to Casa Grande a week after "the incident." The wound of his betrayal had not diminished. Instead it had festered in her heart, and she dreaded facing him. As she watched from a front window, the car rolled to a stop, and he stepped out, looking the part of a dashing, romantic hero. *Why did you have to ruin what we had, Raúl?* She swallowed the ache in her throat and denied herself the right to cry. *Not in front of him. Nor for him.*

Drawing a deep breath, she braced herself. His knock sounded at the door, but Isabel didn't hurry her step. She lingered in the front room for a few moments, letting him wait and wonder. His second knock brought Maria from the kitchen, but Isabel waved her away, not wanting any witnesses to the humiliating scene that would surely follow. She felt glad *Abuela* had taken Manuel for a guided tour of her tropical garden. She would not need to worry they'd overhear.

Just as he rapped a third time, Isabel opened the door. He put on a winning smile and reached for her. "*Mi amor,*" he crooned.

Mi amor. The pet name was more an insult than an endearment after hearing him call another woman the same thing. Isabel shrugged away from his touch and moved to stand beyond the half-opened door, out of his reach. She greeted him with cold, unwelcoming silence.

His smile faded. "Isabel? Is something wrong?" He placed a well-manicured hand against the door and pressed it open a little wider. "You look pale. Are you sick?"

"You could say that." She turned and walked toward the living room, leaving him to decide whether or not to follow her.

The door clicked shut, and she heard his steps on the tile behind her. In the living room, she avoided the couch and chose a chair made for one. Her choice brought a frown to his features, one she understood all too well. He liked to touch her and hold her. Recent events had helped her realize how much he influenced and controlled her with physical contact. He would pet her and she would melt, push aside whatever concerns she had, ignore her instincts in order to keep his affection—the perfect recipe for a dysfunctional relationship. Well, no more.

Looking mildly perturbed, he seated himself on the end of the couch nearest her. "I have been unable to contact you for days, and you've not returned my messages. Do you know how your absence affects me, Isabel? I am lost without you." He moved to lay a hand on her knee, but she shifted so her legs were out of his reach. Surprise flickered over his features at her silent rebuff. "What is it, *mi amor*? Why do you pull away from me?"

She held her tongue for several minutes, allowing the tension to thicken and fill the air between them.

"Isabel?"

"I saw you."

A dark eyebrow quirked upward in question. He obviously did not understand, and why would he? He had been too busy fondling that woman to notice that they weren't alone on the boat.

"I came to the yacht on Sunday to surprise you, and I saw you with her."

His eyes widened with understanding, then his gaze dropped to the floor. For a moment, he had the decency to look embarrassed. But like all cads, he quickly recovered from the surprise and rallied. "Isabel, I am sorry you witnessed that indiscretion, but you must understand. The other women mean nothing to me."

Anger ripped through her, and every muscle in her body clenched with the surge. "Women? You've been with more than one?"

He held his hands out to his sides and shrugged. "Isabel, this is the way of Venezuelan men. You will be thankful for my experience when you finally surrender to me. I am an accomplished lover."

Her disgust and fury grew. For the first time she saw him for what he was. *You arrogant, unrepentant womanizer!* "So am I supposed to thank you for being unfaithful to me? You did it to please me? Is that what you're saying?" Isabel wanted to claw his eyes out. No wonder he was able to sweep her off her feet so easily. He'd had so much practice, and she was totally naive.

"I am a man. You have denied me your full affections for months. How did you expect me to contain my passions?"

She gasped in outrage and shot to her feet, ready to send him on his way.

His hand snaked out and he grabbed her wrist, pulling her onto his lap. She fought against him, but his arms locked around her like a steel vise.

"I could have seduced you, Isabel, or taken what I wanted at any time. You were putty in my hands. But I chose to respect your wishes, to honor you by waiting."

"Let go of me!" She jerked and flailed, trying to free herself.

"I didn't mind. It seems right that I should wait for the one I want to marry." He hooked one hand behind her head and tried to kiss her while Isabel struggled against his advances. But she was losing the fight. He was so much stronger than she.

"Is there a problem here?"

Raúl's grip loosened at the sound of the deep masculine voice in the doorway. Isabel leapt from his lap and backed away from him as a wounded animal might shrink from a fight. Raúl's gaze shifted from her to the doorway, his soft, brown eyes turning hard in anger. "Mr. Santiago, your timing leaves something to be desired."

Manuel crossed his arms over his chest, glaring. "I'd say I have perfect timing, Raúl."

Isabel felt a surge of gratitude as Manuel stood his ground, playing her protector.

Doña Montez appeared in the arched doorway beside Manuel, her back straight, black eyes flashing with outrage. "How dare you treat my granddaughter this way in my house?" For a seventy-eight-year-old woman, her grandmother proved to be very intimidating when angered.

For the first time, Raúl lost a little of his bravado. "I uh … forgive me, Doña Montez." He looked to Isabel, as if the ask for her help.

Isabel lifted her chin and met his pleading look with a defiant one of her own. "Leave. Now."

He glanced about the room as if looking for an ally. Finding none, he walked toward the door, his back still rigid with pride.

No one spoke until the front door clicked shut and the roar of his engine had faded from their hearing. Only then did her grandmother break the silence, her voice soft with compassion. "The blinders are off and you see with your own eyes now, *Nieta*. But not all men are like Raúl." The old woman turned to stare at Manuel, a slow smile spreading across her aristocratic features. Isabel watched the color creep past Manuel's collar and spread upward over his face.

"I'll leave you two to sort this out." Manuel turned and hurried away.

Tears burned Isabel's eyes and spilled down her cheeks, bringing her *abuela* to her side. When warm, motherly arms pulled Isabel into a comforting embrace, she allowed all the pain of the last week to bubble to the surface and spill out.

Seven

Manuel glanced into the office. Finding it empty, he headed for the living room in search of Isabel. After the scene with Raúl, she had retreated to her bedroom to nurse her wounded heart. Though he hated to burden her with another concern, he needed to make some decisions regarding his future. As much as he would like to, he couldn't live on hopes and dreams. He needed an income. Living off the generosity of an old woman left him feeling emasculated, and he knew he couldn't stay at Casa Grande much longer.

The living room sat empty, leaving Manuel to wonder where she could have gone. Since he'd looked in every room of the house, he decided to continue his search outdoors. He let himself out the front door and found her standing a short distance away. She leaned against a split-rail fence on the other side of the gravel driveway, facing the neatly spaced rows of avocado trees. The wind toyed with the hem of her skirt, causing it to flutter around her knees. The movement drew his attention to her shapely calves, and he studied their smooth, firm lines. His reaction unsettled him, and hoping to avoid further temptation, he forced his gaze to her face.

Gravel crunched beneath his feet as he walked, but if she heard his approach, she didn't acknowledge him.

"Hey, Isabel. Do you have a minute?"

She blinked a few times and glanced his direction. The afternoon sun warmed her features and outlined her full lips when she offered him a faint smile.

"Want to go for a walk with me?" She gestured toward the aisles of the grove. "It's been years since I've explored the orchards."

He moved to her side, resting his elbows on the rail as he studied the trees. The gnarled trunks branched out and mushroomed into full, leafy treetops that met their counterparts to either side, creating arched canopies of shade. "Looks inviting."

"Come on then." She stepped between the rails and bent to maneuver her upper body through to the other side. Manuel followed, his broad shoulders and heavier frame not fitting between the rails as easily as hers.

As they started down the lane of trees, Isabel scanned the area. The forlorn look on her face caused Manuel to wonder if she was searching for her lost happiness.

"You okay, Isabel?"

"I came to Venezuela a few times with my parents in my youth. This country, this place, seemed so magical back then. I was certain I could be happy here."

"You're not happy?"

She sighed, a sound that seemed to testify to the deep weariness in her soul. "I've never been happy anywhere." She stopped and leaned against the trunk of a tree, the rugged background enhancing her soft beauty.

Manuel draped his hand over a low branch and waited.

"My dad is a professor. That's how he met my mom. He came to Venezuela to teach English for a year at Central University. They met and fell in love. But a cross-cultural marriage isn't without its difficulties. His teaching contract ended, and he needed to live where he could find steady work. They ended up in the Northwest. He taught at a junior college for a while then moved into a position at a larger private college after he'd established himself in the field. We lived in a conservative, white neighborhood, and I attended a private school. I can't begin to tell you how difficult that was for me."

"Private school was difficult?"

She laughed, but there was no humor in the sound. "My cultural differences were so exaggerated in that setting. My skin was darker than anyone else's, and I talked with a slight accent because we spoke primarily Spanish at home. My mother used to pack *arepas* and foods the other kids couldn't even pronounce in my lunch sack. Some of the students found me interesting—in the same way a science project is interesting. For a while I thought I could make friends, but in the end they kept me at a distance. I never fit in there, and I don't really fit in here either. Maybe that's why I grew so attached to Raúl. He never made me feel different. Only cherished and accepted."

Color stained her cheeks when she glanced at him. "I don't know why I'm telling you all this. I guess it's part of the pity party I'm throwing for myself. Sorry, I'm not good company." She pushed away from the tree and continued down the path.

As he watched her go, shoulders drooping and steps sluggish, something inside prodded him to try and cheer her. He jogged to catch up. "Nothing wrong with talking about your feelings to a friend."

"Yes, but I'm not talking. I'm whining and moping. I'm mature enough to realize that fact, just not mature enough to quit."

He chuckled. "Would it make you feel better if I whined to you about my parents and my childhood?"

She stopped and faced him, her hands on her hips. "You mean you have parents? You were such a grumpy bear the first few times we met, I was certain you'd simply crawled out of a cave somewhere." Her lips twitched, breaking the stern look she tried to maintain.

He grinned. "I prefer you being ornery over whiney. At least it's a change."

She playfully swatted at his sleeve. "Okay, tell me about your parents."

They resumed their stroll, walking elbow-to-elbow, their arms occasionally brushing together in comfortable companionship. "My father was a simple man, a farmer who inherited a small piece of land from his father. He worked long, hard hours in the field and never really reaped much for his labor. He told me once that, as a boy, he'd dreamed of becoming an architect, but his parents didn't have money for schooling. He settled for farming the land instead.

"My father made sure I went to college. I know he wanted to give me the opportunity he never had. When Dad died a few years ago, he seemed ancient. All those years of struggling to earn a living from the land wore him down, made him old before his time." Manuel paused, feeling regret spring up with fresh energy. "I wish I could have made something of myself before he passed, showed him what his sacrifice meant to me."

Isabel studied him with her intense blue gaze. "What about your mother?"

"She's still on the farm. In fact, she's asked me to come home and run it for her. She can't seem to find a decent foreman, and the place is sinking deeper and deeper into debt." His fingers curled into fists as he battled the argument that raged inside him. "I don't think I'd survive it, Isabel. To me, it would seem like a slow death. A part of me would rot away each day. I'm not made for long-term attachments, not to people or places. The boredom of facing the same scenery and the same tasks day after day would drive me insane. I could hardly bear teaching for a few semesters. Facing a lifetime of drudgery would kill me.

"My father understood that feeling, suffered that exact fate. But he did what life required of him, and now my mother needs that same sacrifice from me. I have to choose between my dreams and my family responsibilities. The choice should be simple, but it's not. Maybe I'm selfish, but I don't want to let go of my career, pitiful as it is."

When he looked down at Isabel, the compassionate expression on her face made him uncomfortable. "So there you have it," he quipped, covering his emotion with sarcasm. "My contribution to our pity party."

The corners of Isabel's lips twitched. "You win. Your sordid history beats mine by a mile."

"A mile? Don't you mean a kilometer? We use metrics here." The attempt at levity fell flat.

She sobered. "I'm glad you trusted me enough to share your story with me."

He stared at the ground, shuffling his feet, kicking up little clouds of dirt. "Think we can talk about something else now?"

They'd reached the edge of the orchard, and Isabel stepped in front of him. "Look over there. See that river in the distance? That's one of the boundaries of the property, and the other is the crest of that far hill."

He stood behind her, trying to follow the direction of her hand as she pointed out the boundaries of the hacienda, but a more inviting sight caught his gaze. She'd fastened her hair up in a clip, leaving the silky skin of her shoulders and neck invitingly bare. Manuel felt his thoughts slipping again, drawn by the feelings of attraction that pulled at him. Before he succumbed to the urge to plant a kiss on the delicate arch of her neck, he placed his hands on her shoulders and turned her to face him.

"Isabel, we need to talk about the project."

Her sculpted eyebrows lifted in question. "Okay. What's up?"

"As much as I want to continue the work we've started, I can't impose on your grandmother's hospitality any longer."

"But we're nearly finished with the translation. Why give up now?"

"Because I assume we've lost our sponsor."

When her mouth dropped open, he knew she'd not considered the ramifications of her break with Raúl. She lifted her hands to her cheeks and moaned. "Oh no. I didn't even think about the project, Manuel. I was so hurt and angry ... and you counted on his support. I did too."

She turned away and began to pace. Manuel waited while she wrestled with her issues, not daring to voice his opinion lest he reveal his desperation.

"Maybe we can still work together." Her finger pressed against her bottom lip as she thought aloud. "I'm mature enough to maintain a working relationship with him despite what happened. He saw this project as a business investment, so I don't see why he wouldn't agree to continue as planned."

She pinned Manuel with a penetrating stare. "What are you thinking?"

"I'll agree to proceed if everyone else does, but I need a firm decision soon. My mother...."

She laid a hand on his arm, her gentle touch setting his nerve endings afire. "Don't give up on your dream yet, Manuel. If your mother's farm can hold out a few more months, we may be able to solve her problems and yours for good. I'll call Raúl tomorrow." Her smile looked confident and reassuring.

He returned her smile with one of his own, deciding that bearing his soul to her hadn't been such a bad idea after all. Sympathy could serve as a powerful motivation.

Pearls

~ * ~ * ~ * ~ * ~

Isabel cradled the phone in her hands, trying to summon the courage to dial the number. The prospect of talking to Raúl terrified her, not because of the pain and hurt he had caused her, but because on some level she feared she still loved him and worried she would succumb to his deceptive charm. Even knowing what he'd done, she couldn't stop her heart from beating erratically at the thought of him. But did she love him, or did she simply need to feel she belonged somewhere and to someone?

Isabel tried to remember the exact emotions she felt when she found him with another woman. As she rolled the memories around in her mind, she realized she was not as upset about his unfaithfulness as she was about what she would lose as a result. She'd depended on him to meet a deep emotional need, and he'd failed her. In the midst of her self-pity, a niggling voice told her she bore part of the blame for misplacing her trust and trying to draw strength and satisfaction from the wrong source.

"I know, Lord. I should depend on You for these things, but I haven't figured out how to do that yet. My head and my heart are in conflict. Please, change my heart, God, because I don't know where to start."

Squaring her shoulders, she picked up the phone and dialed Raúl's work number. "Raúl Guerrero, *por favor*."

Raúl picked up the extension and plunged into an apology before she could say a word. "Isabel, *mi amor*, I am so glad you called me. Before you say anything, I must beg your forgiveness for my lapse in judgment. I have spent much time considering your words, and I realize I have wronged you. Can you forgive me?"

Isabel bit her trembling lip and swallowed down the emotions lodged in her throat. He always knew just the words to touch her heart. His ability to play on her emotions had caused her trouble before. This time she would proceed with more caution.

"I forgive you, Raúl, but you have to understand, I can't forget. What you did hurt me deeply."

His disappointed sigh carried through the phone line. "And I will regret causing you pain until the day I die. Tell me how to repair the damage I've done. I cannot bear the thought of spending a lifetime apart from you, Isabel. You are the only woman I've ever really loved."

At that moment, Isabel felt grateful for the miles of distance between them. He sounded so sincere, so bereft, that she might have been tempted to dismiss the whole matter in order to regain the blissful perfection of their earlier relationship. But deep down she knew they could never go back.

"What happened between us changed my feelings. I won't subject myself to the pain of living with an unfaithful man. I want love, and true love comes with trust and loyalty and commitment. I don't want to spend my life wondering and worrying if you're romancing other women. I don't want to end up bitter and angry like your mother."

"My mother has nothing to do with us!" His earlier penitence evaporated, replaced by anger.

"Raúl, whenever a man cheats on a woman or vice versa, someone ends up suffering the way your mother did all those years. Those stolen moments of secret passion are never worth the final price. In the end someone always pays, usually with a piece of their heart, and I don't want anything to do with it."

A long silence followed her statement, and she wondered if anything she said had had an influence on him.

When he cleared his throat and spoke, his voice sounded carefully controlled. "You have given me much to think about, Isabel. In my country, men are judged by their *machismo*. We are expected to have relationships with multiple women. I never considered that my way of life would disturb you. I will reconsider."

His statements forced Isabel to recognize the vast differences between them. For all his claims to a belief in and respect for God, he appeared completely ignorant of godly principles and values. Yet Isabel couldn't place the blame solely at his feet. She'd chosen to involve herself with a man before ensuring his beliefs matched her own before she'd really prayed about the decision. She had suffered for her arrogance. "I'm glad, Raúl. I truly believe there's a better way to live, and I hope you'll experience that someday."

"So what happens now, Isabel? Will I see you again?"

His question reminded her of the reason for her call. "I think that depends on you. Our romantic days are over, but we had a business arrangement too. I'm willing to continue working with you on the journal project if you're still willing to sponsor Manuel and I."

"Of course. I would not consider backing out for even a moment. I believe you have a good chance of finding the pearls, and I want to help. In fact, I'd like to hear a progress report. Could I come out to the hacienda and talk with you?"

Isabel recognized bait when she saw it, and she refused to fall into his trap. "Manuel and I would be happy to update you." She stressed Manuel's name, hoping Raúl would realize she had no intention of spending time alone with him. Keeping her heart under control would be hard enough without fending off his romantic overtures. She knew all too well how persuasive he could be.

"Manuel. Yes." Raúl didn't sound too happy. "When would you like to meet?"

"How about next week? We should have the journal fully translated by then, and we can base any plans we make on all the information available."

"Very good. I'll call you next week to set up a definite day and time."

With business finished, all that remained unsaid was goodbye. Isabel felt the significance of this farewell. More than just the end of a conversation, it represented the official close of her relationship with Raúl. From this moment forward, they would share no interests beyond business.

Drawing a deep breath, she summoned the courage to sever their ties. "Well, you probably need to get back to work."

"Yes, I suppose." He sounded as reluctant as she felt.

"Goodbye, Raúl." The finality of the words settled deep into her heart.

"Goodbye, *mi amor.*"

~ * ~ * ~ * ~ * ~

Raúl set the phone in its cradle and smiled. Women. He knew how to persuade them, to charm them, to control them. Isabel would present a challenge, but a worthwhile one. While he listened to her protests, he'd also heard the longing in her voice. She wanted him to woo her back. Why else would she insist on continuing the project with him? She couldn't bring herself to break away completely.

He would play the role she'd handed him, and in the end, he would win back her her heart. And the victory would be sweet.

Pearls

Eight

Isabel entered the kitchen, feeling as fresh as the sunshine that had poured through her window while she'd dressed. "Morning, all." She flashed a brilliant smile to Manuel, Maria, and her grandmother.

Manuel glanced up from his food and gave her a questioning look. "You look nice." He scooted his chair over to make room for her at the table. "Special occasion?"

She glanced down at the cream-colored capris and soft coral t-shirt she'd put on that morning. "No. I woke up in a good mood and felt like dressing to match."

"I don't know how you ladies do it." Manuel shook his head in mock pity. "You have to match your clothes, shoes, purses, makeup, and now you tell me you have to match your mood too? I'd never get it right."

Isabel nudged him with her elbow as Maria set a plate in front of her. "You know what I mean, you … you man."

His smile sent a wave of anticipation through her. Had he always been so adorable and fun? Isabel opened her breakfast *arepa* and breathed in the delicious aroma. "Mmm. Ham and cheese. My favorite." She closed her eyes and said a quick prayer.

"What are you young people planning to do today?" her grandmother asked as Isabel lifted the food to her mouth.

Isabel nodded to Manuel, signaling him to answer since her mouth was full.

"I thought I'd spend most of the day working. We need to finish the translating soon. Though I enjoy Maria's cooking, I can't stay here forever. I have other obligations to consider."

Maria, who stood at the counter kneading a fresh batch of dough, tossed a coy smile over her shoulder. The flirtatious behavior didn't escape Isabel's notice, and she felt a rise of irritation. *Maria's at least ten years older than Manuel. Would he even be interested in her?*

She turned to study him, as if seeing him for the first time. Manuel's eyes were the deep, rich brown of the fresh-tilled soil on her grandmother's land. In contrast to Raúl's finely sculpted features, Manuel appeared more rugged and durable—handsome in his own way. He kept his black hair cropped short, and he'd recently grown a short, thin mustache. Isabel liked the new addition to his face, thinking it made him look more masculine, if that was possible.

His glance shifted her way, and he grinned. "Are you looking at something in particular, Isabel?"

Embarrassed, she averted her gaze. "Your mustache is new."

He reached up and smoothed his fingers over his lip. "Yes. Do you like it?"

"It's fine," she murmured, hoping to sound casual despite the sudden rise in her pulse rate. Isabel felt his eyes on her but refused to look his way.

"Well then, I think I'll get started on our work." He stood and carried his plate to the sink. "Delicious meal, Maria. Thank you." On his way out of the kitchen, he stopped behind Isabel's chair. "Will you be joining me?"

"Yes, when I'm finished with breakfast. I intend to work all day too."

His fingertips brushed over her shoulder as he left. "I'll save you a chair."

~ * ~ * ~ * ~ * ~

Manuel scanned the same page three times and still had no clue what he was reading. Giving up, he laid the book aside and allowed his thoughts to drift where they chose. They went to Isabel. He couldn't help but wonder about the look he'd noticed in her eyes at breakfast. Did he see interest, or even attraction?

This isn't the time for a romantic entanglement, especially not with her, he reasoned. The Raúl fiasco was still fresh in her memory. He had no desire to be her rebound guy, nor did he have any use for a relationship. A woman would interfere with his career plans. He still had many years of work ahead of him before his career was established and his achievements recognized. He needed to pay his dues, and a woman would only hinder him. He'd accepted long ago that his career choice required him to live a solitary life.

His decision to remain a bachelor was based on more than just his own selfish interests. He wouldn't subject a woman to the unreasonable demands his life would impose on a marriage, either living apart for long periods or roughing it in crude accommodations on a dig site. No woman would enjoy that. And even if he found a wife who would travel with him, children would likely follow. He couldn't imagine raising kids in that lifestyle. Some of his colleagues had opted for boarding school, or simply left a wife at home and only visited the family on occasion. God never intended families to live that way, and Manuel knew it.

Occasionally, someone beautiful and intelligent like Isabel came along to capture his interest and test his convictions. Twice he'd started to care for a woman and consider a more permanent relationship, but each time, his career choice created a conflict of interest. Both attempts ended in heartbreak for him and the female involved. After that, he had sworn off women.

He liked Isabel too much to involve her in a romance destined for failure. Besides, he didn't need a wife and children. His career would offer him fulfillment. Isabel needed a man who could make her happy.

Yet, the thought of her with another man curdled the breakfast in his stomach. As if his thoughts had summoned her, she appeared in the doorway. "Hi," he said, patting the chair beside him. "Saved you a seat."

She came and sat beside him, bringing with her the pleasant scent of her perfume. He shifted in his chair, moving closer to enjoy the fragrance.

"Before we get to work, can we talk?" Isabel's gaze met his, and her vulnerable expression caused his firm resolve to crumble.

He wanted to smooth his fingers over her cheek and chase away her troubled look with a kiss. Instead, he crossed his arms over his chest to keep from touching her. "Sure, Isabel. What's on your mind?"

"I spoke to Raúl yesterday."

Manuel's stomach tightened in reaction to the sadness in her voice. Or was his desperation to retain Raúl's support causing the indigestion? Not wanting to appear callous, he chose to direct his question toward her welfare and let her bring up the sponsorship when she felt ready. "Did you settle the issues between you?"

"We talked, but I don't think we settled anything. I told him I wouldn't date him anymore. I can't trust him, and I don't want to live with doubt and suspicion. His views about marriage and fidelity are very different than mine."

"The world is full of men like him. You deserve better."

She offered him a wan smile. "If a crop of good men exists, I've never been able to find them. I think my radar has faulty wiring. I can't seem to tell the difference between the good ones and the bad ones. Maybe I'm not meant to marry."

"Don't give up hope just yet. God will send you the right man in His perfect time. You're a beautiful, caring woman, and you'll make some lucky guy very happy."

A pale blush bloomed on her cheeks, and she studied the floor intently. "I'm not sure why I'm talking to you about this. The sordid details of my love life don't really pertain to our business arrangement."

He gave in to his urge and reached out to cup her cheek in one hand. Her creamy skin felt even smoother than he'd imagined. "I'd like to think we've become friends over the last month. You can talk to me about anything, anytime." He trailed his fingers along her jaw, enjoying the delicate lines and textures he encountered.

Her eyes widened in surprise, and she searched his face. Embarrassed at having revealed more than he intended, he withdrew his hand and turned to the work spread out on the table. "So what about all of this? Is Raúl still willing to support us financially?"

"He is." Isabel scooted her chair closer to the table and picked up a pencil. "He'll call us next week for a progress report. Hopefully by that time, we'll have some solid leads."

"Not if we don't get to work," he said in an unintentionally gruff voice. He didn't want to sound angry, but he didn't know any other way to disguise the emotion she stirred in him.

If Isabel noticed his discomfort, she didn't show it. "Bet I can translate faster than you can." She flashed him an impish grin, then pulled a notepad toward her and bent over her work.

Manuel picked up the reference book he'd been reading before she arrived and tried in vain to concentrate on the pages.

~ * ~ * ~ * ~ * ~

July 26, 1505

The slavers prowl the shores of the mainland with regularity. To avoid them, Karwa and I have moved inland and taken shelter in a great cavern. A river flows through our underground city, providing us with water for drinking and bathing. My love for Karwa deepens with each sunrise. The cave lacks the comforts and amenities of a real dwelling, yet Karwa manages to provide the feeling of home wherever we rest our heads. In her tenderness, she has become my home, and so long as she remains by my side, my joy is complete.

~ * ~ * ~ * ~ * ~

Later that afternoon, Manuel flipped through the journal's pages, jumping several entries ahead of their work. "Look at this, Isabel. The entries are less frequent after they reach the mainland. He wrote only a dozen or so over the course of the next year. Let's see …." He scanned several pages, looking for the information he needed. "I'd say they stayed at this cave location for a while. Maybe a year."

"You sound excited. Is this significant?"

"Possibly. People follow a pattern when they hide valuables. They choose a familiar place, study the location for a while, look for a good hiding spot, and make sure no one else is nosing around the area before they finally hide their possessions."

Isabel rested her chin on her hand. "That makes sense. I wouldn't stash something precious just any old place. I'd feel more secure if I took time to evaluate my options and make my decision. A person can't do that if he's just passing through."

"Exactly. So we want to look closely at the areas where Rodrigo and Karwa lived for longer periods of time. We'll most likely find our clues there."

"This cave they mention, do you think we can find it?"

"I think I already know which one they're talking about. Only a few caves in Venezuela contain underground rivers. Maybe the next few entries will give us more clues, but *La Cueva de la Quebrada El Toro* is nearest the shore. It's near La Taza, about three hundred kilometers west of here."

"The Cave of the Bull's Ravine? I think I've heard of it. Isn't it part of a national park now?"

"Yes. Grab a fresh sheet of paper and take notes, Isabel. This location is worth some preliminary investigation. When we've finished with these next few entries, maybe we can find some information about the known history of the cave on the Internet. The university gave me access to some online archives."

"Sounds good to me." Isabel's blue eyes twinkled with excitement, and she flashed a smile that sent his heart knocking around his insides.

Manuel scrambled to gather his thoughts before they completely escaped his control. She definitely had a way of interrupting his concentration.

~ * ~ * ~ * ~ * ~

Isabel studied the skyline of Caracas looming on the horizon as Manuel drove them into the city the following week. Caracas was not unlike New York or other large cities in the United States, except for the palms and tropical vegetation that graced the medians and green areas in the middle of the concrete jungle. The ever-present heat challenged the car's air conditioner to maintain a comfortable temperature. She smoothed a hand over her neck where beads of perspiration gathered.

She was uncomfortable, but more so because of their mission than the weather. They would meet with Raúl later in the afternoon, but first they needed to visit the police station. One of the detectives who had come to talk to her shortly after the fire had called and asked her to come in for more questioning. Apparently, they had stumbled onto some new leads, and they wanted to talk with her about them.

The police station bustled with activity, telephones and computers providing background noise to the conversations of officers and their charges. With Manuel at her side, Isabel waited her turn at the front desk and asked for directions to Ramirez's office.

When she stepped into the area that housed the detectives,

Officer Ramirez looked up from his desk and smiled. "Señorita Palmer. Thank you for coming." After offering Manuel a chair in the waiting room and giving him a cup of coffee, Officer Ramirez led her to a smaller room where they could speak in private.

He didn't waste any time getting to the point. "We found an eyewitness who saw this man letting himself into your apartment." The detective slid a mug shot toward Isabel for her inspection. "Recognize him?"

Isabel lifted the photo and studied the rugged face. A large man with greasy hair and a cruel sneer on his lips stared back at her. The coldness in his piercing black eyes made Isabel's skin crawl. What could he possibly want with her or her apartment? Thoughts of the journal flashed through her mind, and she wondered again if there was a connection. But she had only mentioned the book to a handful of people, and she thought each was trustworthy. It couldn't be that.

She handed the photo back to the officer. "I'm sorry, sir, but I don't know the man. I'm sure I've never seen him before."

The officer nodded. "Unfortunately, we know him well. He's a member of an organized crime ring we'd love to bust. They deal in drugs, black market goods, stolen valuables—anything illegal and lucrative. Do you have any idea why someone like that would be interested in you, Señorita Palmer?"

Isabel pressed her fingers to her mouth, fear prickling in her chest. Organized crime? This situation was getting more serious by the minute. "I'm sorry, I don't. Am I in danger?"

The officer took a long swig of his coffee. "Until we know why he was in your apartment, we can't really say. Could have been a coincidence or mistaken identity. Then again, maybe not. You'll let us know if you think of anything, won't you?"

Isabel tugged her purse strap onto her shoulder as she rose to go. "Yes, if you'll let me know about any developments in the case."

The officer followed her to the door, pausing before he opened it. "Just in case this wasn't coincidence, you'd do well to exercise caution. Keep your eyes and ears open. If you see anything suspicious, call us."

"I will." Her heels clicked against the tile floor as she walked to the waiting area where she'd left Manuel. When she poked her head in the doorway, he rose to greet her.

With a gentle hand on her elbow, he steered her toward the front doors and the parking lot beyond. "So, how did it go? Any new leads?"

The officer's warning rang fresh in her mind, and she wondered if Manuel's interest stemmed from friendly concern or something more sinister. With fear rolling around inside her, she hurried ahead of him. "We can talk about all that later. Let's just focus on business right now. Raúl's probably waiting."

Nine

Manuel couldn't help but notice the lines of anxiety creasing Isabel's forehead. The meeting with the detectives had obviously disturbed her, but she seemed reluctant to talk to him. Unable to reassure her with words, he resigned himself to escorting her in silence.

They parked and walked toward the little coffee house in Sabana Grande where they'd agreed to meet Raúl. As they approached, Isabel stopped and clutched at Manuel's arm. "You can't leave me alone with him," she blurted. He felt her fingernails dig into his flesh through his cotton sleeve and realized how difficult this meeting would be for her.

He gently pried her fingers loose and moved her hand into his. Entwining his fingers with hers, he gave her hand a reassuring squeeze. "I promise, I'll stay with you the whole time. It'll be all right, Isabel."

For a moment, she followed along like a scared child clinging to a parent for support. Then, as if she realized her lapse of courage, she snatched her hand away from his and crossed her arms defensively over her chest. "I just don't want to be alone with him. I'm not sure he's accepted our break up, and he may try to charm me out of my convictions."

"Charm is prohibited," Manuel repeated to let her know he'd heard and understood her concerns.

"Yes. No touching, either. You'll run interference for me, won't you?"

"Interference at your service, ma'am." He grinned and offered her a wink.

Isabel stopped walking and propped her hands on her hips. "This is serious, Manuel. If you're going to treat it like a game, then

Pearls

I'm leaving."

"You can't leave. I drove you here, remember?"

Defiance flashed across her features, and she turned on her heel and started away from him. He reached out and grabbed her elbow before she could escape. "Isabel, I didn't mean to anger you. I was just trying to lighten the mood. You look like you're on the edge of an anxiety attack."

She stared at the pocket on his shirt. "I thought I could handle this, but now I'm not sure."

Manuel stood beside her, caressing her arm while she gathered herself. "Raúl can't hurt you unless you let him. I'll do what I can to keep the pressure off you. If the meeting becomes too difficult, just excuse yourself and go to the ladies' room. I can handle Raúl myself."

She released a long breath and nodded. "Thanks, Manuel. I owe you one."

He placed a finger beneath her chin and urged her to look at him. "We're friends, Isabel. It's no problem."

The interior of the coffee house boasted modern decor in subtle neutrals, and the low lighting provided a relaxing atmosphere. Polished chrome countertops lined the coffee bar, and tall potted plants added color and warmth to the setting. Raúl waved to them from a booth near the back, and they headed his direction. Manuel sensed Isabel's tension as they neared the table.

Raúl stood to greet them, his gaze sweeping over Isabel, taking in the breezy summer dress she wore. "Isabel. How lovely you look." When he bent and tried to kiss her cheek, she stepped backward, bumping into Manuel's chest. Manuel reached out to steady her, placing a hand on each shoulder.

When she didn't move away from Manuel's touch, Raúl frowned. "Come, *mi amor*. Sit by me."

Isabel glanced to the booth then turned and rolled her eyes at Manuel. "I need to use the ladies' room."

As she hastened away, Manuel glanced at his watch and chuckled. *She lasted all of thirty seconds. That didn't take long.* He sat down, fully aware that Raúl hadn't bothered to acknowledge him yet.

Raúl stared after Isabel's retreating form, wearing a look of frustration. When she disappeared behind the restroom door, he stalked to the coffee bar.

Manuel sighed, thinking maybe he was crazy. No amount of money was worth the hassle these two were sure to cause him.

He waited several minutes in solitude until Isabel finally returned.

"Scoot over," she hissed, urging him to make room for her beside him. "I don't want to sit by Raúl."

Obliging her, Manuel shifted to make room. As soon as she took her place beside him, Raúl appeared, carrying two steaming mugs of cappuccino. He set one cup in front of Isabel and grazed her cheek with his fingers before taking his seat opposite her. "I bought you a hazelnut—your favorite, Isabel."

"Where's Manuel's coffee?"

Raúl shrugged, not even looking Manuel's direction. "I didn't know what he liked."

Isabel's gaze turned hard, and she pushed the mug toward Manuel. "I quit drinking coffee, Raúl. Manuel can have mine."

Amusement turning his lips, Manuel lifted the mug and tasted the bittersweet brew. "Mmm. Thanks, Raúl. Hazelnut is my favorite too."

Raúl made eye contact with Manuel, staring as if he were an apparition that suddenly appeared at the table. Manuel couldn't resist the urge to wink. His carefree attitude only increased Raúl's frustration, and for some reason, seeing irritation plastered across Raúl's face gave Manuel great pleasure.

As they sat in awkward silence, Manuel couldn't help but appreciate the comedy of the situation. Raúl had come solely to pursue Isabel. Isabel, in turn, sought protection and support from Manuel, which he gladly provided. Yet Manuel couldn't bring himself to release her from the painful obligation of dealing with Raúl because they needed the money. Together they formed a ludicrous love triangle.

My life has turned into a soap opera, he thought with resignation. Sighing, he took another swig of the coffee.

~ * ~ * ~ * ~ * ~

Isabel did not intend to sit in the booth suffering Raúl's unwanted attention a single moment longer than necessary. The sooner they talked business, the sooner she could leave. "Raúl, Manuel and I have finished translating the journal, and we have an update for you. Would you like to hear it?"

"Of course, *mi amor*. We can discuss whatever you like."

His tone suggested he only intended to humor her, and Isabel bristled at the condescension. "Manuel and I have translated all but a few Indian words. We couldn't find definitions for all of them, but it's clear that Rodrigo Velasquez did not directly reveal the whereabouts of his treasure."

Raúl nodded, and Isabel felt certain he faked the look of disappointment.

"However, we found that Rodrigo and Karwa lived for long periods in three different locations. He included enough description of these places to allow us to identify them with reasonable certainty."

"Why does it matter where they lived?" Raúl asked.

Isabel looked to Manuel, deferring to him to make this explanation.

Manuel set his coffee down and leaned his elbows on the table. "Past finds of buried treasure have taught us that people usually hide their valuables in a place intimately familiar to them. Rodrigo did not mention the hiding place of his treasure. However, it stands to reason that he would have left it in one of three locations, possibly with the intention of returning and recovering it later after his treason was forgotten. Then he could safely use the pearls for trade."

"This doesn't seem like much to go on." Raúl sounded skeptical.

"There's more. The final line of the journal states that he buried his treasure in his home. We don't know which of the three places he's referring to, but it's possible that if we find and explore the areas they lived in, we will uncover the treasure or at least other clues. With the modern technology used in archaeology today, we could fully explore the areas with a minimum of bother and expense."

"What will this adventure cost me?"

Seeing Raúl's skepticism, Isabel jumped back into the conversation, knowing she stood a better chance of convincing him than Manuel did. "We've been gathering figures and putting together a cost sheet. We can rent most of the equipment for a more reasonable price than if we purchased it. And Manuel and I are prepared to forego the luxuries and make do with simple accommodations. Equipment rentals, camping gear, and basic supplies add up to about twenty grand for a two-month search."

Isabel held her breath while Raúl sat in pensive silence. If he said yes, she and Manuel could have their gear packed and ready to go by the end of the week. She needed to put some distance between herself and her problems, namely Raúl. Time apart would be good medicine for them both.

Raúl reached across the table and took Isabel's hand before she had a chance to pull it away from him. "I would not deny you anything you asked, Isabel. Do you want to search for the pearls? Would it make you happy?"

His touch unsettled her, but she forced herself to endure it. Now that she'd distanced herself from him emotionally, she saw him much more clearly. She'd once admired his elegance and influence, but now he appeared base and conniving. The games he played to control her and his need to maintain a position of superiority irritated her.

Now he was turning his unscrupulous behavior on her. Well, if he wanted her to ask for his assistance, she could do that. A simple request for help seemed a small price to pay to rid herself of him for two months. She pushed back the inner turmoil and forced herself to give a polite answer. "Yes, Raúl. This project is very important to me. I'd like very much to proceed with our plans."

"Then it's settled. I'll have a contract delivered tomorrow, and the funds will be available by the time you sign it. I only ask that you keep receipts and records for my financial reports."

Isabel flipped her hand over and grasped his in a businesslike handshake. "Great! We can handle that. Now, Manuel and I have some work to do, so we need to go." She slid out of the booth, hoping Manuel would take the hint and follow.

Manuel moved slower than she would have liked, but he did rise. Standing by the table, he paused and offered his hand to Raúl. "I appreciate your support, Raúl. If you leave us instructions, we'll be happy to contact you with updates on our search."

Raúl's eyes held a cunning glint. "That won't be necessary, Manuel. I'll be coming with you."

Isabel's mouth dropped open with surprise. "What?" she exclaimed.

"I have a vested interest in this project in more ways than one." His eyes flashed over her with possessive intent. "I intend to accompany the two of you and oversee my investments."

Isabel's stomach seemed to fold in on itself. *He laid the trap and we walked right into it.* She tried to gauge Manuel's reaction, but he'd masked his response with a carefully neutral expression.

"We'll be in touch," Manuel said. Suddenly in a hurry to leave, he propelled her toward the door with a firm hand on her back. When they were out of Raúl's earshot, Manuel expelled a noise that could only be described as a growl.

"My sentiments exactly," she agreed. The car ride home was long and quiet.

~ * ~ * ~ * ~ * ~

He didn't want to make the call, but he knew that if he didn't, he'd have even more trouble on his hands. Forcing himself to the task, he dropped a coin into the payphone.

A gruff voice answered the other end of the line.

"Listen, I'm calling to let you know I'll be out of touch for a while."

"You're not trying to escape your commitments, are you?"

"No, of course I wouldn't try anything so foolish." A sweat broke out on his forehead.

"Good because your grace period is almost up. When can I expect a payment?"

"As soon as this bit of business is complete, I'll have your payment in full, I swear."

"I certainly hope so, for your sake." The line clicked, cutting off the connection.

He stared at the phone, willing his panicking heart to slow to a normal rhythm. "Yes, I understand. My life depends on it."

~ * ~ * ~ * ~ * ~

"So, you will be going away soon?"

Isabel smiled. Doña Montez never bothered with trivial small talk. Somehow Isabel had guessed that her grandmother had a mission when she had suggested a walk in the garden. With arms linked, they strolled the flagstone paths, enjoying the sweet fragrances and vivid colors of the tropical blooms. "Yes, *Abuela*. Just for a month or two."

"Your decision to interrupt your schooling surprised me."

Isabel patted her grandmother's arm. "The university will be there when I return. Right now, I need a change."

"Something has been bothering you, I think."

"That business with Raúl was pretty upsetting to me."

"I think something was disturbing you before that."

Isabel sighed. Her grandmother was so perceptive—sometimes too perceptive for comfort. "You're right. I've struggled with discontent for years. I've never really felt like I belonged anywhere, you know? I'm always an outsider."

Her grandmother nodded. "Every heart needs to find a place of belonging."

"So, you understand, *Abuela*?"

"More than you know."

The old woman's cryptic smile puzzled Isabel. "I think you're talking riddles again."

Doña Montez winked. "Do you think you will find what you are searching for on this journey?"

"I hope so. Are you worried about me?"

Her grandmother cocked her head to one side, her face pensive as she considered her answer. "I trust Manuel to keep you safe."

"What about Raúl? I'm sure he'll look out for me too."

Her grandmother snorted, as if the idea was preposterous. "He will have enough trouble taking care of himself. You will depend on Manuel for support if you are smart."

The comment piqued Isabel's curiosity. "You never liked Raúl, did you, *Abuela*? We never had a chance to discuss my relationship with him. I'm sorry I didn't listen to you sooner, but I'd like to hear your thoughts now."

"Your Raúl, he is beautiful to look at, but inside, he has no substance. This is the way of many men, not just in this country, I think. Beauty and wealth are double-edged swords. They can offer tremendous advantages to those who wield them correctly; however, skill with a sword does not make one a victor."

Pearls

"What are you saying, grandmother?"

"Success can be measured in many ways. God measures a man by his fruit—fruit of the Spirit, that is. Despite Raúl's many favorable attributes, he lacks godly character. You could not see it at the time, *Nieta*. You looked with your eyes, and his beauty deceived you. Now you know to look with the discerning eyes of the Spirit. They are more reliable than your natural vision."

Though her grandmother spoke with compassion, Isabel felt the sting of the rebuke. "I was having trouble adjusting at school. I wanted so much to make friends and feel like I belonged. I think I let my loneliness get the best of my judgment. When Raúl came along, I was vulnerable." Isabel fell silent, still wrestling with the fresh wounds of her failed relationship.

Her grandmother seemed to sense her need for solitude and remained quiet for a while. After they rounded the back corner of the garden and began the walk back to the house, she spoke. "Do you think this Manuel has the character to match his attractive face?"

Isabel pondered her grandmother's words in silence for a moment. "I don't know, *Abuela*. I guess I haven't really talked to him much, at least not about personal issues. He's shared a little about himself, but we mostly talk about the journal or archaeology."

"Perhaps he feels reluctant to discuss personal matters with you because of your relationship with Raúl."

"Maybe."

"You should talk to him sometime, Isabel. I mean really talk. You would like him very much."

"Why do you say that?"

"He is a good man. Loyal, hard-working, committed. And he is a Christian."

Isabel stopped near a rose arbor and turned to face her grandmother. "How do you know all of this, *Abuela*?"

"While you hide in your room, he sits in the kitchen and talks with me. Sometimes we walk in the garden, or he drives me to the store. I enjoy his company. You would too." Her grandmother's lips parted in a mischievous smile.

"Just what are you saying, *Abuela*?"

"You have my blessing if you want to date him, Isabel."

A hot flush climbed Isabel's neck and face. "I don't think I'm ready for another relationship, and even if I was, what makes you think Manuel would be right for me?"

Doña Montez lifted her chin to a defiant angle. "I am old, but I am not blind. I see what you refuse to acknowledge."

They resumed their walk and soon the back wall of Casa Grande came into sight. Bending, Isabel laid a kiss on her grandmother's cheek. "I love you, *Abuela*, even when you talk in riddles."

Her grandmother tipped back her head and laughed. "You will see when you are ready, Isabel."

Pearls

Ten

Isabel hefted the last box into her arms and carried it to Manuel, who arranged the supplies in the cargo bed of one of the jeeps they'd rented for the journey. Still groggy from rising before dawn, she yawned as she handed over her load.

"Is this the last one?" He lifted the box from her grasp as if it weighed nothing. Since meeting her for breakfast at five o'clock in the morning, he'd shown no signs of weariness or fatigue. Isabel might find his energy irritating if she were awake enough to care. Rubbing the sleep from her eyes, she ambled toward the house, wanting to nurse a cup of black coffee while they waited for Raúl to arrive.

"Wait, Isabel. I need your help tying down the supplies." He held a coiled length of rope aloft. "I don't want our gear bouncing out of the jeep when we hit the rougher roads."

"Okay, sure." When she walked back toward him, she stumbled over a root hidden by the grass and fell against Manuel's chest, clutching at him to steady herself.

His arms wrapped around her as his deep, pleasant laughter met her ears. "Falling for me, are you?"

She lifted her face until she met his gaze. The look in his eyes set her pulse throbbing in her neck, and embarrassment about her clumsiness faded away. The tenderness in his eyes wreaked havoc with her heart.

When she didn't move to break the contact, he tightened his embrace, his gaze shifting from her eyes to her lips. Isabel felt the breath leave her lungs as he lowered his face toward hers. Wanting to experience his kiss, her eyes fluttered shut, and she surrendered herself to the moment.

The blare of a horn startled them both, and they jumped apart as Raúl's car skidded to a stop beside them. His eyes blazed fire.

Raúl climbed from his car in silence, though the looks he flashed their direction spoke volumes. With tight, jerky movements, he pulled his suitcase from the trunk and thrust it into Manuel's hands. "Go pack this in the jeep."

Manuel seemed to take the incident in stride, appearing almost amused at Raúl's behavior. Isabel did not feel so charitable. The condescending way her ex-boyfriend ordered Manuel around infuriated her, and she wondered how long the two men would be able to work together before Raúl's attitude caused a fight. She felt partly responsible for the animosity, yet helpless to amend the problem.

Men! Maybe I'm crazy for even considering this trip.

As soon as Manuel turned his back, Raúl grasped her hand and pulled her out of hearing distance. He turned her to face him, his hands caressing her upper arms. Before her eyes, his angry mask transformed into one of sympathy and concern. "Has he been bothering you, *mi amor?*"

Isabel stepped back, moving out of range of his touch. "Who? Manuel?"

"Don't worry, Isabel. I won't let him pressure you in any way. I'll have a talk with him when we reach our first location."

She scowled at Raúl. "I think you misunderstood."

"I misunderstood nothing," he snapped. "Manuel is trying to gain your affections so he can use them to his advantage. If we find this treasure, you stand to gain a great deal of money. Men like him, *los pobres*, the poor, they will do anything to attain wealth, and that includes taking advantage of a woman's heart."

"Is that what you're trying to do, Raúl? Are you using me?"

"No!"

Isabel had to give him credit. The outrage reflected on his face looked genuine.

"I love you, Isabel. I only want to see you safe and happy. As your fiancé, caring for you is my duty."

Isabel shook her head in disgust. "You were never my fiancé, Raúl, and we are no longer even dating. So I'd say your duty is to mind your own business."

She tried to stalk away, but he grabbed her arm and pulled her back. "I can see that Manuel has confused you. I was unwise to allow you to spend so much time with him these last weeks."

Isabel's shoulders tensed with fury. "*Allow* me? Since when are you in charge of my life? I will do what I want, when I want."

He smiled down at her as he might a small child. "Calm down, Isabel. Hysterics won't solve our problems."

"*I* don't have any problems, Raúl. *You* do. That's why we're not dating anymore." A hundred angry and cruel comments rushed into her mind, but she clamped her lips together and refused to say more, recognizing that despite her anger she wanted to conduct herself in a manner that upheld her values.

Manuel chose that moment to interrupt their conversation. "Hey, you guys ready to go?" he called from his position near the jeeps.

"Yes!" Isabel hurried to his side before Raúl had a chance to protest.

Manuel gave a final tug on the rope securing the load and turned to face her. "You riding with me?" he asked.

Before she could answer, Raúl stepped in between them, and hissed a reply through gritted teeth. "No, she'll ride with me."

Manuel reacted like a bull with a red flag waved in front of him. His hand snapped out and latched onto the collar of Raúl's designer shirt. "Why don't you let her decide?"

Isabel stepped between them before punches started flying. "It's all right, Manuel. Raúl and I have some issues to discuss." She gave him a pleading look and hoped he'd understand her intentions from the businesslike tone of voice she used. For some reason, she wanted to assure Manuel that no romantic feelings remained between her and Raúl, at least not on her end.

Manuel released his hold on Raúl's collar and shoved his hands into his pockets. "Let's go then."

She climbed into the passenger seat of Raúl's jeep, trying hard to ignore the smug smile on his face. *God help me. I think these men will kill each other before a week passes ... if I don't beat them to it.*

~ * ~ * ~ * ~ * ~

The jeep's engine and the rush of air through the open cab created too much noise for conversation. After several failed attempts at shouting her thoughts at Raúl, Isabel resigned herself to riding in silence. They would have to discuss their relationship later.

On their way to the main road, they passed through several villages. Most consisted of little more than a few tumbledown buildings arranged in haphazard proximity. Isabel thought the modest villages were quaint, like still lifes from another era. She especially liked one in particular. A run-down shack served as a general store to the inhabitants of the countryside. The old-fashioned gas pump beside it offered the only fuel for miles around. As they approached, Isabel leaned against the door of the jeep, preparing to enjoy the picturesque setting.

Instead of the rush of pleasure she expected, she felt a jolt of terror. Lounging atop a rusted-out truck in front of the general store sat the man whose mug shot the police had shown her, the man involved in organized crime.

Their eyes locked across the distance.

Recognition rolled across his features, and his lips curled into a sneer. He raised one hand and pointed at her, a simple but thoroughly threatening gesture.

A chill of fear rippled down her spine. It appeared as if he'd been waiting for her. But how could he know she'd be driving this road ... unless someone had told him of their plans? She glanced at Manuel's jeep just ahead of them on the road, then to Raúl beside her. Would one of the men do such a thing? Both claimed to care for her on some level, and yet, she didn't know either one of them very well.

Her vulnerability assailed her, and she questioned her wisdom in embarking on this trip. Once out in the wilderness, help would be far away and there would be nowhere to hide from danger. What had she gotten herself into?

~ * ~ * ~ * ~ * ~

His hands gripped the steering wheel of the jeep until his knuckles turned white from the strain. *What's he doing, sitting by the side of the road like he's been waiting for me?* Panic seized him at the sight of the man, eerily pointing at their caravan. He'd told them he was leaving town. Was this their form of a sendoff, a reminder, or an overt threat?

~ * ~ * ~ * ~ * ~

After six hours muscling the jeep over rugged roads, Manuel

led their mini-caravan inside the boundaries of the *Parque Nacional* and followed the directions sent by the park rangers to a site not far from the mouth of the cave. He had called ahead and received permission from the park board to do some exploration in and around the cave. His references from Central University garnered him the respect he needed to obtain unrestricted access.

When he found the clearing the park employees had suggested as a campsite, he pulled his jeep off the rough access road that served workers in the wild, beautiful area. Tall trees surrounding the clearing would provide them with shade most of the day, while dewy ferns and flowering plants offered a palette of colors and smells to please the senses.

The location was not perfect, lacking amenities such as electricity, water, and restrooms, but they could make themselves comfortable and accomplish their goals. Besides, this would provide a good trial run before they moved to the other locations, remote enough to make this one seem luxurious. He had some reservations about his partners' abilities to endure the conditions they would encounter in the field. Isabel and Raúl were still close enough to civilization to make a quick return if the going was too rough for them.

The other jeep rolled to a stop behind his, and Isabel climbed from the vehicle with slow, stiff movements. Placing her hands on her lower back, she leaned side to side, stretching out the kinks inflicted by the rough ride. "I would kill for an iced tea and a recliner chair right now."

Manuel chuckled, reached into the back of his jeep, and pulled out a few items. "I can offer you a canvas chair and a bottled water. Will that do?"

"My hero!" she quipped, flashing him a mega-watt smile as she accepted the proffered items.

Manuel watched her walk to the clearing and set up her chair. She looked beautiful in a campy sort of way. Though wrinkled from the long drive, her khaki shorts and a pale-blue sleeveless shirt complemented her slender figure. She'd pulled her hair into a ponytail, accentuating the fine lines of her features. Even without makeup, her skin emanated a healthy glow. Thick, dark lashes framed her eyes.

Snapping off the bottle cap, she tipped her head back and took a long drink, unwittingly displaying the curve of her neck. He could stand and watch her all day, yet she seemed oblivious to the effect she had on him.

"What are you staring at?"

Raúl's angry words hissed into Manuel's ear and rankled his nerves. If they hoped to attain any peace in the camp, he and Raúl would need to settle some issues.

"I'm enjoying the view, Raúl. Do you have a problem with that?"

Raúl didn't flinch at Manuel's threatening tone. "You will stay away from her, or I will make you sorry."

"Isabel is her own woman. She'll associate with and date whom she chooses. If she doesn't choose you, that's your problem. I have no pity or patience for a man who mistreats a woman the way you did Isabel. She deserves better than you."

Raúl jabbed a finger into Manuel's chest. "What do you know of it?"

Taking a step closer, Manuel glared at Raúl. "Who do you think comforted her when she discovered your unfaithfulness?" The murderous look on Raúl's face brought Manuel a measure of satisfaction.

"I'm funding this little camping trip, and I won't hesitate to send you home."

Manuel snorted. "Only a fool would do that. You'd be lost without my expertise."

"I can hire another expert."

"Not one that has Isabel's allegiance."

Raúl gritted his teeth. "You will show me the respect I deserve, or I will make you sorry."

Manuel snickered at the threat. "If you try, you'll find yourself with a fight on your hands, and I think you're too much of a coward to risk it. I suggest you direct your energy toward getting these jeeps unloaded." Pulling one of the heavier boxes from the pile of supplies, he thrust it into Raúl's chest.

Raúl staggered under the weight for a moment before recovering his balance and shoving the box back at Manuel. "I am not a slave. I will not carry your supplies like some kind of pack mule."

"They're your supplies, too, and you're not going to sit around and fan yourself like a prissy prima donna while we work. Now, get moving."

Manuel forced the box into Raúl's hands again, and this time Raúl seemed to concede defeat. He stomped away, leaving Manuel to gloat over the minor victory.

After Raúl stalked past Isabel, she rose and joined Manuel by the jeep. "A prissy prima donna?" she asked, laughing under her breath.

"You heard that, did you?" Their fingers brushed together as he handed her a lightweight bundle. She made no move to pull away, so he allowed the touch to linger, enjoying the softness of her skin against his.

"Thanks for defending me, Manuel. I don't think he understands or accepts that I've cut him out of my life in a romantic sense. He's using this project to try to get me back."

"Any chance of that happening?" Manuel tried to sound casual, but the answer to her question held incredible importance for him.

She searched his face. "I don't think so. I hope not."

He grabbed a box and followed her toward the clearing. Only a mild unease over Raúl's threat interrupted the pleasant warmth in Manuel's breast. Despite his earlier bravado, he still harbored concerns. While his heart told him to defend and protect Isabel, his head reminded him of his financial problems. As much as he wanted to plant his fist in Raúl's smug and egotistical face, he needed the funding Raúl offered. He'd simply have to find a way to deal with them both.

Pearls

Eleven

Excitement coursed through Manuel's body as his paddle cut into the dark, swift water, urging the canoe further into the limestone tunnels and caverns of *La Cueva*. A battery-powered light attached to the front of the boat cast a glowing orb before them to guide their way. The high ceilings of the cavern lay obscured in inky blackness, hiding the Guácharo birds from sight, though the cave echoed with the haunting whisper of their wings.

A park ranger had escorted them past the tourist sections of the cave, allowing them to bypass the guide ropes and turnstiles that forced the cave's visitors to maintain orderly processions. When they'd passed the gawking tourists, Manuel couldn't help but feel sorry for those confined to walking the designated path. The euphoria of exploration and discovery would be squelched as the bored park ranger, who had led countless tours in his years of service, spouted information about the cave in his sleepy monotone.

For Manuel, the urge to explore never ebbed. Today he could satisfy the relentless hunger for adventure that gnawed at him when he found himself trapped in a classroom or buried in research. He couldn't have tolerated a guided tour and was glad for the freedom to explore on his own.

Once beyond the boundaries and barriers of the tourists' domain, the park ranger left them to their own devices. Manuel, Isabel, and Raúl, set out on the water in a canoe on loan from the park. After half an hour, they approached the place where they'd left off searching the day before.

In addition to a river, the cave housed two giant reservoirs in miles of underground terrain. Manuel intended to explore every nook and cranny possible. For three days they had searched for a rocky shelf Rodrigo mentioned in his writings. Manuel's intuition told him they would find it today. He dug his paddle into the water one more time before laying it beside his feet in the bottom of the canoe. "Anybody want a pair of night-vision goggles?" he asked. He delivered a pair into Isabel's outstretched hands before snapping off the light at the front of the canoe. With the aid of the goggles, they could search the dark caverns without the bother of hauling in bulky searchlights.

She slid the eyewear into position on her face and adjusted the strap behind her head. "At first these things creeped me out, but now I think I like them."

"Creeped me out?" Manuel and Raúl asked in unison.

Despite Manuel's years of English classes, Isabel frequently stumped him with her odd phrases. Looking at her through his goggles, Isabel glowed a phosphorescent green. She smiled and stuck out her tongue.

"I saw that." He laughed.

Raúl leaned forward, squinting. "Saw what? How can you see anything in this place?"

"You need to wear a pair of goggles, Raúl." Isabel offered him a pair. "It's almost as bright as day with the goggles on."

He pushed them back at her. "I wore them the first day. They made my face itch."

Through his goggles, Manuel had a clear view of Raúl's petulant expression. He couldn't decide what Raúl hoped to accomplish in coming along on their daily journeys. He had no experience, no knowledge of the journal, and no desire to help. He'd been whiny, disagreeable, and uncooperative, and Manuel wanted nothing more than to toss him overboard.

Isabel, on the other hand, seemed unaffected by Raúl's attitude. Manuel wasn't sure if she was unflappable or a great pretender. Maybe she still loved him and couldn't see Raúl's hideous faults for the stars in her eyes. The idea perturbed him, and he compensated by barking orders.

"Everybody remember what to look for? We want to find a rocky shelf shaped like the bow of a ship. If we see any rock formations that look like they might be candidates, we'll stop and explore to see if we can find the other identifying markers. Since we finished covering the left side yesterday, we'll start on the right today."

Raúl sighed with boredom, and Manuel wondered why he bothered trying to include the man. Maybe he did it for Isabel's sake.

Oblivious to Manuel's inward battle, Isabel scanned the cave walls and rock formations to the right of the canoe. He decided to follow her strategy and concentrate on work, not Raúl. The sooner they found what they were looking for, the sooner they could go.

A few minutes later, Isabel pointed. "Look, Manuel. What is that?"

~ * ~ * ~ * ~ * ~

Isabel nearly tipped the boat in her excitement. The outcropping emerged from the darkness, exactly as Rodrigo had described in his journal. Grabbing a paddle, she helped Manuel steer the canoe alongside the ledge.

He hopped out, and holding the mooring line firmly in his hand, he glanced around. "Amazing."

"What? What do you see?" Raúl's impatient questions echoed off the stony walls of the cave, magnifying his obnoxious behavior in Isabel's mind. If only he would try to cooperate.

A surge of frustration dampened Isabel's enthusiasm. "Would you like your goggles now?" she asked.

"No. Didn't we bring battery-powered lamps?" Isabel heard him fumbling through the supplies near his feet, followed by the click of a switch. Her goggles flooded with blinding light that seared her retinas. With a disgusted huff, she yanked them off and sat waiting for the halos to fade from her vision before she moved again.

Manuel came and knelt in front of her, one strong hand holding the boat steady, the other extended to her. "Let me help you out."

His firm grip filled her with a sense of security, and she let her hand linger in his after she stepped onto the ledge beside him.

"Careful, the rocks are slippery." Manuel squeezed her hand, seeming to enjoy the contact as much as she. Their gazes met and held, shared enthusiasm passing between them.

Raúl plunked the lamps at Isabel's feet and hoisted himself up beside them, disrupting the moment. "This is it? It doesn't look any different than the other ledges we looked at the first few days. How can you be sure this is the right place?"

Manuel heaved a sigh and spoke as if addressing a child. "The small opening in the wall back there, and the natural pool right here. The journal explained it all. Plus, Rodrigo described the shape of the ledge." Manuel glanced around. "It really does look like the bow of a ship. I can see why a sailor would feel comfortable here."

Raúl snorted in disgust. "How could anyone be comfortable in this damp, dark place? And what is that smell?"

Digging his fingers into his hair, Manuel turned away mumbling to himself. Isabel thought she heard him mutter an insult, but she couldn't be certain. Sensing Manuel had reached the limit of his patience, she answered Raúl's question. "I think it's the Guácharos."

"The what?" Raúl stared at her, his nose wrinkled in disgust.

"The oil birds that live in the cave. Remember? We talked about this on our first day of exploration."

"I don't recall anything about birds."

"Well, you were a little busy checking your cell phone for a signal and combing your hair, so maybe you didn't hear that information." Her voice was rising now too, but by the look on Raúl's face, he had no idea why everyone was acting so testy toward him.

He opened his mouth to respond, but before he could get a word out, Manuel intervened, turning the conversation to matters of business. "I don't see any place to tie the boat, so I think we need to pull it up onto the ledge. Raúl, grab that end. I'll take this one, and Isabel, you get the middle."

For once Raúl showed a modicum of cooperation, and together they lifted the lightweight canoe out of the water.

"Let's have a look around and see what we can find," Manuel suggested, grabbing a lamp.

"What's there to look for?" Raúl asked.

Manuel appeared ready to explode with impatience, so Isabel fielded the question. "We'll see if we can find any nooks or crannies big enough to hold a small chest. Rodrigo said he buried the treasure in his home, and this was where they lived for the first year of their marriage."

"How could anyone live here?" Raúl argued.

"They were hiding from slavers. The cave supplied Rodrigo and Karwa with water and shelter, and they carried supplies and firewood in on their boat. People can be very resourceful under difficult circumstances. Now are you going to look around with us or not, Raúl?"

Raúl crossed his arms over his chest. "I'll stay here."

"Fine." Isabel grabbed Manuel's sleeve with her free hand and pulled him toward the opening of a small chamber at the back of the ledge. The journal recorded that Isabel's ancestors had used the chamber as a bedroom, pounding pegs into the rocky walls and hanging hammocks from them. Isabel wondered if the cave walls still bore the scars of Rodrigo's handiwork.

"Raúl is driving me crazy," she whispered as they ducked under the low opening of the chamber. "I've never been a violent person, but he's really testing my patience. If he was a child, I'd spank him."

"If he keeps acting like a child, I will spank him." Manuel's mustache twitched, and a smile appeared below it. "Don't think about him for the next few minutes. I need a break."

"Agreed." Isabel examined the new surroundings, noting the ample size of the room. Approximately twelve by fifteen feet, the chamber would have made a nice-sized bedroom. Markings caught her attention. She crossed to the far side and held her light close to the wall. "Look, Manuel, there are some pictures carved into the rock. I wonder if they mean anything."

"I found some over here too. Mine looks like a calendar, probably Rodrigo's way of keeping track of the date. We'll study them in further detail to see if they lend us any clues about the pearls."

Smiling, Isabel ran her fingers over the cave walls, feeling an overwhelming sense of connection with her long-dead ancestors. Five-hundred years earlier, they'd stood on the exact spot she now occupied, driven from their people and all that was familiar, yet the journal told how they were completely at home in their love for one another. Would she ever find that sense of belonging in her own life?

After studying that spot for a few minutes, she continued her search of the chamber, inching slowly around the room, careful to take in every detail. Manuel seemed equally absorbed in the exploration, spending most of his time studying the pictures and markings on the walls.

"What's taking so long back there?"

Isabel startled at the sound of Raúl's voice. She'd forgotten all about him in the blessed peace created by his absence. She stepped to the opening. "It's a good-sized chamber, and there are interesting markings on the walls. Would you like to have a look?"

"No. I'm ready to go back to the camp."

Isabel sighed. *We should have sneaked away from camp without him this morning.* "Just give us a few more minutes."

She moved back inside the chamber. "Why don't we quit for the day and come back tomorrow without him. That way we can spend the whole day looking around. This is too interesting to hurry."

Manuel nodded. "Our job will be easier if we're not babysitting."

A startled shout came from the main chamber, and Manuel and Isabel rushed to the opening.

Raúl held a lamp aloft with one hand while the other flailed wildly at the air. "Get away from me!" he shrieked. "Get away!"

Isabel heard the flap of wings and the odd squawk of the Guácharos as they shifted about, obviously disturbed by Raúl's interloping. He continued to shout and shake his fist, only aggravating them more. Isabel watched with morbid fascination as a group of birds descended on Raúl, diving and circling with malicious intent, threatened by what they viewed as an intrusion.

Raúl dropped the lamp, throwing his arms over his head in an attempt to ward off the attack. His head snapped from side to side, looking for an escape. He made a run for the chamber opening, but his attempt to escape was thwarted when his feet slipped on the slick surface of the rocky floor. With a dull thud, he sprawled in a most ungraceful fashion on the ledge then rolled to his side and curled into a fetal position. Having neutralized their enemy, the birds lost interest and flew back to the dark ceilings above.

As Raúl pushed to his feet, a string of curses poured from his lips, surprising Isabel. He'd never talked that way in front of her—yet another reminder that she'd been in love with an ideal and not with the heart and soul of the man.

Behind her, Manuel shifted, and she realized his arm had slipped around her waist, a gesture both protective and possessive. She leaned back against him and felt his chest shaking in suppressed laughter.

"What's so funny?" she whispered.

"Look at Raúl." His lips brushed against her earlobe as he spoke, his warm breath fanning across her neck. "He's covered in droppings."

She noticed the slimy gray sheen that coated Raúl's designer shirt and pants.

He brushed at his clothes, trying to remove the offending substance, then held his hands in front of his face, his features twisting in disgust. "The slime on the cave floor smells terrible."

Manuel, who'd shown reluctance to speak to Raúl all day, suddenly became a fount of information. "Now, Raúl, we told you about the oil birds that inhabit this cave. And where there are birds, one will generally find bird droppings."

A look of horror spread across Raúl's face. "Do you mean, this is—"

"Yep. You found the bird poop." Manuel slapped Raúl on the back, managing to avoid touching the soiled sections of the shirt.

Raúl's unmanly shriek echoed through the large chamber. He rushed to the water's edge and frantically tried to wash away the smelly substance.

Knowing how upset Raúl was, Isabel tried desperately to suppress her laughter, but the harder she tried to hide her amusement, the more her urge to laugh grew. Manuel's uninhibited chuckle sent her over the edge. A giggle escaped and grew into a full-blown belly laugh until tears poured down her face.

Divine justice. Raúl had tortured them all day with his surly disposition, and in one glorious moment, God had issued vengeance. And only God could have served up a retribution so fitting.

Pearls

Twelve

Isabel's stomach growled as they neared the campsite. The light meal they'd eaten at lunch hadn't satisfied her appetite for long. Hunger had gnawed at her middle for over an hour. After Raúl's misfortune in the cave, they'd returned to camp for a quick lunch, then spent the afternoon hiking some of the trails in the national park. Isabel and Manuel had tried to slip away, leaving Raúl at camp while they enjoyed time alone. But Raúl responded like an animal defending his territory and refused to allow them any privacy.

The jeep bumped over the last stretch of road, and Manuel steered it into the makeshift parking space. While he exited the driver's side, Raúl jumped out of the passenger seat and moved to help Isabel down from her perch in the back of the jeep. She accepted his hand and hopped to the ground. The moment she landed on her feet, Raúl wrapped her in his arms and pulled her against him. Before she could launch a protest, his lips covered hers in a demanding kiss.

She stiffened and struggled against the hold he had on her, finally convincing him to release her. "What are you doing?" she hissed.

A devilish grin spread across his face, causing his dimples to appear full force. "If you couldn't tell, perhaps I need to do it again." His gaze dropped to her lips, and he moved toward her.

Pressing her palms hard against his chest, she backed away from him. "No, you don't!" She turned toward their tents in time to see the dark look Manuel flashed her way.

Undeterred by her rebuff, Raúl kept a possessive hand on her back as they joined Manuel at the tents.

Manuel's accusing stare flustered and embarrassed her, but

Raúl seemed not to notice. He grabbed his bag of toiletries and a fresh shirt. "I'm going to that visitor's center to wash in the restroom. Anyone else want to come?"

Isabel squatted by the box of food supplies. "Not me. I want to start supper before I starve."

Manuel retrieved the miniature camping stove and set it on the ground near Isabel. One burner atop a small canister of fuel provided an efficient way for campers to cook. "I'll help Isabel. We can clean up in the creek later."

Raúl's lip pulled up in disgust. "I don't know how you can tolerate these living conditions. It's unhygienic." He stalked to the jeep, not waiting for a reply.

Tension drained from Isabel's shoulders as he drove away. She hadn't realized how much stress Raúl caused her until she had a moment away from him. She glanced up and caught Manuel staring at her. "What?"

He dropped his gaze to the matches in his hand. Taking one from the box, he struck it and lit the burner. "Hungry for something in particular?"

"I'm not picky." She held up a can and studied the label. "I can make do with anything."

"Yes. I've noticed." He accepted the canned ham she offered him and attacked it with the can opener.

His tone and attitude confused her. He seemed to be referring to something more than dinner, but she couldn't fathom what he was insinuating. She studied his face. "Are you angry?"

A muscle in his jaw flexed. "No."

"You are! You're mad." She moved closer in order to study his face. "What's wrong?"

He dumped the ham into a small pan and set it on the burner, refusing to look her in the eye.

Upset by his withdrawal, she reached out and touched his arm. "Manuel, please talk to me."

He heaved a sigh. "He's a pathetic excuse for a man, Isabel. I can't understand your attachment to him. You seem like the type to look beyond a pretty face."

She lowered herself to the ground and sat cross-legged, propping her elbows on her knees. Understanding dawned in her mind, and she smiled at him. "You're jealous."

His answer was part growl, part grumble, and fully incomprehensible. Moving like a robot, he continued to cook, refusing to give her any more clues about what he was thinking.

His reticence intrigued her, and she wanted nothing more than to question him until he'd revealed the depth of his feelings. The very idea that he might have feelings for her sent a shiver of anticipation through her. But if she questioned him, fairness would dictate that she reciprocate and share her feelings about him. In no way ready for that discussion, she dropped the issue, choosing instead to refute his earlier claim. "Do you think I'm still interested in Raúl?"

"I don't have to think. I saw you kissing."

"He kissed me. I didn't kiss him. There's a difference."

Manuel's "hmmph" suggested he disagreed.

Feeling suddenly defensive, she crossed her arms over her chest. "Look, Manuel, I'm in a tough position here. I've tried to explain to him that it's over between us, but he refuses to accept it. I'd love to blast him when he pulls that Romeo stuff, but we need Raúl's support to continue this search."

"Or maybe you still care about him."

Isabel laughed with derision. "Honestly, I can't figure out what I saw in him in the first place. Why didn't I notice how selfish and petulant he is?"

The endearing smile lines at the corners of Manuel's eyes threatened to appear. "You'd never seen him under adverse circumstances. In Caracas he controlled his environment. Now that he's not able to dictate every detail, you see him without the advantage of familiar territory."

"Yeah, I noticed he's out of his element here. But I don't know how much more I can take. He's really starting to annoy me. Will you hate me if I clobber him and alienate our only sponsor?"

Manuel grinned. "Not if you let me watch."

She giggled, glad to feel the camaraderie between them restored. While she could endure Raúl's complaining and unwanted advances, she couldn't bear Manuel's scorn and disapproval.

Isabel handed him another can then went to find the plates and silverware. They worked side-by-side, preparing a modest meal of *cachapas*, heavy corn pancakes filled with ham, beans, and cheese.

The jeep returned just as they dished up plates. Sporting a fresh shave and damp hair, Raúl looked as if he'd stepped from the pages of a fashion magazine. He caught her staring and flashed her a dimpled smile.

Her breath caught in her chest. No wonder she'd fallen for him. He was the very image of the Latin lover. What woman could resist such beauty when taken at face value?

Raúl sat beside Isabel, and she couldn't help but enjoy the enticing scent of his cologne. His faults aside, she could give him credit for immaculate hygiene and impeccable taste in clothes. Isabel handed him a plate and a fork. He promptly cut a bite and lifted it to his mouth.

Manuel winked at Isabel and bowed his head. "*Padre Santo*, we thank you for this meal we are about to eat, and for your hand of blessing on our lives. Amen."

"Amen." From the corner of her eye, Isabel saw Raúl shake his head and stuff the bite into his mouth. Obviously, he saw no need to delay the meal to say a trivial prayer.

Isabel and Manuel settled into their canvas chairs and began eating. With the sun setting in the west, the forest creatures began their evening song. Isabel marveled at the peace and beauty around them, but the moment was short-lived.

"What is in this sorry excuse for a meal?" Raúl stared at his plate with disgust.

Isabel felt slightly offended by his insensitive comment. "It's *cachapas*. You don't like it?"

An insect biting at his arm interrupted his answer. He dropped the fork to his plate and smacked at the offending creature. A curse escaped his lips. "We haven't had a decent meal in days."

"I've enjoyed all our meals," Isabel disagreed. "Maybe you're being too picky."

Raúl waved his hand in the air around his head. "Where are all these insects coming from?"

Isabel looked up and noticed the unusual number of bugs hovering in the air around him.

Manuel cleared his throat. "I told you several times already that the insects are attracted to fragrances. If you'd forego the cologne and hair products, you wouldn't have a problem."

Raúl glared at Manuel. "And then I would look like you, Manuel, barely more civilized than the animals that live here."

Just then, a large fly landed on Raúl's neck and bit him, eliciting a pain-filled yelp. He slapped at the offensive pest, but the bug had already inflicted its damage.

Manuel shrugged. "At least I won't be covered with bug bites. You're going to look beautiful with welts all over your body."

Raúl jumped to his feet, sending his plate tumbling to the ground. "I will not stay in this godforsaken place a minute longer! How do you expect me to endure these conditions? I've not had a real shower in days; the bugs and mosquitoes are eating me alive; and that cot you expect me to sleep on could be classified as a torture device!"

Manuel shook his head as if he'd known all along that Raúl wouldn't be able to endure more than a few days of rough living. "What did you expect, Raúl? You knew we wouldn't be staying at five-star hotels."

Isabel stifled a giggled, but couldn't hide her amusement. Raúl had maintained a bad attitude since the moment of their arrival, and Isabel wondered if God had added to his difficulties because of it.

Manuel had the bravery to say what Isabel had thought all along. "Roughing it is part of the job. If it's too much for you, you could always go back home."

"I've heard enough of your smart remarks!" Raúl ducked into the main tent and came out holding a set of keys and his suitcase. "Come on, Isabel. We're leaving."

Surprise rippled through her at the unexpected order. "Me? I'm not going anywhere, Raúl. If you want to leave, that's fine. I want to stay here and continue working on the project."

Manuel set his plate aside and stood. "Just let me get a few supplies out of the jeep, and you can be on your way, Raúl."

Glaring from one to the other, Raúl must have realized he wasn't going to gain any sympathy. He stomped to one of the jeeps and slung his suitcase in the back. No sooner had Manuel lifted the spare box of food supplies from the vehicle than Raúl gunned the engine, spinning the tires and kicking up a cloud of dirt in his hasty retreat.

Manuel coughed and waved the dust away.

Isabel observed the hasty departure, relief spreading through her at being given a break from his tantrums. She recognized that eventually she would have to confront the issues between her and Raúl, but for now she intended to enjoy the reprieve.

~ * ~ * ~ * ~ * ~

Manuel watched Isabel fight her drooping eyelids and decided it was time to send her to bed. They'd sat by the campfire talking and laughing for hours after Raúl left, relaxed and carefree for the first time since the beginning of the journey. Despite her yawns and heavy eyelids, she seemed reluctant to say good night. He'd been afraid to suggest it, not wanting to end the magical evening. Years had passed since he'd spent hours talking with a woman for the sheer pleasure of it, and even then, he didn't remember enjoying anyone's company like he did Isabel's.

When her eyelids closed and her head started to nod, he knew he couldn't prolong the evening any further. He knelt beside her chair, laying a hand gently on her arm. "Time for bed, Isabel."

Her eyelids fluttered, and she fixed sleepy eyes on him.

"You're not holding up your end of the conversation anymore," he teased.

Full lips curved into a lazy smile that wrapped around his heart and squeezed it like a vise. He closed his eyes against the onslaught of emotion. "Go to bed, Isabel."

She nodded and let him pull her to her feet. He felt her hand squeeze his bicep. "Tonight was fun, Manuel. More fun than I've had in a long time."

Summoning all his restraint, he suppressed the desire to hold her in his arms and kiss her soundly. There would be time to show her his feelings later. Turning her toward her tent, he gave her a gentle push. "I'll see you tomorrow morning."

"Sweet dreams," she answered, her voice barely above a whisper.

He knelt and tossed dirt over the coals of the campfire, aware of her every movement as she zipped the flap of her tent closed.

~ * ~ * ~ * ~ * ~

Isabel focused the beam of the electric lantern toward the small pool, trying to see into its depths. The light reflected off the surface, decorating the crude cave walls with nebulous, swirling patterns in pale shades of blue.

"Are we really going in there, Manuel?"

"You nervous?"

"A little. I've never tried anything like this."

"I'll go first and make sure it's safe." Manuel dropped to one knee and pulled at the strings of his sturdy hiking boots. "I'm going to tie that rope around my waist. If I'm not back in two minutes, you pull me out. Okay?"

"Um, why don't you just make sure you come back."

He laughed. "I almost get the feeling you like having me around. Am I growing on you?"

She knelt down and covered his work-roughened hand with hers. "Please, don't take any chances."

The look in his eye caused her breath to quicken. He leaned toward her and brushed a kiss across her cheek. "I promise."

As he lowered himself into the pool, he sucked a breath sharply through his teeth. "Cold," he gasped, sinking until only his head and shoulders remained exposed. "I'm touching bottom. Hand me a lamp."

Their fingertips met when she passed him one of the lights. He gave her hand a gentle squeeze. Turning, he dunked the lamp under water, and Isabel was glad to see it lived up to its reputation of being waterproof. He walked along the edge of the pool, holding the lamp close to the sides and feeling around the rocks with his free hand. "I found it," he announced after a few minutes.

He shot a smile her way before ducking under water. Isabel leaned over the edge, trying to monitor his progress. His activity disturbed the water's surface, distorting her view.

A few moments later he emerged, his hair plastered to his head and water running down his face in rivulets. He ran a hand over his face and smiled. "This is the passageway, all right. I can't see the other side from here, so I'll have to swim in and investigate. Feed the rope in a few feet at a time. I'll give it a tug when I'm through."

She nodded and took the rope in her hands. A trail of bubbles rose to the surface as he submerged and fit himself into the underwater passage. Eerie silence enveloped her as the seconds ticked past, the rasp of the rope sliding across the rocky ledge the only sound in the isolated cave. Isabel realized she was holding her breath and exhaled with a loud huff. She didn't know which made her more nervous, waiting on him or thinking about making the trip herself.

The rope jerked and she startled. He was through, safe and sound on the other side. She forced her tense shoulders to relax as she secured the loose end of the rope to the canoe. Knowing he'd soon be back for her, she slipped off her shoes and the cotton shirt she wore over a tank top. She sat on the edge of the pool, and shuddered when her warm feet dipped below the surface.

Bubbles floated up and tickled her legs just before Manuel emerged. He grinned and splashed water her way. "Ready for a swim?"

She moved her lamp to the edge where she could reach it then slid into the pool.

Manuel stepped up to help her, wrapping an arm around her waist and lowering her into the water beside him. "You're shorter than me. I don't think you can touch without your face going under."

Accepting his help, she slid her hands onto his shoulders, allowing him to cradle her against his chest. His body felt warm in the frigid water, and she snuggled a little closer.

"How far is it?" she asked, her voice breathless as she adjusted to the temperature.

"The tunnel is just a few meters long, and it's plenty wide to allow for maneuvering around. We can't swim side-by-side, but you can follow close behind me and hold the rope to keep us connected, okay?"

"Okay." She grasped her lamp tightly in her hands. "I'm ready."

He moved closer to the opening and released her. She perched one forearm along the edge of the pool to help her stay afloat while he prepared to make the trip a second time.

Manuel fumbled with the rope and handed it to her. "Hold on right here, and you'll be able to follow about two meters behind me. Just give me a few seconds' head start. You can do this, Isabel. It's just a short swim." He brushed his fingers across her cheek and

110

smiled. "Ready?"

She nodded.

After drawing in a deep breath, he plunged under the water and slid into the opening in the rock. Clutching the rope in one hand and her lantern in the other, Isabel followed his lead, her heart thundering in her ears.

Her lantern seemed to lose some wattage in the pervasive darkness of the watery tunnel, lighting only a foot in any direction. Lack of goggles or a mask further blurred her vision. After only a few feet, the closeness of the rocky walls encroached on her comfort, seeming to narrow in on her with alarming malice. She tamped down panic and flutter-kicked harder, allowing the rush of adrenaline to propel her forward.

Manuel pulled on the rope, aiding her progress, and she glided through the last few feet of the tunnel with a speed that brought relief. She broke the surface of the water on the other side and found herself once again enfolded in Manuel's embrace.

Resting her forehead against his chest, she drank in deep breaths of damp, stale air. "Thanks for the extra help. I was a little panicked in there."

His chest rumbled with quiet laughter. "You did fine. Second time is much easier." His voice echoed off the rock walls with a strange hollow ring, and the water dripping from their wet hair and shoulders plopped into the pool with exaggerated loudness.

Recovered, she moved away from him and found she could touch bottom. "Let's don't talk about the second time just yet. I still can't believe I swam through that hole the first time. How do you suppose Rodrigo did it? He didn't have underwater lights like we do. He would have been swimming blind."

"It took some courage, no doubt. But you have to admit, his bravery was worth it. This is the best hiding place I've ever seen." Manuel held the lamp over his head and glanced around the small room, which Isabel guessed to be about eight feet in diameter. The dome-shaped ceiling that arched a few meters overhead seemed to shift and sway with patterns of light dancing over it.

Isabel watched the fascinating display for a few moments before turning her attention to Manuel. He had hoisted himself up onto a small shelf indented in one side of the cavern. She waded through the chest-deep water and allowed him to pull her up beside him, thankful for a moment's relief from the cool temperature of the pool. Lifting her feet out of the water, she wrapped her arms around her knees to conserve warmth.

"Look at this, Isabel."

She turned and saw the small rivulet of water seeping from a crack in the wall.

Manuel ran his fingers over the fissure. "I'll bet this trickle becomes a small waterfall during a hard rain. The running water probably carved this niche we're sitting on over hundreds of years, maybe even this chamber and the tunnel to the main cavern. It's a good source of fresh water."

Isabel shivered and leaned closer to him, seeking his warmth.

His arm wrapped around her back and pulled her closer. "This is kind of nice. Our own private room; dim, romantic lighting; a reason to hold you close; what more could a man want?"

The tone of his voice gave her a new reason to shiver, and she tilted her chin to look up at him. With his free hand he traced the lines of her face—her cheekbones, her brow, her jaw—his fingertips finally coming to rest on her lips. She closed her eyes, every one of her senses going haywire. He explored the curves of her lips with a slow, deliberate touch, awakening needs she didn't know she had and leaving her dizzy with anticipation by the time he dipped his head to claim his reward.

His skill surprised her. Someone, somewhere had taught Manuel to kiss.

"I've been waiting to do that for a long time," he sighed when he lifted his head. The dim lamplight didn't hide the fire in his eyes.

"How long?"

"Since you walked into my office that first day and mesmerized me with those beautiful blue eyes."

Isabel looked away, a blush burning her cheeks.

"Then when I learned you're as smart as you are attractive, I wanted to kiss you even more." He ran his hand lightly down her arm, making her skin tingle with electricity. "Is it all right that I kissed you, Isabel?"

She felt the weight of anticipation behind his question. It was a request to take their relationship to the next level. His friendship had become invaluable to her. She looked forward to sharing his company for long hours each day, appreciated his gentle manner toward her, found herself craving the warmth of his touch and the comfort of his smile. He'd come into her life unexpectedly, took his place in a quiet, unassuming manner, became the pillar of strength and stability she needed, offered her comfort and support, and asked nothing in return.

Her heart said to trust him, love him. But her mind cautioned her against a rash decision, taunting her with foolish choices of the past, reminding her of the unanswered questions concerning the break-in and fire at her apartment.

Wiggling away from him, she slid into the water and grabbed her lamp. "Shouldn't we be looking for the treasure or something?"

His face registered disappointment, and she wasn't prepared for the pain it caused her knowing she'd put it there.

He followed her lead and slipped into the water. "Yes. It shouldn't take long to make a sweep of the area. Not many square feet to cover in here, and no place to hide a chest of pearls except under the water."

"I'll start at that end and you start here. We'll meet in the middle." Isabel turned and waded to the far side of the cave, glad to put distance between herself and the awkward situation she'd created. For now, she would busy herself with work. Later, she would consider whether she was ready for a relationship and if the feelings she was having for Manuel were real or just another way to fill an emotional void.

Pearls

Thirteen

After half an hour of probing the walls and floor of the hidden chamber, Manuel knew they'd hit a dead end in their search for the pearls. In addition, he was trying hard to conceal his disappointment about Isabel's rejection—and failing miserably. He'd growled at her twice in the space of ten minutes and hated himself for causing the wounded looks that appeared on her face.

She couldn't control how she felt any more than he could. Besides, he didn't have any business making a play for her heart when he had nothing to offer. His home, job, and income were all uncertain. She deserved someone who could care for her in style, someone with Raúl's looks and affluence. He only hoped she would find a man who would treat her well, like he would if circumstances were different and he could offer her that life.

He dismissed the thought. Better to accept that they would never be a couple so he could salvage the friendship and business partnership. "Isabel, I think we've done all we can here. Let's go back to camp and change into clean, dry clothes."

She nodded and walked toward the entrance to the underwater passageway. He'd never untied the rope fastened to his waist, and it tangled around Isabel's foot as she walked. She stumbled and he instinctively reached out to steady her as she scrambled to regain her balance.

"Sorry," she mumbled, not looking his way. She started to pull away from him, but he grabbed her hand and gave it a squeeze.

"I'm all right, Isabel." He put as much emotion as possible into the simple phrase, hoping she'd understand his double meaning.

Her thick, wet lashes looked lustrous when she turned his way. "Are you sure? I didn't hurt you?"

He smiled. She really was a smart woman.

"Manuel, can we talk when we get back to camp?"

Pearls

His gut clenched as he wondered whether this would be a good talk or a bad one. He didn't really want a lengthy discussion about why she didn't want a relationship, but he couldn't deny her when she turned those eyes on him. Keeping his face placid, he agreed. "Okay." While hoping for the best, he prepared for the worst.

~ * ~ * ~ * ~ * ~

They made the trip back to the camp in tense silence, and Isabel knew she'd worried Manuel by asking to talk. She was worried too. During the time they spent searching the chamber, she couldn't stop thinking she'd acted in haste. Despite the fact that Manuel and Raúl were entirely different men, she made the same mistake with them both. She relied upon her eyes and her heart to make the decision when she should have asked for God's direction.

They reached the camp, and Isabel slipped into her tent to change, using the moment of privacy to unload her burdens on her heavenly Father. After changing into dry clothes, Isabel picked up the small Bible she had brought with her on the journey. Just holding the leather-bound pages between her hands infused her with confidence. If she allowed Him to make decisions for her, she wouldn't need to worry about the outcome. Like a benevolent parent, He wanted the best for her life and offered advice and guidance that would lead her to His perfect will. She had not bothered to talk with Him about Raúl and felt the stinging consequences.

Abuela had pointed it out to her with such clarity. *You looked with your eyes, and his beauty deceived you. Now you know to look with the discerning eyes of the Spirit. They are more reliable than your natural vision.*

"God, I want to see beyond the limitations of my eyes. Your Word says that if I acknowledge You in all my ways, You'll direct my paths. I need Your direction right now."

Further words didn't seem necessary to express the turmoil raging inside her. She simply closed her eyes and opened her heart, offering Him access to her doubts and fear. She knew He would see the desire of her heart, and He would lead her to the best course of action. To Isabel, dating Manuel seemed a natural progression in the relationship they'd begun over a month ago. Friend, companion, and confidant—he'd weathered each marker in the course of their relationship, and she longed to continue the journey, seeing where the path would take them. But as she prepared to offer her heart this time, she wanted divine assurance.

"Is Manuel a part of Your plan for my life?"

As she sat quietly waiting for an answer, warmth washed through her and settled a deep peace in her heart. The touch of His presence brought with it a greater clarity of vision, and she began to view Manuel in a different light. Gone was the fear that had plagued her earlier. In its place lay a quiet assurance that her Father, who could see the future, had granted her His blessing.

Manuel was nothing like Raúl. Though Manuel's comments about his relationship with God had been brief, he had spoken with sincerity. He wasn't a man to talk endlessly about his relationship with God when displaying the fruits of it was so much more effective. And when she considered his behavior toward her, he had displayed the values that filled his heart. Daily, Manuel offered her consistency, honesty, and a willingness to show her his weaknesses as well as his strengths. Manuel allowed her a realistic view of himself. She preferred to see a real picture—flaws included—rather than a false pretense like Raúl's carefully crafted façade. A decision based in truth was a sound one. And a safe one.

Safe. Fear concerning the unanswered questions about the apartment fire crept into her mind, sliding under the warm blanket of newfound peace that enveloped her and running its cold fingers up her spine. She wanted to snatch her burdens out of God's capable hands. *No, Isabel.* With effort she pushed the fear away and clung to God's reassurances.

"I'm leaving that in Your hands. I know You wouldn't mislead me." Besides, she had no real reason to suspect Manuel's involvement in the more sinister events of the last month. In fact, she couldn't find any logical reason to relate the events back to him. Perhaps the fire was a fluke, a coincidence that had touched her life by accident.

Knowing she was wasting energy worrying about problems she had no control over, she put the unpleasant thoughts out of her mind. Through the thin canvas of her tent, she heard Manuel stirring around the campsite. No doubt he was feeling confusion and disappointment over their earlier encounter, and Isabel wanted to set him straight.

When she stepped outside, he was sitting by the fire pit, coaxing up a blaze. Isabel sat in the canvas chair across from him and tucked her hands between her knees.

He glanced up at her. "Time to talk?"

She nodded. "You caught me by surprise earlier. I wasn't prepared to talk about my feelings, and I think I hurt you."

He prodded the campfire with a stick, clearly uncomfortable. "It's all right, Isabel."

"No, it isn't because now there's this awkwardness between us, and that isn't what I want at all. I like you a lot, Manuel, and the idea of being more than friends ... well, it appeals to me."

"But?"

She could see by his expression that he'd assumed the worst and was waiting for the final blow to strike. His pain became hers, and the urge to reassure him overwhelmed her. "I need to go slow so I can work out some issues."

"Raúl?"

"Among other things. I have a bad habit of rushing in and making a mess of my life. I don't want that to happen again."

He dropped the stick into the fire and leaned back in his chair, assuming a more relaxed posture. "What does 'go slow' mean to you?"

"I like how things are between us now. We've become good friends, and sometimes, we hold hands or you put your arm around me. We're just a little ways beyond friendship and that feels right for now."

He smiled. "Feels right to me too. I've wanted to ask you on a date for some time, but circumstances never seemed right."

Laughter welled up in Isabel's chest. "Does *now* seem like the right time to start dating? In case you haven't noticed, we're hours from the nearest theater or restaurant. I have a sneaking suspicion you were waiting until the cost of dating went down."

He smiled. "There may be some truth in that, but I'll never admit it."

"It's all right. I'm a simple girl. I don't expect extravagance."

"I might surprise you."

"You already have, Manuel."

His gaze swept over her, and the warmth in his dark eyes spoke volumes.

"And in answer to your earlier question in the cave, it's okay that you kissed me, Manuel. Going slow can include an occasional kiss."

His white teeth contrasted with his dark mustache when he smiled. "You have the softest lips of anyone I've kissed in years. Of course, it's been two years since I've dated anyone, so there wasn't much competition."

"Thanks a lot!" Giggling, she snatched up a can of bug spray and tossed it at him.

He caught it with little effort and dropped it to the ground beside him. "Don't worry, you'd have probably won even if there had been other competitors."

"What do you mean *probably*?"

"It's hard to be sure when you've only kissed me once."

Isabel tried to look affronted. "I didn't kiss you! You kissed me."

"If we're officially taking this relationship beyond friendship, maybe it's time you kissed me, Isabel."

"You're flirting with me," she accused.

"Is that allowed?" He circled the campfire and pulled her out of her chair.

Adrenaline raced through her as he folded her into his arms. "I suppose." Her voice came out in a breathless whisper.

"Are you going to kiss me?" His eyes issued a challenge she couldn't resist.

Standing on tiptoe, she attempted to plant a chaste peck on his cheek, but he turned his face at the last second and captured her mouth in a deep kiss. Isabel melted against him, deciding she liked his way better than her original plan. He held her captive for several beats of her racing heart before ending the kiss.

He didn't seem in any hurry to let go of her, so she rested her cheek against his chest and reveled in the wonder and excitement of the new closeness they had found. Even more exhilarating was the sense that she had somehow connected with destiny. The peace and rightness she felt in his arms could surely be trusted.

Pearls

~ * ~ * ~ * ~ * ~

Manuel finished loading his personal possessions and gear into the back of the jeep and decided to start on the general equipment. After determining the hidden chamber was empty, they spent two more days probing every nook and cranny of the area in the cave once occupied by Rodrigo. The markings on the cave wall proved insignificant to their search and the area yielded no further clues. Deciding to move on to the next location, they drove to the visitor's center and called Raúl's cellular phone to let him know of their decision.

Since his hasty departure from camp, Raúl had been staying at a motel an hour's drive from the cave. He promised to meet them and help transport the gear to the next location—after griping and criticizing their lack of a find.

A reluctance to leave invaded Manuel's thoughts. The last few days alone with Isabel had been the closest to perfection he'd ever experienced. At first she'd been shy and a little awkward, as if uncertain how to act around him, but soon they relaxed into a comfortable rhythm, finding the right mix of work and play. The transition seemed as natural as breathing to Manuel. He could quickly grow addicted to her company.

The sound of her tent flap unzipping drew his attention. She stepped out into the early morning light and lifted her arms over her head in a deep stretch. The scene reminded him of a butterfly emerging from a cocoon and stretching its wings in preparation for flight, only his butterfly had tousled hair and sleepy eyes.

"Morning, beautiful."

She dropped into one of the canvas chairs, a slow smile spreading across her face. "Why do you insist on getting up so early?"

"Habit." He figured the half-truth was safer than telling her that he enjoyed seeing her first thing in the morning, looking soft and vulnerable while sleep still had a hold on her. He wondered what it would be like waking up beside her every morning. Blissful, no doubt. But that sort of speculation was premature. They had a lot to learn about one another before he could consider an arrangement that included matching pillowcases. An explorer at heart, he intended to enjoy every moment of their journey.

She finger-combed her hair and rubbed her eyes, banishing the last traces of the morning look he admired. "How long is the drive to Santo Domingo?"

"Around five hundred kilometers. We'll be on the road most of the day. I'm hoping we can make camp before nightfall. You riding with me this time?"

"Definitely. I don't intend to get trapped with Raúl again. He can throw a fit if he wants, but it's time he accepts that I'm not dating him anymore."

"If he needs convincing, you'll let me know, won't you?" Manuel kept his tone light, but he couldn't have been more serious. He'd held his feelings in check during the last month, knowing it wasn't his place to interfere with Isabel's private life. Now that she had invited him into her inner circle, he didn't intend to let Raúl bully her.

"Raúl might be difficult to deal with, but I don't think he's going to give me any real trouble." She slipped out of the chair and stood in front of him, resting her palms against his chest. "But thanks for sticking up for me. It feels good to know you're there for me if I need you."

Holding her close felt nice, and Manuel decided he might like to have a good morning kiss. He leaned toward her, but she dodged his advances and wiggled away from him.

"Not before I've brushed my teeth," she laughed.

Smiling, he let her get away, confident he could collect from her later.

~ * ~ * ~ * ~ * ~

Isabel finished packing the last of her gear just as Raúl drove up. Grabbing the straps of the nylon case holding her tent, she toted it toward the waiting vehicles.

Raúl met her halfway. "Good morning, Isabel. Let me carry that for you."

"Thanks, Raúl." She handed it over and watched him hustle to the jeep.

The temperamental disdain that drove him from the camp days earlier had vanished, and he helped load supplies into the jeeps with more intensity than Manuel and Isabel combined. In addition, Isabel noted something in his appearance had changed. He looked as if he'd been drinking, but it was more than that. Perhaps a casual acquaintance wouldn't notice the difference, but because they'd dated for months, Isabel saw the glint of fear in his bloodshot eyes. His features were set in hard, serious lines, making him seem drastically different from the carefree playboy she had dated.

The skin on her neck prickled with apprehension.

Catching her eyes on him, Raúl scrubbed his hand over his face, as if trying to erase the evidence of a night of heavy drinking. She'd known him to drink a glass of wine with dinner, but he'd never shown signs of bingeing, so why now? Had something or someone driven him to the bar, seeking a temporary escape?

The speculation frightened Isabel, and she hovered close to Manuel, drawing comfort from his presence. They made little conversation as they finished loading. Isabel climbed into the passenger seat of Manuel's jeep, and they left the park with Raúl following in the other vehicle.

As miles of highway stretched out before them, Isabel tried to relax, told herself she was worrying without any real cause. Despite her internal admonitions, she couldn't ignore her feeling that danger prowled the shadows, waiting for an opportune moment to strike.

Fourteen

The road to Santo Domingo led them under a swollen canopy of storm clouds. Traveling without the jeep's canvas top and sides allowed a breeze to blow through the vehicle. The airflow warded off the tropical heat, but rain would cause problems. Too much water could damage some of the equipment they carried, and Manuel didn't relish the idea of getting soaked. A roadside sign told him the next town lay only minutes away.

"Let's stop here and zip the top on the jeep. We can take a restroom break and get a bite for lunch too."

"Sounds good." Isabel turned and waved at Raúl, signaling him to follow them off the highway.

The exit took them to a quaint town situated on the side of a mountain. Stucco buildings nestled into the rise of the landscape, each red-tiled roof standing slightly higher than the one before it. Bold lettering painted on the salmon-colored storefronts identified the wares of each shop. A colorful array of fruit decorated the doorway of the *frutería*, while clothes and housewares filled the windows of other stores.

Manuel spotted a street vendor and turned the car into a gravel parking lot. "Why don't you see what kind of food that woman is selling while I find the top and zip it on?"

Isabel nodded and climbed out, moving slowly at first, no doubt working the stiffness out of her muscles.

In uncharacteristic compliance, Raúl climbed from his jeep and followed Manuel's lead without comment. Manuel felt relief that, for once, Raúl didn't criticize or question his leadership. In minutes, both jeeps were enclosed in canvas, and Isabel returned with beefsteak and egg sandwiches and bottled waters.

She smiled when she handed Manuel his lunch.

"Thanks, Isabel." He leaned against the side of the jeep and unfolded the foil wrapping on his sandwich.

"Welcome."

She turned her back to give Raúl a sandwich, and Manuel wondered if she offered Raúl the same smile he'd received. A touch of envy plagued him whenever he saw her with her former beau. She had loved Raúl once. Maybe she still did. Knowing she had wasted months of devotion on a man who viewed her as nothing more than a trophy gouged at Manuel's sense of decency. If he could, he would roll back time, give her the months she'd lost, love her the way she deserved. He wanted to erase Raúl from her life. Maybe then she would look at him in the starry-eyed way he'd seen her look at Raúl.

The sky thundered, echoing the rumble of jealousy in Manuel's heart. He crumpled his sandwich wrapper and tossed it in a nearby trash bin. "Better eat fast. We need to keep traveling. This rain may slow us down, but we can still arrive at our destination by nightfall if we make steady progress."

Isabel nodded and lifted her sandwich to her mouth, her eyes smiling at Manuel as she took a bite. He relaxed and felt the jealousy ease. She'd made her choice, walked away from Raúl's manipulations and opened herself up to the possibility of a relationship.

But gaining her trust and her love would take time. With deadlines and responsibilities pressing in on his life, Manuel didn't know if he could afford to wait.

~ * ~ * ~ * ~ * ~

Isabel snuggled into the bucket seat of the jeep, enjoying the relaxing patter of rain falling on the roof of the vehicle. Manuel sat beside her, his hands on the wheel and eyes on the road, seemingly content with the companionable silence. His presence comforted her, wrapped her in a cocoon of safety, removing the weight of problems and worries from her mind.

He had a quality about him that she'd grown to admire, a rock-like stability that anchored him and those around him. She wondered if his inner strength stemmed from his relationship with God. Manuel had never openly discussed his faith, but she saw him pray at meals. More importantly, she witnessed his character and integrity. If his life was any indication, he was firm in his convictions.

"Manuel, tell me about your faith in God."

He shot her a crooked grin that made her heart do acrobatics.

"What is that smile about?" she asked.

"Your conversation starter. You've been quiet for an hour then you ask a deeply personal question like that."

She realized how abrupt she must have sounded. "If you don't want to talk about it, I understand."

"I want to tell you, Isabel. You just surprised me. So what do you want to know?"

She thought for a moment, searching for a good starting place. "Do you go to church?"

"Every week. Sometimes more, depending on where I'm living and what my current schedule is like. Unfortunately, my career has prevented me from perfect attendance."

"How long have you believed?"

He kept one hand on the wheel while the other stroked his mustache. "Hard to say. I think I always believed. My mother made sure we attended Mass every week and raised us with a healthy measure of reverence for God. Later, when I went to college, I hooked up with a Bible study group that helped me learn the value of having a relationship with God."

Isabel liked his answer. It revealed his depth and maturity, but she still felt a need to probe his convictions in a few other areas. "How do you feel about fidelity?"

His expression suggested he'd expected the question. "I'm not like Raúl if that's what you're asking." He paused, and Isabel thought she saw a blush creeping beneath his tan.

She couldn't remember seeing him flustered before. "Manuel?"

He gave an embarrassed laugh. "I might as well be honest with you. If we start dating, we'll talk about it sooner or later. Truth is, my experience with women has been pretty limited. I had a few experiences in high school that I'm not proud of, but after I joined the college study group, I recommitted to Christian dating principles. Since then, I've never dated more than one woman at a time and I've honored the boundaries God set out for male-female relationships."

His statement washed over her like a warm ocean wave. In a

country where men judged one another by their conquests, finding a man like Manuel was rare. No. More than rare—a treasure.

"That must have been a tough decision. This culture puts a lot of emphasis on *machismo*."

His expression grew thoughtful. "I guess my belief in God influenced me, but I had other reasons too. Rodrigo's journal entries, the way he viewed the Indian women, reminded me so much of my own experiences."

Intrigued, Isabel waited.

"I have three sisters," he explained. "I would be furious with any man who took advantage of them, so how could I justify my behavior if I did the same to someone else's sister? Besides, anyone can see Rodrigo and Karwa had something special. There's only one way to build a love that endures, and they found it."

As she pondered his answer, the reservations she'd built up inside her heart softened a bit. "You're a good man," she whispered, slipping her hand into his.

He wove his fingers with hers and lifted her hand to his lips. After pressing a kiss to the back of her hand, he flashed her a devilish smile. "What about you, Isabel? Any confessions you'd like to make?"

Her face heated. Why did this subject always make her feel so awkward? But she couldn't avoid answering him, not after he'd spoken so honestly about his experience—or lack of it.

"When I was fifteen, my parents sat me down and talked with me about the choices I would confront when I started dating. They were very candid about the pressures of dating and the options available to me. At the end of our talk, they shared from their hearts that they wanted the best for me, and their experiences had led them to believe waiting until marriage was the best option. Every other choice has risks and consequences. My dad pulled a ring out of his pocket and asked if I would wear it as a symbol of my promise to wait."

She lifted her hand and showed him the ring. "I still wear it."

"It's beautiful."

"I'd like to give it to my daughter someday—if I have one."

"Do you want children?"

"Yes, a few. How about you? Do you like kids?"

"I love them. They're born with an insatiable curiosity and a sense of adventure. Natural-born explorers—my kind of people. But I don't know if I'll ever have any. My career isn't conducive to family life."

Faint stirrings of disappointment registered in Isabel's mind. She felt as if he'd just pointed out the limits of their budding relationship. They could date, have fun, but could there ever be more between them? Before she allowed her feelings to grow serious, she needed to consider whether she could deal with the unusual demands of an archaeologist's lifestyle. His career would preclude any sort of normal life. Maybe she was crazy for even considering dating him. On the other hand, perhaps God had arranged for her to tag along on this expedition to give her ample information on which to base her decision. If she wasn't sure by the end of their journey, she never would be.

Turning her thoughts to work, she rehearsed the information she knew about the next location they intended to explore. Santo Domingo was a small town nestled in the mountains only thirty kilometers from the Columbian border. Their destination lay another twenty kilometers south of the town in the sparsely populated mountain range.

"You got quiet." Manuel's gentle voice interrupted her thoughts.

"I was thinking about our next location. Reviewing facts and details, trying to prepare for what's ahead."

"Why don't you get out the journal and read the entries out loud. We both need to review our homework."

"Good idea. Did you pack the working copy in this jeep?"

"I think so. Look in the box underneath my bedroll."

Isabel undid her seatbelt and turned around. Kneeling in her chair, she reached between the seats. The road curved sharply, and she tottered off balance, leaning heavily on his shoulder for a moment before she righted herself. "Oops, sorry, Manuel."

He laughed at the apology.

She caught the amused glimmer in his eye. "You did that on purpose, didn't you?"

His grin gave him away.

"Try and keep your attention on the road," she scolded with a smile.

Shifting the bedroll and a few other items, Isabel uncovered the three-ring binder holding their notes. Once they had completed the journal translation, they used a word processing program to compile their translation, observations, and notes into a logical and functional notebook. The working copy was more practical than the journal and saved wear and tear on the artifact.

Isabel settled into her seat and flipped through the pages. Finding the one she searched for, she began to read aloud.

~ * ~ * ~ * ~ * ~

> *January 15, 1506*
>
> *Karwa's belly grows round with the coming of my child, filling my breast with emotions too powerful for words. At night I lay beside her, rest my hand on the swell of her abdomen, and feel the child move within her. She carries a precious and priceless treasure, one I would stop at nothing to protect. By our best estimate, she will give birth late in the dry season.*
>
> *This cave is not a fit habitation for an infant, and in truth I grow weary of the dark, damp atmosphere. The walls of this great cavern have offered us shelter and protection, but our time here draws to a close. I wish for my child to be born in a home, one safe from the far-reaching menace of slavery.*
>
> *The slavers encroach further into the interior each day, and we must go far inland to make a life free from the threat they impose. We will travel now, putting distance between the enemy and ourselves while Karwa can still endure the difficulties of a journey. Perhaps it is idealistic of me, but I hope to find a home where peace abounds, a place where attributes such as greed, cruelty, and prejudice are intolerable. If such a place exists, I will find it and give it to my children for their inheritance.*

~ * ~ * ~ * ~ * ~

One paved road snaked through the town of Santo Domingo, following the curve of the landscape. Houses and shops in pastel shades of stucco flanked either side of the street, stretching a line of civilization through a valley of green wilderness. In the background, a heavy mist lingered midway up the slopes of the mountains while low-slung clouds snagged against the higher peaks.

In the muted light of early evening, men leaned against the fronts of their homes, smoking pipes or playfully tussling with their children. Women pulled wash off the clotheslines and chatted with neighbors over vine-covered fences. The poignant vignettes spoke of life lived at a slower pace, and Manuel felt a sudden craving.

What would it be like to settle down—buy a house, marry a woman, have children? Some days, the unrelenting pursuit of his dream wore him down, and the sacrifices he made to follow his heart seemed too great a price. But could he find happiness in a common life, one he'd spent years trying to avoid? He glanced at Isabel, who was sleeping in the passenger seat. Maybe. Exploration took on many forms, and he could only imagine the discoveries he could make with the right woman by his side.

A hand-painted sign advertised a general store, and Manuel steered the jeep into a parking space. During the long drive, he and Isabel had compiled a list of supplies they needed to purchase before leaving the comforts of civilization, and this looked like as good a place as any to buy them.

Manuel placed a hand on Isabel's shoulder and gently shook her. "Wake up, sleepyhead."

Her eyelids fluttered open, and she stole his breath away with a sleepy smile. "Where are we?"

"At a general store in Santo Domingo. Want to help me buy some supplies?"

She nodded and pulled down the mirror on the sun visor, trying to smooth her mussed hair into place.

"No need to bother with primping," he said, tugging a strand of her hair. "You look beautiful."

She snorted. "Yes, sleeping in the front seat of a jeep does wonders for a person's appearance. I have a horrible crick in my neck."

"You looked comfortable enough while you were snoring."

"I don't snore."

"Okay." He rolled his eyes, knowing the simple expression of doubt would rile her.

Her wicked grin surprised him. "Those canvas tents we sleep in are pretty thin, Manuel. I've discovered you talk in your sleep, and I can hear you from my tent on the other side of the camp. You'd be amazed at the things I've learned about you."

She giggled and hopped out of the vehicle, leaving him to wonder if he'd been spouting secrets while he dreamed. He certainly had plenty to conceal.

Raúl had parked behind them and now leaned against his jeep, looking as exhausted as Manuel felt. The drive had worn them all down, and Manuel looked forward to making camp and relaxing. The storekeeper greeted them at the door and promptly snatched up the list. He waved Manuel away and bustled off to assemble the items.

"There's something to be said for small town service," Manuel commented.

Isabel shrugged and smiled. "Since I'm not needed, I think I'll find a restroom and freshen up."

After Isabel left, Manuel struck up a conversation with an old man who sat on a bench in front of the shop. Though wrinkled and bent with age, the man still possessed a keen intellect. He answered Manuel's questions about the area, seeming eager to talk of the land he had called home all his life.

When the supplies were paid for and loaded into the vehicles, Manuel walked to where Raúl and Isabel waited.

Manuel nodded toward the old man. "This local says it's too dangerous to drive out of town tonight. A heavy fog covered the mountains around three in the afternoon, making the road dangerous for travelers."

Raúl nodded. "Let's find some rooms tonight, have dinner, and sleep in a real bed. We can head out early in the morning."

"Agreed." Manuel scanned the street for signs of a hotel or restaurant. Seeing a group of locals gathered outside a building a block away, he decided that might be a good place to start. In his travels he'd found that the residents of a town would lead him to the best eateries if he simply followed the crowd.

The building turned out to be a cantina that served mouth-watering dinners in addition to drinks. They took a booth near the back of the one-room tavern. The rowdy laughter of men—and a few women—enjoying an evening out frequently drowned out the music of the guitarist in one corner of the room.

A sultry young waitress sauntered over to their table, wearing a look that suggested she had a target clearly in her sights. Manuel watched with interest as she engaged Raúl with a come-hither smile and flipped her lustrous dark mane over her shoulder with red-nailed fingers. Raúl's gaze roamed her figure before he turned on the charm, and the two fell into flirtatious conversation.

Manuel thought it a good sign that Isabel showed no interest in the romance playing out before her. She glanced around the bar, taking in the activity, studying faces. Occasionally, she would nudge Manuel with an elbow and point out something that caught her interest.

After a harsh word from her boss, the waitress managed to tear herself away from Raúl's side and take their order to the kitchen. As she walked away, she tossed a coy glance over her shoulder as if to ensure she'd not lost Raúl's attention. She wasn't disappointed. Raúl demonstrated extreme flexibility, craning his neck to admire the exaggerated swish of her hips as she crossed the room.

Manuel thought they'd make a perfect pair, but he didn't want to see Isabel hurt by Raúl's distraction. In a surge of protectiveness, he draped an arm along the bench behind her and rested his hand on her shoulder. She leaned into his touch and sighed, a pleasant, contented sound.

Raúl's attention seemed to distract their waitress and slowed their service to a ridiculous crawl, or maybe the woman intentionally delayed their meal to keep Raúl at her table. Manuel didn't know and didn't care. He just wanted to eat and find someplace to bed down for the night. He took a swallow of his lemonade and prayed for patience.

After an unreasonably long time and many frivolous visits from their waitress, the food arrived. The steam rising from the hot plates smelled delicious, and Manuel muttered a quick prayer before digging in with gusto. After concentrating a few minutes of attention on his meal, a fork invaded his territory and skewered a piece of chicken from his plate. He glanced up and caught Isabel's mischievous smile as she waved the bite between them.

"Hey, this is my food," he scolded, holding a hand over his plate as if to fend her off.

"I know, but you looked like you were enjoying it so much I wanted to try a bite."

"You ordered the exact same meal."

The chicken disappeared into her mouth while her eyes issued a challenge.

He laughed. "That bite's going to cost you."

"How much?"

"I'm not sure, but you can bet I'll collect later."

Isabel smiled and went back to eating. Manuel glanced up and caught the cold-burning flames of jealousy in Raúl's hard stare. *Unbelievable!* The man had spent the last hour ogling the waitress and still had the nerve to act possessive where Isabel was concerned. Manuel refused to be sucked into the challenge. He concentrated on his meal.

When they finished dinner, the three of them exited the cantina and stood outside, discussing where to go next.

"The bartender said there's a place a block down the road that rents rooms. Where are you parked, Raúl? You can follow us."

Raúl shook his head. "You go on. I'm going to wait for Esperanza to get off work."

Manuel hesitated. "All right. We'll reserve you a room."

"Don't bother. I won't need one." Raúl flashed a cocky smile.

Manuel realized with dismay what Raúl was implying. Was the man really so bold, or was this some sort of revenge aimed at Isabel? One glance at her carefully distant expression told him all he needed to know about her feelings. Although angered that Raúl would parade a conquest before Isabel, Manuel held his reaction in check for her sake. "Let's get moving then."

Raúl reached into his pocket and pulled out the keys. "Do you want to take both vehicles? I'll get my bag out of the jeep and plan to meet up with you tomorrow."

"Fine." Manuel snatched the keys from Raúl and reached for Isabel's hand.

Just then, a man pushed his way between their group, knocking Raúl into the wall of the cantina and jostling Isabel backward into Manuel's arms. The stranger disappeared before they had a chance to recover and protest.

"That was rude," Isabel commented. She rubbed the shoulder the man had slammed into. "There was no need to run us down like that."

"Probably drunk," Manuel offered.

Uttering a few profanities, Raúl ran a hand through his hair and straightened his clothes. He dragged his hand across the front of his shirt, catching it on a note poking out of his pocket. Frowning, he pulled out the slip of paper and opened it. His face paled.

"What's wrong?" Manuel asked.

His expression smoothed over, and he wadded the paper and stuffed it in his pants pocket. "Nothing."

Manuel knew he was lying, but he didn't want to pursue the matter in front of Isabel. "Let's get going then."

Raúl headed down the street toward the jeep, and Manuel started to follow. When he realized Isabel wasn't with them, he turned.

She knelt on the sidewalk, holding a rumpled piece of paper in her hands. Her hair fell loosely around her face and hid her expression from his view, but her back was rigid.

"Coming, Isabel?"

She jumped as if he'd startled her then shoved the paper into her pocket. "Yes."

He took her hand as they walked through the darkened street. "Want to tell me what's the matter?"

"Not now."

"When?"

"Later," she promised as they arrived at the jeep.

Raúl slung the strap of his leather suitcase over his shoulder and turned on his heel. "I'll find you in the morning."

Pearls

Fifteen

Isabel stared out the window of the modest bed and breakfast and admired the moonlit garden. The proprietress had bragged about her gardening skills as she'd shown them to their rooms, and even in the fading light, Isabel could see the woman had not exaggerated. Flagstones carved a path through flowering bushes and large ferns. Fruit trees hovered above them, branches outspread as if to protect their smaller charges.

She and Manuel had settled in an hour ago, and though tired, Isabel couldn't seem to relax. Too many worries swirled around her mind, and she decided a walk in the garden might benefit her. She slipped on her shoes and left her room. Passing Manuel's door, she thought some company might be nice.

She knocked softly, heard the creak of bedsprings, and the rustle of clothes being pulled on. His tousled hair and half-buttoned shirt told her he'd been more settled in than she had.

"I'm sorry. Did I wake you?"

"No. I was reading in bed. What's up?"

"Can't sleep. I thought I'd take a walk in the garden. Want to come?"

"Love to. I'll get my shoes."

They met at the back door and slipped outside. Isabel wrapped her arms across her chest, fending off the cool night air. She filed the information away, making a note to wear a jacket in the evening while they worked in the mountains. They ambled along the path in silence, surrounded by the heady scents of the plants.

Near the back of the property, they came across a bubbling marble fountain surrounded by a ledge thick enough to sit on. Moss had grown up in the cracks of the brick pathway surrounding the fountain and released an earthy smell when crushed underfoot. Isabel sat on the marble edge and drank in the pleasant fragrance.

"You're quiet tonight." Manuel wore a concerned expression on his face. "You okay?"

"Yes."

"Are you thinking about Raúl?"

"A little."

"You have a right to feel hurt and angry. You were involved with him for a while. It must be hard to watch him—"

His voice trailed off, and Isabel was grateful for his discretion. She'd seen Manuel's worried glances when Raúl announced he intended to spend the night with Esperanza. The concern had touched her. His arm slid around her back and urged her to sit closer. She accepted the invitation and laid her head against his shoulder. The sounds of the night enveloped them as he held her, stroking her back and her hair. "To be honest, Manuel, I wasn't hurt at all by what happened tonight. As soon as I saw her coming our way, I expected it from him. I think I just feel sorry for him."

"Not the reaction I expected. Care to elaborate?"

"I remember my mom and dad sitting on the couch holding hands. I'd catch them staring at one another with soft smiles on their faces. Then Dad would wrap his arm around Mom's shoulders and pull her close. She'd snuggle against him, and he would sigh with contentment. I loved seeing them like that."

"Sounds like a nice memory."

"Yeah. They taught me that love doesn't have to be flashy or exciting. "

"You were fortunate, Isabel. God put parents in your life who modeled a healthy, loving relationship. Not everyone experiences that."

"Guess I never thought of it that way. I only knew that I wanted that kind of love for myself."

"I think everyone does, but it's hard to find what's missing in your life when you don't know what to look for."

Isabel paused. "Maybe you'll think I'm crazy but I want Raúl to know that kind of happiness and satisfaction in a relationship."

He shrugged. "Noble, considering what he put you through."

Heaviness tugged at her heart. "It's hard to blame him. Raúl had an unhappy childhood. His mother never knew true love or a happy marriage, and Raúl never had the love of his father."

"It must be hard for him to understand God's love when he's had such poor examples."

Isabel sighed. "I never talked to Raúl about God. Not much anyway. Whenever I mentioned anything related to my beliefs, he would change the subject. I could tell he didn't want to hear about it, so I never pressed the issue. Now I wish I would have said more."

Manuel slid his arm around her shoulders and gave her a gentle hug. "Don't beat yourself up over it."

"But maybe I could have done something or said something to help him understand."

The corner of Manuel's lips curled into a smile. "I think God will find a way to get the message across. If not through you, then He'll send someone else. Let Him deal with Raúl and you quit worrying about it."

She thought about his words a moment and realized he was right. It was time to let go of the past, leave Raúl in God's capable hands, and move forward. She tilted her head and smiled up at Manuel, liking the way the moonlight touched his hair with a gentle glow. "You're pretty wonderful, you know that?"

He gave her a roguish wink. "I thought you'd never notice."

"I noticed."

He bent and brushed her lips with a kiss. "Now, don't forget it."

When he gave her shoulder a gentle squeeze, she winced.

"Sorry, did I hurt you?"

She rubbed at the ache. "That guy plowed into me pretty hard. I guess it's still a little tender."

He frowned. "That reminds me, what did that paper say? You promised to tell me later."

She dug the note from her pocket and smoothed it against her leg. She held it up in front of them and let the bright moonlight illuminate the message.

"I'm watching you."

Isabel felt Manuel stiffen.

Her own body iced with fear at seeing the sinister message again. "I think I recognized him."

"Who?"

"The man who ran into us. I only caught a glimpse of his face, but I think he may be the one from the pictures."

Manuel's eyes narrowed. "What pictures?"

She sucked in a breath. They'd never discussed the details of her police interview. Unsure who to trust, she had kept her suspicions to herself. Now she felt the time had come to share the burden. "The police showed me photos of the man suspected of burning my apartment building. He's connected to an organized crime ring the police are investigating. I saw him again as we drove out of Caracas, sitting by the roadside. Now this. It was too dark to be certain, but I think he might have followed me to Santo Domingo."

Manuel stared at her with disbelief. "And you're just now getting around to telling me? Isabel, do you realize how much danger you could be in? Why would you keep this a secret?"

She looked away, not wanting to admit the reasons. So much had changed between them in recent weeks that now her reservations seemed silly.

He cupped her chin and forced her to face him. "Why didn't you tell me?"

The genuine concern written on his face coerced a confession to the surface. "I wasn't sure I could trust you. If this has to do with the journal, then someone told them about it. The list of possible conspirators is pretty short."

Disappointment registered in his eyes, but he didn't pull away. Instead, his thumb traced hypnotic circles over her cheek. "I didn't realize what you'd been through in the last month. I'm sorry, Isabel."

"It's not your fault. I just wish I knew why a criminal would be interested in me?"

"I'm not sure." He took the note from her hand and slid it into his pocket. "But I intend to find out. I think we should consider contacting the Caracas police about this incident."

Isabel shook her head. "It was dark, and he moved so fast. I couldn't be sure I recognized him, not enough to justify alerting authorities."

"Well, I can still have a talk with Raúl in the morning. Maybe he can give us some answers."

Isabel tried to laugh. "Listen to us, sitting here fretting like a couple of scaredy-cats. Some clumsy stranger bumps into us on the street and suddenly we're certain an organized crime ring has us in their targets. Why should we automatically assume the worst? Now that I think about it, maybe that waitress slipped the note into his pocket. This might be her way of flirting or something."

Manuel's sober expression didn't change. "That's possible. Don't worry about it any more, Isabel. I'll take care of everything tomorrow."

Isabel faked a smile, but his reassuring words didn't penetrate the unease in her gut. The matter had grown more complicated than she ever expected, and she was tangled in the center.

~ * ~ * ~ * ~ * ~

Manuel turned off the jeep's engine and took a moment to collect himself. The forty-five-minute drive had done nothing to abate the irritation he felt, and he didn't want to unload his frustration on Isabel. Maybe he should be relieved Raúl hadn't showed up this morning and that he failed to answer their repeated calls to his phone. Manuel had no desire to endure his sponsor's peevish behavior on another excursion. In fact, he preferred that Raúl find something else to occupy the time, but he could have sent word instead of letting them wait and wonder for hours.

And the one time Manuel actually wanted to see Raúl and speak with him, the man managed to be conveniently absent. Leaving a heated message on Raúl's voice mail hadn't felt nearly as rewarding as blackening an eye would have. But Raúl would turn up sooner or later.

Isabel's jeep rolled to a stop behind his, and the engine fell silent. He watched in his rearview mirror as she slid from her vehicle and cast a glance about the area. As she approached his jeep, the look on her face questioned his reason for stopping. Fumbling with the door handle, he stepped out to explain.

"We're not there yet, but the jeeps can't take us any further. We'll have to hike the rest of the way, backpacking our supplies. It might take several trips to get it all, but we can take our time if we want."

Isabel nodded. "Let's get the camping gear first. We can set up our tents and rest before we come back for more."

Pearls

Manuel sorted through the back of his vehicle, pulled out items he wanted to take on the first trip—including the GPS system he'd need to navigate the jungle—and set them in a pile off to the side. As he prepared for the trek, the thrill of exploring the wild and unknown pulsed through him. It had been years since he'd hiked so deep into untamed wilderness like this. He wondered if Isabel felt the same sense of anticipation.

When they had assembled all they could carry, they began the vigorous hike through thick forest jungle to the site of an ancient village. Able to see no more than ten feet in any direction, they stumbled over the uneven terrain, blazing a trail through the thick underbrush that competed for space in the rich soil beneath their feet.

Leafy plants and thorns snagged at their clothes as they pushed through; roots rose up to catch at their feet, as if trying to keep them from secrets hidden deeper in the wilds. The area offered a good place for Rodrigo and Karwa to hide from the slavers. The vegetation was so thick, a man could be hiding in the brush ten feet away and would not be visible.

Then without warning, they stepped out of the vegetation.

Smoothed by centuries of weather and use, gray stones crowded together to form a meter-wide path that stretched out a winding line in either direction. A two-foot-high retaining wall formed from the same gray stone ran along one side of the path, holding back a rise of land.

Manuel stepped onto the lichen-coated rock and studied the handiwork of ancient Indian tribes, admiring the imprint they'd left on the land. He threw a glance at Isabel and smiled at the wonder written on her features. Yes, exploration definitely appealed to her.

He looked at the GPS he carried and pointed to the left. "We want to go this way." Digging his thumbs under padded shoulder straps, he adjusted the weight of his pack to a more comfortable position before continuing the hike. Isabel traipsed behind him, the sound of her labored breathing reminding him to temper his eager stride.

The path sloped gradually for a time, curving and undulating with the flow of the land, but soon they reached the foot of a mountain. The stone path did not end, but simply compensated for the incline, forming a crude staircase that climbed the side of the mountain.

"Let's leave our packs here and see how far a climb it is to the terraces. We might be wiser to camp down here closer to our water source. And we won't have to lug our gear 1,000 feet up the mountainside."

She wriggled the pack off her shoulders and lowered it to the ground. "Fine with me. I hate the stair climber at the gym."

He dropped his pack beside hers and flashed a grin. "Race you to the top."

Manuel ran toward the stone stairs, slowing only to glance back and ensure she was following. Their rubber-soled sneakers created a muted clatter as they rushed up the incline. Manuel defended his lead, pushing to stay a few feet ahead. After a few dozen steps, he felt the effects of the exercise. A minute more and his leg muscles burned with strain. Their ascent slowed to a walk then a painful crawl. He heard Isabel's ragged breathing close behind him.

"Manuel," she groaned.

He glanced behind him and noticed she'd stopped moving.

"I concede. You win." She dusted off a stone step with her hand and sat down, panting.

Manuel bent over, his hands on his knees, giving his lungs a moment to catch up. When his heart rate slowed and his breathing evened out, he went and sat beside her. "Quite a workout, isn't it?"

"How much further?"

"I think we're less than a quarter of the way up."

She moaned and dropped her face into her hands. "Did I volunteer for this job?"

"As I recall, you insisted on coming along. Are you sorry?"

"My thighs are sorry that I'm going to have to climb this hill every day, but overall, I'm really glad I came." Her expression sobered. "Your work is fascinating, Manuel."

He brushed a loose strand of hair off her cheek. "Just my work? What about me?"

Her gaze flicked over his face, and she laid her hand on his. "Let's just say I'm liking each new discovery I make."

"The thrill of exploration is the best part."

She leaned closer to him. "I don't know about that. This part is pretty exceptional too." Her lips brushed over his, and his senses jumped to full awareness.

He reached out to pull her closer, but she slipped through his grasp.

Laughing, she darted up the steps. "Look who's in the lead now!"

He jumped up to follow. "No fair. You conceded defeat."

"All's fair in love and war."

He paused on a step and stared at her retreating form, wondering if she realized what she'd just said. Did she love him, or was this another American cliché? He wished he could see her face, search her eyes for the answers to questions he was afraid to ask openly. She still acted skittish at times, as if frightened by the thought of letting him close to her. Maybe he didn't have the right to expect more than a warm friendship, but the better he got to know her, the more he wanted to know. His resolve to stay single was crumbling as his heart plunged forward, intertwining itself with hers beyond hope of retrieval.

Sixteen

The path led Isabel up to higher altitudes of the mountain where the air seemed thinner, making each breath more difficult. She was considering asking Manuel if they could take another rest stop when the trees opened up, and she stepped onto a terrace like the ones she'd seen in pictures. Centuries ago, Indians had cleared a section midway up the mountain and transformed the rough slope into a series of circular platforms that ascended like giant steps. A stone retaining wall fortified the edge of each grass-covered level. Stone-lined ditches and underground sluices ran along the ridges to keep the water from eroding the terraces.

The place had a timeless quality that captivated her. Bending, she touched one of the rocks and felt the warmth of the sun radiating from the smooth pink-tinged stone. A tap on her shoulder made her glance up.

"Take a look at this." Manuel gestured to a point behind her shoulder.

She turned and caught her breath at the beautiful scenery. Green mountain peaks and shadowed valleys stretched as far as the eye could see. Low-slung clouds lingered so close overhead that Isabel felt the urge to reach up and try to touch one.

Magnificently grand, the view humbled Isabel with its majesty. "This explains how Rodrigo drew that topographical map so accurately. It's a stunning view."

They stood in silent awe for a moment.

Isabel sighed. "I think I'll sit down. My legs are tired." She walked to a meter-high wall bordering the next terrace and found a comfortable perch. Manuel followed and dropped onto a rock a few feet away.

"Aside from the view, what do you suppose influenced the tribe to build so high on the mountain? I can't imagine this location was convenient for the Indians."

Manuel smiled. "From a military standpoint, it's a highly defensible position."

"I should think so. No doubt, the enemy was ready to drop from exhaustion by the time they climbed to this height. I know I am."

He chuckled. "Since the rain at this altitude is sufficient for agriculture, the Indians grew food on these terraces. There are settlements like these all over the mountains, connected by the stone paths and stairs. Some of the larger colonies supported as many as 3,000 people."

Isabel studied the area. "I can't believe it's still here after so many centuries. Erosion hasn't impacted the landscape much, if at all."

"The tribes who built these were incredible engineers. Some of the modern coffee plantations that plant in the higher altitudes have tried to reproduce this kind of construction, but they haven't been able to build anything that compares with what the Indians accomplished."

"How long do you think it will take us to search this area?" Isabel cast a skeptical look around. More than twenty terraces sprawled across the mountain side, making for a large search grid.

"The ground-penetrating radar equipment is fairly efficient. I think we can cover one or two terraces a day. But I suspect this direct sun will make us uncomfortable if we work during the heat of the day. I suggest we hike up here first thing in the morning and work until lunch. Then we'll spend the warm afternoon hours in the valley looking for that well Rodrigo mentioned."

Isabel nodded. "Judging by the quality of the Indians' work here, I expect we'll find the well intact."

"Ready to hike down?"

Isabel pushed to her feet, weary but willing. "I guess we better get moving if we hope to get the camp set up and settled by nightfall."

As she walked toward the stone stairway, Isabel's legs felt like noodles. After backpacking the gear from the jeeps, her back and arms would probably offer some complaint, as well. No doubt her limbs would be stiff and sore in the morning. Despite the discomforts, she had no desire to abandon the search. In fact, she had never felt more exhilarated. She didn't think of herself as an explorer or adventurer, but after a week of trekking the wilds, she couldn't imagine anyplace she'd rather be.

~ * ~ * ~ * ~ * ~

Isabel stepped from her tent several mornings later, glad to leave its close confines. She slept well in the small tent, but it seemed claustrophobic when she was awake and trying to move around. She lifted her hands over her head and indulged in a languorous stretch, thankful the soreness she'd experienced the first few days had subsided.

Often when she awoke, Manuel was already busy fixing breakfast, his close shave and fresh clothes making him look as if he'd been up for hours. Today, the camp appeared empty. She peeked into the larger tent they used as a workstation and storage area for their supplies and equipment, but it sat empty and quiet. A few feet beyond the main tent, the flap on his sleeping tent hung open, hinting that he'd risen before her and set out on his own.

Rather than wait for him, she decided to go to the stream and wash up. She grabbed her bag of personal items and headed for the designated "facilities."

Along the way, she spotted Manuel sitting on a large rock jutting from the mountainside. Its smooth surface provided a tempting, if unusual, place to sit. A book lay across his lap, and when he shifted, the sun glinted off the gold-leafed pages. A Bible. Before he could look up and see her, Isabel turned away, feeling as though she'd intruded on a private moment.

She'd seen him perched on the rock once before, reading and meditating on the scripture. Seeing his devotion filled her with guilt. When had she stopped taking time for God each day? At some point during the hectic move from the United States to Venezuela, she'd forgotten about the peace, strength, and direction God offered to those who would come and sit with Him daily.

Her spiritual life had suffered neglect for years, and no doubt, this contributed to her lack of judgment where Raúl was concerned. Even though she now realized her error, she'd done nothing to correct the problem or ensure she wouldn't repeat the same mistake again. She hadn't change her habits or sought healing for the reason she'd made the poor decisions in the first place. She sensed God tugging at her heart. Maybe the time had come for her to renew her own commitment.

After washing up, Isabel returned to her tent and pulled out her worn Bible. As she opened to a Psalm and began to read, a comforting presence wrapped around her like a blanket, and she felt the joy of returning home.

~ * ~ * ~ * ~ * ~

Before the trip, Isabel had never seen radar equipment that scanned underground. Now, after four days of working the machinery, she felt like a seasoned expert. At first, the images she'd viewed on the monitor looked like confusing blobs to her. Manuel had taught her to see the images, lines, and shapes in the sonar feedback displayed on the screen. Some pottery, a hammer-like tool, and an eating utensil had appeared on the screen over the last few days. Each discovery amazed her, helping her better understand Manuel's passion for his career.

She and Manuel finished their breakfast and climbed to the terraces to begin another day's search. They'd started with the highest terrace and were working their way down, fully scanning each level before moving down to the next one. Because of the cumbersome weight of the equipment, they left it on the terraces each night instead of hauling it up and down the long staircase.

Isabel pulled at the tarp draped over the supplies and began to uncover their equipment. When she realized Manuel hadn't joined her, she turned to find him staring into the distance, a frown creasing his handsome features.

She followed his line of vision and tried to identify what had drawn his attention. "What are you looking at?"

He pointed into the distant sky. "See that? Is it smoke?"

She tipped her head and studied the faint gray curl hovering over the treetops. "Yes, I think so. Probably some other campers making their breakfast or maybe someone lives on this mountain. The area isn't completely isolated, is it?"

"No. I imagine a few people live out here."

"They wouldn't have electricity this far out, would they?"

"Probably not."

"Smoke from a campfire or stove isn't so unusual then, is it?"

"Maybe." Manuel looked unconvinced and continued to study the smoke curl. "But last night the smoke was further west. Residents wouldn't be moving around."

A chill swept through Isabel, making the roots of her hair tingle and stand on end. Was it the man who'd burned her apartment then waited for her along the road out of Caracas? Maybe she had seen him in Santo Domingo, but why would he follow her across the country? She could not fathom any motive to justify the extreme behavior.

"I'm sure it's nothing to worry about." Her voice sounded strangely calm. She turned her back to the distant fire, but as they went about their daily routine, the ominous curl of smoke never left her thoughts.

~ * ~ * ~ * ~ * ~

The bristly rope pricked Isabel's palms, but she refused to loosen her grip. She vowed to have a thorough mental evaluation upon her return to Caracas because no sane woman would agree to put herself in the precarious position in which she now hung—literally.

"How you doing down there?" Manuel's steady voice bounced over the stones, taking on a hollow ring before it reached her ears.

Isabel rolled her eyes and resisted the urge to say something snide. "Fine. Can you lower me more quickly, please? This harness isn't very comfortable."

She heard him chuckle, but the rate of her descent did increase. Why she'd let him talk her into being lowered into the old well was a mystery. Maybe the warmth that radiated from his eyes or the way his mustache twitched when something amused him had influenced her decision. She'd remember not to look him directly in the face the next time he proposed something outrageous.

"Can you see the bottom yet?" Manuel called to her. "I'm running out of rope up here."

"Oh, that's comforting." She aimed her flashlight downward and leaned to see if anything materialized in the dark abyss. The change in position caused her to sway, and she instinctively reached out to brace a hand against the stones lining the circular wall of the well. Her fingers slipped on the slimy rock, and she cringed. Moving carefully, she took another hesitant look down.

"My light is reflecting off the water table. I'm almost as low as I can go without getting wet, but I can't tell you how deep the water is."

"I'll lower you a few more feet. Holler when you're almost touching the water."

Isabel clung to the rope as he worked the manual winch, which allowed him to handle her suspended weight with ease.

"Stop! My feet are just about to get drenched."

"Can you see the bottom now?"

She aimed her light into the water, but the beam was absorbed after only a few feet.

"No, I'm sorry. It must be deep."

"Let's find out how deep. I'm going to tie something heavy to the end of another rope. You lower the weight into the water until it stops sinking then mark the waterline on the rope. We'll measure from the weight to the mark and get a depth."

"Okay. That sounds like it will work."

"I need to find a weight. I'll be right back."

The sound at the top of the well ceased and, except for the creak of the rope, Isabel waited in silence. The rope sling chafed her hips and thighs, and she shifted to relieve some of the discomfort.

A shadow moved across the top of the well accompanied by the sound of scuffling. She glance up into the point of light at the top of the tunnel and saw the glint of sun on metal.

"Manuel?"

Suddenly, the rope went slack, and Isabel dropped into the icy water, the impact plunging her under the surface. She righted herself and gave a powerful kick, thrusting herself to the top. When her head emerged, the length of rope that had held her aloft wrapped itself around her shoulders and arms. The harness tied around her midsection slid downward and tangled her legs. She coughed and choked, trying to clear the water from her throat. Her thrashing entangled her in the rope, and her heavy shoes and clothes began to suck her down.

"Manuel!"

No answer.

Panic flooded through her, and Isabel wrestled against the

dangerous restraints tangling around her. She sank into the dark water and fought her way to the surface again, desperation overtaking her senses.

"Isabel?"

She heard Manuel's horrified yell but couldn't call to him. Keeping her face above water long enough to breathe took all the effort she could muster.

He must have heard her thrashing because he continued to yell down to her.

"Isabel, I brought another rope. When I drop it down, you grab on."

He kept talking, but her splashing and frequent dips under the surface muffled his instructions. She worked to free a hand from the tangle, wondering how she would find the strength to hold onto the rope long enough to reach the top of the well. She pushed away the frightening thought and forced herself to relax and think.

She stopped fighting the ropes winding around her limbs and worked instead on freeing herself from their hold. When she forced her legs to still, the harness slowly drifted down to her shoes. Fluttering her feet, she freed her legs. Able to tread water more easily, powerful kicks kept her afloat while she untangled her arms. Almost free, she felt something brush against her head. She startled then realized it was the rope Manuel had sent down. Relief flooded through her as she grabbed hold of her connection to the surface.

"Get a firm grip!" Manuel ordered, "And let me know when you're ready."

"Can you lower it a few more feet?" she called.

The rope dropped down a little further, giving her the extra length she needed.

Isabel pulled her knees to her chest and slipped her foot through the loop he'd tied at the end of the rope. Grasping hold with her hands and locking her other leg around the rope, she called up to him. "Get me out of here, Manuel."

The rope went taut. As Manuel hoisted her out of the water, her weight caused the rope to twist and spin, bumping and banging her against the rock walls. She adjusted, taking more weight on her hands and using the foothold as a counterbalance. Her arm muscles strained with the task and were soon shaking violently and burning like fire. The light at the mouth of the well grew larger and brighter, but not as quickly as Isabel would have liked.

"Hurry, Manuel, I don't know how much longer I can hold on!"

"You can do it, Isabel. Hang in there, girl." His voice sounded strained, and Isabel realized how much effort he was expending in cranking the winch.

She closed her eyes and gripped the rope, trying not to think about the pain in her muscles or the raw skin on her hands. Soon, two strong arms wrapped around her waist and pulled her over the rock ledge that surrounded the well. She and Manuel collapsed to the ground, panting and clinging to one another.

"What happened?" he asked between jagged breaths. "I left for just a minute and when I came back you were in the water."

"I thought I saw someone, but when I called out your name, no one answered. The next thing I knew, the rope gave." A chill of terror ripped through her and left her whole body shaking violently. "I thought I was going to drown. The rope got tangled around me and—" Frightened sobs broke off her words.

Manuel pulled her closer and stroked her back. "Shh. You're safe now."

She pressed her face into his shoulder and wept until the emotion abated. "I can't go back down there, Manuel."

He planted a gentle kiss on her forehead. "I wouldn't ask you to."

She swiped at her eyes, feeling foolish. "I don't think we'd find anything anyway. The bottom of the well is too deep. It's not accessible enough, and there were no loose rocks or niches in the walls. The pearls aren't down there." She met his eyes, begging him to agree. Another trip down that shaft was out of the question no matter how much she wanted to help.

He nodded and pulled her to her feet. "I trust your judgment, Isabel. You have a knack for this sort of thing. Rodrigo seemed fascinated with that well, but maybe that's all it was—a fascination. We'll concentrate on the terraces."

She picked up a length of rope and stared at it. "I can't believe the rope broke. It was almost new, wasn't it?"

Manuel's face darkened. "It didn't break; it was cut. The edges were clean, not frayed."

Isabel stiffened. "Someone followed us here?"

Manuel looked away, his profile tense. "I didn't see anyone, but that would be my guess."

Her gut tightened and twisted into a knot. "I'm scared, Manuel."

He turned and gathered her in his arms, heedless of the water dripping from her clothes and hair. "I'd never let anyone hurt you, Isabel. You can trust me."

His strong arms offered comfort and safety, and she allowed herself to relax. She would let him bear the burden of worry until she had time to recover.

As if sensing her need, Manuel tightened his hold. "From now on, we'll be more cautious. But don't worry. I'll protect you."

Pearls

Seventeen

As she neared the jeeps, Isabel startled and ducked behind a tree. She'd been so lost in thought that she hadn't noticed the person sitting on the hood of the vehicle until she was almost upon him. She peeked around the trunk of the tree and breathed a sigh of relief. Raúl. Chiding herself for being so jumpy, she went to greet him.

"Hi, Raúl."

He smiled as if he'd been expecting her.

She walked to the jeep and leaned against the hood next to him. "How did you get here?"

"I had one of the locals drive me this far. We found the jeeps, but I didn't know where you'd gone from here."

"Our camp is a ten-minute hike away. Have you been waiting long?"

"Two hours, maybe."

"Sorry. If I had known you were coming, I would have met you. Maybe we should have invested in a satellite phone for the expedition. It's probably the only way to get a signal this many miles from civilization."

Raúl smiled, flashing his dimples. "It's okay. I didn't mind the wait, and you're here now."

"Which reminds me, I came to get another jug of fresh water. We can use the ground water for washing up, but it's best to use processed water for cooking and drinking. If you'll help, we can carry back twice as much. That will save me a trip later this week."

"Sure, I'll help."

She pushed away from the hood, but Raúl's hand on her arm stopped her.

"Before we go, could we talk?" The tone of his voice suggested a serious conversation.

Pearls

Despite a sudden wariness, she nodded. "Okay."

He turned his warm brown eyes on her, and his pleading expression pulled at something inside her. "Is there any hope for us?"

So, he wanted to go there? Well, maybe it was time they talked. He needed to know there was no chance of a further romantic relationship. Yet having experienced the kind of pain he now suffered, she tried to find a gentle way of relaying the message. "There is no 'us' anymore."

Agony filled his eyes and lined his face. "I miss you, Isabel. I miss you so much it hurts."

His vulnerable admission grated against the barely healed damage he'd inflicted on her heart. Why couldn't he have realized his error sooner and saved them both the pain? "I thought we agreed to move on. From what I've witnessed, I'd say you have. How is Esperanza, by the way?"

He shook his head, shame and regret clearly displayed on his handsome features. "I admit I've tried to distract myself in an attempt to forget you, but it's no good. No one measures up."

His quiet declaration mocked her, tainted her emotions with the bitter reminder of his betrayal, and she couldn't keep the hurt from her voice. "You forget, Raúl, I've seen your other women. If anything, I'm the one who can't compete."

He trailed a finger over her cheek, his eyes begging for a word, a sign, a scrap of hope. "You don't know how beautiful you are. Your beauty was what first attracted me to you. That day in the coffee shop, your shy glances and blushing cheeks—you were so surprised when I paid you attention. At first I thought you were toying with me, acting demure to pique my interest. After our first evening together, I realized you had no idea the effect you have." He smoothed a lock of her hair between his fingers, a look of wonder on his face. "I wanted to be the one to offer you that revelation, to watch you blossom as you discovered yourself."

His raw honesty opened her soul and probed until it found the wonderful memories of times they shared. He'd played the knight in shining armor and rescued her from her struggles, feeding her self-esteem and filling the lonely void in her life. Nothing could erase the elation she'd felt those first weeks and months of their relationship. Even she could not deny the intoxicating effect of his love and affection. But everything changed the day she'd found him on his yacht in the arms of another woman. She couldn't erase the memory, nor could she live as if it didn't matter. It did.

"What are you asking me?" she sighed.

His fingertips trailed over her arms. "Don't abandon me, Isabel. I've never been able to hold onto the good things that come into my life. My father rejected me; my mother despised me; my business practices have not always been ethical. But you are good and moral and pure, and I need some of that in my life. I need you to help me be a better man."

A gentle prompting drew her focus within and beckoned her to search deeper than the memories and longings clouding her mind. Time spent each morning in prayer and meditation had sharpened her discernment to a keen edge. Now, truth cut away her illusions, revealing God's plan with startling clarity. He had brought Raúl into her life for a purpose, just not the one she initially assumed.

Seeing the wisdom of His handiwork, she surrendered to the leading of the Spirit. "You see good in me, Raúl?"

"Yes."

"And you want that kind of goodness in your life?"

He pulled her hand to his lips and kissed it. "More than I can say. Come back to me."

She smiled through the tears in her eyes. The truth had been there all along. Why hadn't she seen it? "You don't really want me, Raúl. You want what's inside me."

His look of confusion prodded her to explain.

"The purity and goodness you feel in me comes from God. It's Him you want—you just don't realize it yet. I don't have the power to give you what you need. No woman does. Only God can satisfy. If you ask, God will heal the hurts of your past and fill you with the peace you're searching for. He offers a satisfaction without compare."

She waited in silence, allowing him to consider her words, silently urging him to recognize and embrace the gift God offered him. She felt the hosts of heaven holding their collective breaths, waiting in expectancy for his answer.

"Does Manuel believe as you do?"

Not the question she'd anticipated, but a fair one. "Yes."

"Do you have feelings for him?"

"I do."

His face registered the blow she'd dealt to his heart. "He'll never amount to anything, Isabel. Women who fall in love with poor men like him sentence themselves to a hard life. I could offer you fine clothes, a comfortable home, travel. Anything you desire, I could give it to you."

She stared at him, perplexed. Maybe he hadn't heard her message, or maybe she'd explained it poorly. Surely, she had not imagined the weight of this pivotal moment. "Some things are more important than money."

"Like what?"

"You just finished telling me you want goodness in your life! Your money hasn't brought you peace or contentment. It won't make me happy either."

"Tell me, what will?"

"I would be very happy if you would ask God to be a part of your life."

"Then would you love me again?"

She smiled softly. "I think we already determined that we're worlds apart on a lot of issues. God is just one of them."

His face clouded with anger. "If you don't love me anymore, then just say so. You don't need to hide behind your God." He slid off the hood and stalked away, leaving her stunned and smarting.

The accusation came as an unexpected slap. She'd offered him the greatest treasure she could give him, something infinitely more valuable than herself, and he'd seen it as a rejection and an insult. She'd felt God's presence in such a tangible way, followed His lead, certain of a successful outcome.

Raúl stopped a short distance away. Hands on his hips, he glanced around in confusion, looking like the lost lamb that he was.

Show him the way. The Holy Spirit's prompting thrust Isabel from her self-pity and made her realize Raúl had not rejected her, but God. If God was still willing to pursue Raúl's heart, she could do her part to help.

She walked toward him. "Look, Raúl, I don't want to argue

with you. I'm hungry and I'm sure you are too. Let's go back to camp, and I'll make you some dinner, all right?"

When he didn't answer, she laid a hand on his arm. "I could still use some help carrying the water." She raised her eyebrows in invitation and offered a conciliatory smile.

The tension seemed to drain from his body, and his shoulders slumped in defeat. "Of course I'll help you, Isabel. Lead the way."

A glimpse of his old charm surfaced. As they unloaded the water jugs, she wondered if Raúl's charm would extend to Manuel and whether Manuel would tolerate Raúl's presence. The men had never discussed the ominous note Isabel found in Santo Domingo, but she knew Manuel wanted answers.

As she led the way to the camp, she dreaded the unavoidable confrontation.

~ * ~ * ~ * ~ * ~

Isabel chopped up a piece of fresh papaya and offered it to her two sullen dinner companions. As she'd expected, Manuel's eyes flashed fire the moment Raúl stepped foot into the camp, and Raúl did nothing to ease the tension. The moment Raúl saw his competition, his penitence evaporated. He slipped into his arrogant persona, taunting Manuel with subtle jabs and insults.

Manuel's tolerance amazed her. Never once did he show any anger at the verbal slights. Though obviously wary and protective, Manuel didn't inflame the situation by responding to Raúl's pettiness. For his admirable behavior, Manuel earned Isabel's respect despite Raúl's attempts to discredit him in her eyes.

After she'd finished her food, Isabel rose and gathered the dirty dishes. When she took Manuel's plate from him, he grabbed her hand and gave her a meaningful look. She knew what he was about to do.

Kneeling beside a plastic tub they used for washing dishes, she watched Manuel stand and approach Raúl. "I need a word with you."

Annoyance flashed over Raúl's face. "I have nothing to say to you."

Manuel crossed his arms over his chest, his face showing determination. "I'd prefer to talk away from the camp."

Raúl stood and jabbed a finger into Manuel's chest. "Let's talk about why you haven't found the pearls."

"We can discuss business if you'd like, but first we're going to talk about a personal issue."

"I am not interested in your personal affairs."

"Someone has been threatening Isabel."

Raúl's gaze darted to Isabel, and she thought she saw a flash of fear. He turned back to Manuel, and anger replaced the expression. "What makes you think I know anything about that?"

"The police showed Isabel pictures of the man suspected of burning her apartment. She saw him again in Santo Domingo when he shoved that note in your pocket."

"What note?"

Manuel slid a piece of paper from his pocket and offered it to Raúl. "If you need to refresh your memory...."

Raúl's Adam's apple bobbed as he stared at the evidence. He snatched it out of Manuel's hand and made a show of looking it over. "I don't know where this note came from or what it means." He wadded it up and tossed it into the fire.

Manuel grabbed a handful of Raúl's shirt and crumpled it in his fist. "Isabel is in danger. This isn't the time for deception and games."

Raúl knocked Manuel's hand away, looking offended at the insinuation. "It's clever of you to try to cast blame on me."

Manuel stepped back, his posture taking on wary lines. "What are you talking about?"

"I looked into your background before I hired you. I should have known better than to do business with you."

Manuel's fists bunched and his shoulder muscles knotted. "You had better have some proof if you intend to make accusations like that."

"You think I don't?"

"I know you don't." Manuel turned to Isabel. "I have no idea what he's talking about, Isabel. I swear."

Raúl sneered. "You can only pretend for so long. She'll find out, you know."

"Find out what?" Isabel walked to their side, unable to stay out of the conversation.

"Manuel has an interesting history. His last coworker ended up dead."

Manuel's eyes narrowed to hard slits. "That was an accident."

"Like the accident at Isabel's apartment?"

She turned to Manuel. "Is this true?"

Manuel looked hurt. "He's lying. I thought you trusted me."

Raúl grabbed her shoulder. "That's what he wants, Isabel. You haven't found the pearls because he doesn't want you to. He'll delay the discovery until he's sure he can control you. If you don't cooperate, he'll arrange an accident."

Manuel looked ready to explode. "I love her. I would never hurt her."

Isabel's eyes snapped to Manuel's face. Did he just say he loved her? Happiness bubbled up inside her like a fountain. She wanted to stop the conversation and linger there in that bit of sweet knowledge, but Raúl's angry voice cut into the moment, shattering the magic.

"How convenient. A woman is always more pliable after she gives her heart to a man."

"You would know, Raúl. You've been using her all along."

With her head and heart reeling, Isabel decided she'd heard enough and stepped between them. "Stop it! All this arguing is getting us nowhere."

Manuel wrapped his fingers around her arm. "You can't possibly believe him. You know he's a liar."

"I have my faults, but I'd do anything to protect Isabel." Raúl slapped Manuel's hand away. "Let go of her!"

Manuel shoved Raúl and a scuffle ensued. Isabel tried to pull them apart but was knocked to the ground. Her startled cry as she thudded into the dirt snapped them out of their fits of anger. They stepped away from each other and stared down at her with similar looks of chagrin.

She bristled. "I want both of you to take a long walk."

Raúl tried to help her up. "Isabel—"

"No, Raúl! Start walking. If you cared so much about my safety, why would you leave me alone with a man you thought to be dangerous?"

Manuel looked pleased, as if exonerated by the question.

His reaction angered her. "And you, Manuel, obviously have

some secrets you should have discussed with me."

"But, Isabel—"

"Just leave, both of you. I need some time to think." She pushed to her feet and dusted herself off.

They stared at her for a moment then looked at one another. She recognized the territorial looks on their faces. Neither wanted to be the first to leave and give the other a chance to plead their case to her.

She glared at them both, disgusted and fed up. "Fine. I'll leave and when I come back, you'd both better be gone."

~ * ~ * ~ * ~ * ~

An hour later the men still hadn't returned. Isabel finished putting away the mini-stove and dinner utensils. Rather than sit and wait for them, she decided to climb to the terraces and view the sunset from a perch near the heavens. After a twenty-minute climb, she settled on a soft patch of grass and studied the fiery brilliance of the western horizon. Birds chirped from the treetops, and Isabel let their songs sooth her. Slowly, her tension dissipated, and she was able to consider the turmoil in her mind with some semblance of reason.

God, what do I do now? I thought I could trust Manuel, but Raúl's accusations suggested otherwise. But can I believe anything Raúl says? Both men have feelings for me, so naturally, they're going to feel like they're in competition and try to discredit one another. How much of this conflict is about male ego, and how much is based on truth?

She wrapped her arms around her legs and dropped her forehead to her knees. *I have invested so much emotion in each of these men that I don't know if I can trust my judgment. Manuel said he loves me, and I think I'm falling for him. He's smart and steady, with that quiet strength that wraps around me and makes me feel secure. He loves You, and I trust his sincerity. But how can I be sure this is right? Abuela would tell me to look with the discerning eyes of the Spirit, but I have so little practice. You'll guide me through this, won't you, Lord?*

His answer came in the form of peace, drifting through her soul like a gentle spring breeze. *Thank you.*

She sat on the hillside, allowing Him to comfort her and fill her weariness with strength until the sun dipped below the horizon, leaving the terrace in shadows. She decided to leave, knowing she should make the climb down while some light remained. Just then, a low percussion sounded across the landscape and built into a dull roar.

The strange rumble made Isabel's hair stand on end. Her instincts screamed danger.

She jumped to her feet and turned in a circle, her head snapping from side to side, looking for the source of the sound. The rumble grew louder, and the trees on the slope far above her began to snap and crackle. She stared in amazement at the mountainside, which shifted and rearranged itself with alarming speed. A wall of sliding rock swallowed vegetation, stripped the color from the slope, and refaced the green mountain with cold gray stone. Large boulders and small stones hurled toward her in a dizzying blur, kicking up a plume of dust in their wake.

She stared with morbid fascination for precious long moments before she realized the monster streaking down the mountainside intended to devour her. In seconds the rockslide would sweep the entire area clean. Horror shot through her, locking her muscles into useless masses of frozen sinew.

Time slowed to a crawl, transforming each second into an eternity of terror. She looked from left to right, seeing no avenue of escape. No chance to outrun the beast, but maybe—

The fear that had paralyzed her only seconds earlier now jolted her muscles with superhuman energy. Her legs pumped beneath her as she ran toward the sliding wall of rock. If she could just get to the cleft in the retaining wall before the avalanche hit. The ground beneath her feet trembled, as if dreading the imminent assault. Her step faltered, and she flailed to keep her balance as she ran.

Pebbles and dirt hailed down on her, stinging her arms and face, obscuring her flight to safety. Out of time, she dove, spending every ounce of strength she possessed in a last attempt at salvation. She rolled until her body slammed against stone with brutal force.

Then the thunder consumed her.

Pearls

Eighteen

For terrifying long moments, the ground trembled and deafening noise enveloped Isabel. She pressed herself into a shallow cleft in the retaining wall, and every muscle in her body tensed as rocks and boulders passed a few feet overhead. She squeezed her eyes shut and held her hands over her face to ward off the spray of dust and stones raining down. The larger rocks vaulted off the terrace above her, their momentum carrying them over her hiding spot and launching them further down the mountain.

After an eternity of seconds, the rumbling faded and eerie silence settled over the area. Her heart pounded hard enough to break her ribs. She let out the breath she'd been holding and drew another only to choke on the cloud of dust swirling in the air around her.

"It's over. I'm alive." Isabel whispered reassuring words to herself and willed her tense muscles to relax and her body to stop trembling. Slowly, the terror of the moment subsided, and her body responded to the relief of safety.

Isabel pushed to a sitting position and leaned against the cleft in the wall that had served as her protector during the onslaught. The small niche was half blocked by debris now, and Isabel wasn't sure she could climb out of the small opening remaining. She shoved at the nearest rock, but it didn't budge. From her position, lying down in the small space, she had no leverage. Better to conserve her energy.

Exhausted from the ordeal, Isabel closed her eyes and allowed herself to rest for a moment. A memory from childhood wafted through her mind. Her father had taken her to see a rock quarry to help with her geology project for a science fair. Isabel clearly remembered the sound of the blasting that echoed across the quarry walls. The sound was strangely like the one she had heard moments ago just before the rockslide began.

The skin on the back of her neck prickled with fear. Was this another accident or an intentional attempt on her life? Isabel suspected someone wanted her dead—but who and why? She lay there trapped and scared while night settled over the mountain, wondering if she'd have to spend the night and asking herself if she might be safer here than in the camp.

"Isabel?" Manuel's frantic call carried across the terraces.

"Here!"

She could hear him scrambling over the rocks and loose scree. She pushed up as close to a sitting position as she could manage and thrust her hand out the opening near the top of the niche. The beam of his flashlight found the hole and directed a shaft of light inside her little cubby.

Manuel appeared in the haze of dust and debris. When he reached her side and knelt in front of the opening, his eyes met hers with relief and fear mingled on his face.

"Isabel! Are you hurt?"

"No. Not really."

"Just a minute, let me get you out of there." He lifted stones and shoved boulders out of the way until he'd cleared a pathway out of the cleft. She crawled out and let him help her to her feet.

"You're bleeding." His fingers gently probed her arm as he examined the source of her injuries.

"Just a few cuts and scrapes. I inflicted them on myself when I slammed into the wall."

Manuel's gaze flicked over the retaining wall and the lack of damage and debris directly beneath it. "You hid here?"

She nodded. "The cleft in the wall was just big enough to shelter me."

"So you were right in the middle of the landslide?"

She closed her eyes and nodded again.

"Where is Raúl?" he asked.

"I haven't seen him since I left the two of you at the camp."

"Me either. As soon as I heard the noise and realized what had happened, I rushed back to the camp. When I couldn't find you, I got scared. I know how you like to come here at sunset, but I prayed that for once you'd gone somewhere else. I didn't see how you could survive if you were here."

A chill skittered down Isabel's spine. Only Manuel knew her evening routine. Had he devised this incident to eliminate her as Raúl suggested he would? She opened her eyes and fixed him with a direct stare. "Are you disappointed this accident didn't kill me?"

He looked stricken. "How can you ask that? Don't tell me you believed anything Raúl said down there. He's trying to tear us apart."

She looked deep into his eyes, searching for reassurance of innocence or confirmation of guilt. His dark eyes revealed no hint of deception. "Where were you just before the avalanche?" she asked him suspiciously.

"Sitting on the rock where I have my morning devotions. I left my Bible there if you want proof."

"I do."

Disappointment lined his face, but he nodded.

"I'm sorry, Manuel. I want to trust you, but someone is trying to kill me. If I put my trust in the wrong person, I could end up dead."

He held out a hand. "Fair enough. Come on. I'll help you down the stairs."

He directed the flashlight a few feet ahead of them, so they could see to find footing in the rubble. Slowly, they descended the stone staircase and made their way back to camp, stopping to pick up his Bible, which was right where he'd said it would be. Isabel relaxed, certain her instincts were right this time. Abuela was a good judge of character, and she'd assured Isabel she could trust Manuel. He'd been nothing but open and forthright in their dealings thus far, so she had no reason to question his integrity.

Raúl occupied a canvas chair when they approached. He jumped to his feet and rushed to her side when he caught sight of them.

"Isabel, what happened? Are you all right?"

"A little banged up but my injuries aren't serious." She studied his face, hating the distrust she felt, but unable to ignore the feeling. He returned the look with openness and concern. Her suspicions eased. Maybe she'd overreacted. Neither man seemed capable of murder. Besides, if they'd brought enough explosives to generate an avalanche, she would have seen them. Obviously, this was an accident—a freak occurrence no one could have predicted.

Still, she'd sleep lightly for the remainder of the trip.

~ * ~ * ~ * ~ * ~

"It's completely ruined, Isabel." Manuel stared at the pile of twisted metal and broken glass. While Isabel had managed to escape the ravages of the avalanche, the disaster pulverized the equipment they'd left on the terraces.

She stared at the pieces of shredded metal, wondering how she would have looked if that wall of rocks had slid over her. Swallowing hard, she tried to focus on the task at hand. "What do you suggest we do?"

"Leave. There's no point in staying here now. The terraces are destroyed." He glanced around the area, angry at the devastation the historical site had suffered. Most of the turf was shredded, and giant gouges marred the once-pristine terraces. Some of the retaining walls had collapsed under the pummeling, and Manuel knew a few heavy rains would wash out much of the terrain. The ancient terraces would slowly erode and disappear. A shame. "We spent three weeks working at this location. If we didn't find it in that amount of time, it's probably not here."

From the corner of his eye, he noticed Isabel studying him. Despite the fact that they had found his Bible exactly where he said it would be, she still didn't trust him completely. Her lack of confidence disappointed him, but he didn't intend to give up. He would simply work harder to earn her faith.

Standing, he turned to face her. "Even if we could keep working, I'd insist on leaving. Since we arrived, it's been one incident after the other. I don't like feeling that you're in danger." He grazed her cheek with his fingertips.

She didn't shy away from his touch. A good sign.

"Come on. Let's put some distance between this place and us. Maybe we'll outrun trouble."

She nodded and slipped her hand into his. "Let's go tell Raúl."

~ * ~ * ~ * ~

While Manuel arranged for Isabel to see a doctor, Isabel leaned against the outer wall of the medical facility and glanced around the streets of Santo Domingo, thinking it strange to be with so many people again after weeks of isolation.

"I need to return to Caracas and see to my business interests. A problem has arisen that I cannot handle over the phone." Raúl's gaze darted over Isabel's features then dropped to the ground. "You don't need me here anyway."

Isabel felt a surge of compassion. Raúl's pride had taken some severe blows in the last few weeks. Though she recognized God's handiwork in progress, she couldn't help but pity the man. When God stripped a person of defenses, the process hurt, even if it was for the best.

"We appreciate all the help you've offered. We couldn't have done this without your financial support."

Raúl shrugged. "You may as well know, the money was irrelevant. I agreed to partner with you so I could continue to see you."

"I know."

His eyes met hers. "I still care. I always will."

She nodded. "I know that too."

He sucked in a deep breath, as if pulling courage into his body. "Is there any chance for us?"

She paused, choosing her words carefully. "Right now friendship and business are all that are possible."

He sighed. "I wish your answer was different, but I'm not surprised. I don't blame you either. If the situation were reversed, my stance would likely be the same."

She held out her hand, and he wrapped his fingers around it. "Take care of yourself, Raúl. And promise me you'll think about our conversation."

"The one about God?"

She tilted her head and looked at him with all the sincerity she could muster. "You might find what you're searching for in Him."

The door of the medical clinic opened, and Manuel stepped out. "They have an exam room waiting. The doctor can see you in just a few minutes."

Isabel drew a deep breath. "Really, I'm fine. I don't need to see a doctor."

Manuel crossed his arms over his chest. "You will see the

doctor or I will drive you back home to your grandmother."

"Please, Isabel. See the doctor." Raúl gave her a look of determination similar to Manuel's, and Isabel knew she had no choice but to concede.

"Fine. I'll go, but it's a waste of money."

"Not in my opinion. I'll see you later. Maybe not until you return to Caracas, but I'd like to hear about the Amazon." Raúl leaned toward her and planted a kiss on her cheek.

Isabel nodded.

Raúl turned and offered a hand to Manuel. "Take care of her."

Manuel looked surprised at Raúl's uncharacteristic gesture but accepted the offered hand. "I will. Have a safe trip back."

The two men stared at one another, and Isabel sensed a message passing through the undercurrents of their gazes. For the first time, Raúl seemed to acknowledge some grudging acceptance of Manuel and his new role in her life.

"I'm leaving then." Raúl turned and climbed into the jeep he would drive back to Caracas. With the loss of equipment in the rockslide, they no longer needed two vehicles to transport gear. With a look of regret in his eyes, he started the vehicle and guided it out onto the road.

Isabel waved until he disappeared around a bend. Turning to Manuel, she smiled. "Guess I can't avoid this medical exam any longer."

He opened the door and held it for her. "After you."

~ * ~ * ~ * ~ * ~

Glad to finish the long drive, Manuel steered the car down the busy streets of Puerto Ayacucho, gateway to the Amazon. The people bustling in the streets wore looks of anticipation as they added colorful decorations to storefronts and windows. The plaza in the center of town was barricaded to traffic, and the area churned with people setting up for an event. Tables and chairs clustered around food vendor stands, and a group of men assembled a stage at one end of the plaza. Bright flags and streamers fluttered in the breeze, adding to the festive picture. Manuel guessed there would be music and dancing in addition to the delicious food and drink.

"I wonder what's going on here." Isabel eyed the activity with the look of one who has spent weeks in isolation.

Her face showed a hunger for some social time, and her interest gave him an idea. "Looks like a festival. I'll ask someone about it."

Manuel found a decent hotel a few blocks from the center of town and paid for two rooms. He walked Isabel to hers and made sure the facilities were adequate. It offered a single bed with a faded blanket, a battered dresser, and a bathroom no larger than a closet. Not the most deluxe accommodations, but they were clean and functional—the best one could hope for in this part of the world.

He left her sitting on the bed and returned a few minutes later with her bags. After placing her belongings inside the door, he leaned against the frame. "I asked the hotel manager about the activity in the center of town. He said it's Carnival Week. They have a big celebration just before Lent, and the festival starts tonight."

She nodded. "I figured it must be something like that."

He met her gaze and summoned his nerve. "I was wondering if you'd do me the honor of attending the festival with me this evening."

She smiled. "Are you asking me on a date?"

"I thought it was time we got around to our first date, since we decided to start dating about three weeks ago."

She glanced down at her clothes and her smile faded. "It sounds like fun, Manuel, but I don't have anything to wear. Every outfit I brought is filthy. I was considering doing something about my dirty laundry when you knocked."

He noticed the dark smudges under her eyes. They'd worked hard for the last two weeks, and she needed a few days of rest and fun. He tweaked her earlobe, unwilling to accept no for an answer. "We can do laundry tomorrow. You clean up and take a nap. I'll see you later."

She nodded, yawning as she shut the door.

"Wait." He put his hand on the door and stopped her. "I forgot to tell you. Don't go anywhere without me. We're only a few miles from the Columbian border. Sometimes guerillas cross over and when they do, Americans aren't safe."

"That's comforting."

"Promise me."

"I promise I'm going to wash up and take a nap. No excursions outside the room."

"Good. I'll see you later."

Manuel listened for the sound of her lock then began to put his plan into action. He would have liked to crawl into bed, as well. Despite hours of inactivity while they traveled, his body felt more fatigued than if he'd labored all day. But he could rest later. For now, he had a mission to accomplish.

Stopping by his room, he dug in his bag for the nicer outfit he'd brought along. Archaeology generally entailed long, hard hours in the field, sweating and working with dirt in one form or another. His wardrobe reflected his practical nature. He opted for functional, durable clothes without concern for fashion. But occasionally, situations arose that required more professional looking apparel. For this reason he always carried one nicer outfit.

He pulled the black pants and shirt from his bag and winced. They were wrinkled and carried a faint odor from having been packed with dirty clothes. Gathering them up along with his supply of cash, he left in search of a laundromat. He found one a few doors down from the hotel and gave the proprietress something extra to have them ready in a few hours.

His next errand forced him onto unfamiliar territory. Even growing up with three sisters had not prepared him for this mission, but if he wanted to make this night a success, he would have to brave it.

As he passed through the open door of a shop with a promising window display, his shoulder brushed against a set of wind chimes, drawing unwanted attention to his arrival. Two saleswomen exchanged knowing glances, and the older lady stepped forward, a smile playing at the corners of her mouth. "Can I help you?" she asked in melodic Spanish.

"I hope so, because I'm certain I won't be of any help to myself." He flashed her a smile and hoped a little charm would buy him extra assistance and cooperation. He needed a female accomplice if he intended to pull this off. "I want to buy an outfit—a dress for a woman."

"This woman, she is special, no?"

He nodded with relief. The sparkle in her eye told him she was a matchmaker at heart. "Very. And I want our evening to be special, so the dress has to be just right."

"Did you have something particular in mind?"

"A dress with a traditional flavor. Colorful, full skirts, a peasant blouse."

She turned and headed for the back of the store, waving at him to follow. "The tourists, they like these so we always keep some in stock. They are perfect to wear to a festival, *sí?*"

She pulled one of the dresses from the rack and held it against her, grasping a handful of the flared skirt and lifting it to show him the fullness. It was feminine without being frilly, possessed a cultural flavor without overdoing it. And she was right—it looked perfect for a festival.

"I'll take it, or at least I'll take one of them." He stared at the rack perplexed. "I don't know what size or color." He realized he hadn't done enough research before he set out on this little expedition.

The saleswoman smiled and patted his arm, obviously accustomed to dealing with addled customers. "Maria!" she called.

The other saleswoman appeared with a look of expectancy on her face.

"Your señorita, she is like Maria, or smaller, or larger…?"

Manuel grasped her plan and decided it could work. Maria looked flustered in her modeling role, evidenced by the blush creeping over her face. Truthfully, he was uncomfortable, too, so he tried to make his perusal brief. His gaze traveled over Maria's frame, his mind making quick comparisons.

"The women are nearly the same size, but Isabel is taller." He held his hand up near his chin, indicating her height. "And she has beautiful blue eyes. Do you have a color that will set them off?"

Maria slipped away while the saleswoman thumbed through the rack of dresses. "This one, I think." She separated a dress from the others and held it out to him.

A vibrant indigo. Manuel could imagine how the hues would play with Isabel's rich coloring. "If that's her size, I'll take it."

The saleswoman carried it to the front counter and proceeded to wrap the purchase in tissue. He paid for the dress, handing over nearly half of his personal spending money on the gift and not regretting a penny. The deal with Raúl had provided Manuel with a modest salary in exchange for his expertise. He sent a portion of the income to his mother, buying a few months' time before her financial struggles demanded he abandon his archaeological pursuits to salvage the family farm. The rest he pocketed for an emergency or occasional splurge.

There was no one he would rather splurge on than Isabel.

On his way back to the hotel, Manuel saw an old man peddling flowers on the corner and veered toward him. The vendor offered a nice selection of fresh-cut blooms, but the only one fitting for Isabel was the orchid. Beautiful, elegant—like her. Manuel laid the flower across the tissue-wrapped package and bounded to Isabel's door, a giddy sensation in his chest adding spring to his step.

He heard her humming as he knocked. When she opened the door, she wore a robe and a towel wrapped around her hair turban style, her face washed clean of makeup.

"For you."

He pushed the gift toward her, and she instinctively reached out to accept it. "What's this?"

"I'll pick you up at six o'clock." He flashed her a smile and pulled the door shut, leaving her to figure out what to do with his surprise.

Nineteen

Manuel arrived exactly on time, looking better than any man had a right to. His black pants and shirt emphasized his dark complexion, and Isabel wondered if he realized how appealing he was.

Funny how she had hardly noticed him when they first met, and now she couldn't take her eyes off him. Maybe he had grown more attractive, or maybe her eyes had learned to see a deeper beauty. Manuel possessed *that* kind of attractiveness in abundance. Patient, gentle, respectful—he'd been the perfect companion during the last few weeks full of wonder and discovery.

He smiled. "You're staring at me."

"You're staring at me too," she pointed out.

He leaned against the doorframe, hands in his pockets. "I can't help it. You're beautiful."

She smoothed her hands across her outfit and flashed him a grateful glance. "Thank you for the dress. It was thoughtful of you."

He lifted a hand and twirled his finger in the air, giving her a silent command to turn and model for him. Blushing, she spun a slow circle, feeling the hem of the full skirt brushing against her calves.

"The orchid looks nice behind your ear, but something isn't right."

"Really? What?" She lifted a hand and touched the flower, making sure it was still in place.

"Come here, let me."

She stepped closer and allowed him to turn her so her back was to him. She felt his fingers on her hair, tugging at the rubber band she'd used to fasten the end of her French braid.

"You're hair is pretty, Isabel. You should leave it down." His

173

breath fanned the back of her neck as he combed through the woven strands. The intimate touch set her scalp tingling, and she closed her eyes. His fingers climbed higher, loosening the braid up to her crown.

When her hair fell free around her shoulders and neck, she turned to face him.

He forked his fingers through her hair and arranged it around her face. "It's so soft."

His velvety touch and voice left her dizzy. He hadn't attempted to kiss her for days, and suddenly she wanted him to. His restraint tormented her. When she thought she couldn't stand another moment of the anticipation building between them, he stepped backward, breaking the spell and leaving her unfulfilled. "Are you hungry?"

She nodded, gaining a tentative control over her senses. "Very. And something smells delicious."

"I think that's *rosquitas*, fried bread sprinkled with sugar and spices. I'll buy you some for dessert." He took her key and locked the door. "Let's go see what's happening in the plaza."

People filled the streets, talking, laughing, eating, and relaxing. Lively music, aromatic food, and street performers vied for the attention of the crowd. Isabel felt the excitement in the atmosphere.

Manuel's fingers closed around Isabel's hand, and he tugged her close to his side. "Let's don't get separated."

They navigated the crowded streets and entered the plaza. Musicians on the bandstand played a lively salsa tune, infusing the area with an irrepressible energy, which manifested itself in tapping toes and bouncing knees. The smells drifting from the food vendors enticed them to that area. They purchased hot sandwiches and drinks and drifted toward the crowded tables.

"There's an empty one." Manuel led the way through the makeshift food court.

Once seated, she inhaled the delicious aroma of her food and smiled at Manuel. "We haven't eaten many meals like this one in the past few weeks."

He raised an eyebrow. "Are you complaining about my cooking?"

"I enjoy your cooking, but even you have to admit there's a difference between fresh food and meals that come from a can."

"I'm just teasing. I'm sick of my own concoctions too. This is a nice treat before we return to the wilds."

Bowing her head, she offered up a silent prayer before taking a giant bite of the steaming sandwich. As they ate, the sun dropped low on the horizon, and the light dimmed to a romantic level. Workers circled the plaza lighting tiki torches, which added to the sultry mood.

The musicians catered to the crowd, playing tunes that beckoned people to their feet. Soon the area in front of the bandstand filled with a laughing, smiling crowd.

Isabel finished her sandwich and sat with her cheek propped on one hand, watching the kaleidoscope of color as the dancers moved in shifting patterns. The music and the steps reminded her of her mother, and she felt a pang of homesickness. Some of her best memories of her mother were related to Venezuelan music and dance.

"Do you know any of the traditional dances?" he asked.

She shrugged one shoulder. "When I was a kid, my mom would put a record on the stereo and dance in our living room. I always thought she was so graceful and beautiful. Over the years, she taught me a few steps, and we would dance together. I think dancing helped her not to feel so homesick."

"Do you miss her?"

She nodded.

"Maybe dancing is the cure for your homesickness too." He rose and held out his hand.

She leaned back in her chair, embarrassed. "I don't think so."

"Come on, Isabel. Dance with me."

She resisted when he tugged at her hand, refusing to move from her chair. "Manuel, it's been years since I tried any of those steps, and even then I was an amateur."

He leaned close, planting a kiss in the hollow beneath her earlobe. "It's like riding a bike. Once you get started, it all comes flooding back."

He had more determination than she did resistance, and after more urging, she allowed him to escort her into the swaying crowd.

Pearls

He turned to her and bowed, brushing a kiss across her fingers. Dropping her hand, he took a step backward and joined in the moves of the dance with surprising skill. Isabel stared because she couldn't help herself. He was good—no, better than good. Excellent. Why hadn't she noticed that agility and masculine grace before now?

"It helps to move your feet!" he called above the music. Isabel felt a blush rising from the neckline of her blouse and realized she looked more foolish standing there gawking at him than she would dancing. Drawing in a deep breath, she tested her feet at a few of the simpler steps, trying to recall the vague memories. A pang of embarrassment accompanied each awkward movement. Maybe if he would look away. The intense glow in his eyes distracted her and increased her struggle.

"Smile, this is fun," he teased.

She flicked a tortured gaze his way before returning her attention to her efforts. Harnessing her discomfort, she channeled her energy into her feet, willing them to remember. Soon rhythms long buried resurrected and infused her muscles with the fire of her Latina blood. Her feet fell in with the rhythm of the music, and her movements grew more confident. She gathered handfuls of the voluminous material of her skirt, and she stamped and twirled, swirling her skirts as she beat out the steps of the music.

Manuel stepped closer, initiating play between them, flirting, chasing, and beckoning with each step of the lively dance. Rising to the challenge, Isabel focused on his smoldering dark eyes and matched her movements to his. Her pulse throbbed in her throat as she allowed him to lead her with nothing more than the intensity of his gaze. The dance built in fervency until the song came to a rousing end. Breathing heavily, her eyes still locked on Manuel's, Isabel applauded the band along with the rest of the crowd.

The musicians drifted into a slow tune, and he held out his arms in invitation. "Like to try something more tame?"

Her stomach flip-flopped. "Looks rather dangerous to me."

He answered with a slow smile and a challenge in his eyes.

Eager to be close to him, she let him take her hand in his. His other arm slid around her waist, coming to rest on the small of her back. Isabel placed her free hand on his shoulder and closed her eyes. His nearness overwhelmed her. The firm muscle beneath his shirt, the spicy scent of his aftershave, and his breath stirring her hair left her senses reeling.

He breathed a contented sigh. "This is nice."

"Mmmhmm."

"You misled me about your dancing skills. You're good."

She smiled to cover her shyness. "You aren't too bad yourself. Where did you learn?"

"I told you I have three sisters. Who do you think had to help them practice?"

"You must have done a lot of practicing, Fred Astaire."

"Who is Fred?"

She laughed. "An American dancer who impressed the ladies with his footwork."

He smiled.

They lapsed into silence. As they danced, Manuel hummed the song. His deep, soothing baritone caused Isabel to tremble.

"Are you cold?"

She dared to look up into his face. "No."

As he stared down at her, understanding flickered over his face and lit a fire in his eyes. Her heart pounded out a staccato rhythm. His gaze dropped to her lips then shifted to a point behind her. "Maybe we should take a walk."

"Good idea."

She followed him from the dance area, still grappling with the feelings he'd stirred. His honorable behavior both delighted and frustrated her. She couldn't remember ever wanting to be kissed more than she had just moments ago. Yet with the specter of danger lurking over her, she wasn't sure she should risk a relationship with anyone. On the other hand, if she couldn't trust a man who showed so much respect and restraint, whom could she trust?

They strolled along the main thoroughfare, fingers entwined. Street performers entertained the festival-goers with circus tricks and magic acts. Manuel stopped at a stand and purchased her the promised *rosquitas*. One bite of the sweet doughy bread transported Isabel to taste bud heaven. A few blocks from the center of town, they found themselves standing in front of a beautiful old church.

Pearls

Thick wooden doors nestled beneath a Spanish arch, and a bell tower stood high overhead.

"Let's go inside." Isabel nodded toward the church.

"Okay." Manuel pulled at the iron handle, and the door swung easily open.

A reverent quiet dominated the interior of the church, unaffected by the revelry on the streets.

Holding hands, Isabel and Manuel passed through a spacious vestibule and into the nave. Cherry wood pews lined either side of a wide center aisle. Their shoes clicked against the marble floors, sending echoes around the ornate room. The front wall of the church captured Isabel's attention with its elaborate decoration. A reredos of a golden cathedral stretched across the wall behind the high altar. Hovering above it, a mural of Christ with arms outstretched beckoned to them. Isabel settled on a pew halfway up the aisle. The deep and abiding presence permeating the atmosphere seeped into her soul, and she felt at peace.

The bench creaked as Manuel sat down beside her. He breathed a deep sigh. "It's funny how a place like this can feel like home. I've traveled all around the world and sat in many churches, some like this one, some very different. But in every place, I felt as if I belonged."

Isabel sat and pondered his statement for a moment, revelation unfolding inside her, answering long-asked questions and filling up places that had felt empty for ages. "I feel it," she whispered in awe. "Belonging and acceptance." She turned toward him, tears brimming in her eyes. "All my life I've searched for a sense of belonging. I wanted people to accept me, but I never felt like I fit in anywhere. It's God, isn't it?"

He nodded. "You were trying to belong to a place or a person, but it's His presence that satisfies."

"I never looked to Him to fulfill that need until the last few weeks." She smiled at Manuel. "You helped me with that."

"Me? What did I do?"

"You impressed me with your inner strength and stability. You set an example by taking time each morning to read your Bible and pray on that rock. I saw you there more than once and realized maybe something was missing in my life. Since then, I've been spending time with God each day, and it's made all the difference. I feel complete and content for the first time in my life."

He smiled. "You always belonged. You just didn't realize it."

She glanced up at his face and saw the look of tender understanding in his eyes. Leaning closer, she rested her head against his shoulder. "Even if we don't find the pearls on this trip, I've made an invaluable discovery. Thank you, Manuel."

His arm dropped around her shoulders and held her tight. "You're more than welcome, honey."

~ * ~ * ~ * ~ * ~

Manuel stopped in front of her door and leaned against the wall. "We'll make our final preparations and replenish supplies tomorrow morning. In the afternoon, we'll fly out to a substation in the rainforest. Our guides will meet us there and help load our *bongos*."

"*Bongos?*"

"Shallow wood canoes."

"Oh. Where will we spend the night? In our tents?"

"Tomorrow night we'll sleep in a *churuata*, which is a small Indian hut with a palm roof. Hammocks encased in mosquito netting hang from the hut's beams. There won't be much privacy, so dress accordingly."

She nodded and smiled. "Sounds like an adventure."

He stared at her a moment, admiring her pretty features and regretting that the date had to end. "I really enjoyed our evening together. I wish we could spend more leisure time together. This trip will be over soon and then...."

Isabel lowered her face so he couldn't see her expression. "I know."

"I don't think you do." He hooked his finger under her chin and forced her to lift her face. Wrapping his other arm around her back, he pulled her close and bent to claim a kiss. Her hands slid around his shoulders, and her fingers curled into the hair at his neckline, sending a chill of pleasure down his back. He lingered a moment longer then broke away while he still had the willpower to do so.

"Be sure to lock your door. I'll pick you up early in the morning."

"I'll be ready."

Her door closed behind her, and the lock clicked into place. Manuel stood there a moment, savoring the lingering effect of her kiss. How had he lived without her all these years? And when this trip ended, how was he going to say goodbye?

Twenty

April 25, 1515

I have discovered the Garden of Eden. We navigated a wide river for many days and journeyed into the heart of a strange and exotic land. The sun is hot, the rain plentiful, so that everywhere I look I see a shade of green. Trees soar to immeasurable heights and plants grow in abundance. I wonder if any European man aside from myself has seen the strange beasts like those scurrying through the trees and prowling across the land.

Karwa grows fearful when the monkeys howl and the large cats roar. Even the water harbors dangerous predators. Yet beasts abound where food is plentiful, and so we will make this land our home. Surely in this wet and wild Eden, my family can settle in peace.

Leafy treetops spread a canopy over the waterway, laying dappled light on the swift current. Isabel admired the tall ferns and flowering shrubs that vied for the coveted space at the water's edge. The peace of the setting seeped into her being and flooded her with a deep sense of contentment. Or maybe the contentment had been there all along, and time afloat the Orinoco River simply allowed her to recognize the sensation.

Manuel seemed equally content as he and his Indian guide paddled their *bongo* alongside hers. Manuel dipped his oar in a steady rhythm while the passing breeze flirted with his hair, lifting the curls off his collar and making them dance.

He caught her staring and smiled. "Hi."

Memories of their kiss last night pushed to the forefront of her mind, filling her with a rush of euphoria. "Hi, yourself." She smiled back at him, tamping down the giddiness certainly plastered all over her features. Their budding romance seemed inherently right in the sensibility of daylight.

"Getting hungry?"

Her stomach jumped at the question. She nodded. "Is this a good time to stop?"

"Good as any." Manuel turned and spoke with his guide. He pointed to a fallen tree trunk. Its massive roots clung to the shore while its length arched from the shore to the murky depths of the river. "We could tie off there and eat."

The Indian who shared Isabel's boat nodded as Manuel's guide gave instructions in their native language. They adjusted their rowing and steered for the shore, slowing to a crawl as they neared their makeshift dock. Grabbing her mooring rope, she shimmied to the front of the shallow canoe, wrapped the line around a sturdy branch, and fashioned a snug knot.

The guides tied the backs of the *bongos* together to add stability then opened their lunch. Manuel joined Isabel near the front of the crafts and handed her a foil wrapped parcel. "It's nothing fancy, but it'll keep you from starving."

She laid the bundle in her lap. "We ate so much in Puerto Ayacucho that I didn't think I'd want to eat again for a week."

Manuel flashed her a shy look. "I enjoyed our time together there."

"You sound as if you're surprised."

"In a way, I was. I've been focused on my career for so long, I forgot how good it feels to relax and have fun with someone special."

She smiled. "I'm glad you picked me to help refresh your memory."

He reached across the distance between them and touched her cheek. "Me too."

For the moment, the sky held back its unending supply of rain, and Manuel shrugged out of his rain slicker. Isabel followed his example then unwrapped her lunch and tasted the meat and cheese-filled pastries. "Good," she muttered through a mouthful.

The sounds of jungle creatures created a symphony while the river rocked the canoes in a gentle rhythm. Isabel finished her meal and leaned over the side of the boat, staring into the river. She trailed her fingers through the cool water, creating a miniature wake.

Without warning, Manuel's hand clamped down on her wrist and yanked her fingers from the water. Surprised, her head jerked up, and she met his intense stare. Disentangling from his grasp, she rubbed away the tenderness left after his unexpected attack. "Why did you do that?"

"If you'd prefer to keep all your appendages intact, I suggest you refrain from dangling them in the water."

His calm demeanor seemed a sharp contrast to his rough treatment of her, and she couldn't help but show her irritation. "What are you talking about?"

He took her hand in his and kissed a trail from her fingertips to her wrist, lessening the sting of his earlier offense. "Crocodiles and piranhas, Isabel. Your fingers are too pretty to serve as fish food."

"You mean there's...." She bent to stare into the water. "In here?"

"Yes." His dark eyes held her transfixed. "So don't put your hands or anything else in the water, please." As if to emphasize his point, he tossed the last few bites of his lunch into the river.

Isabel watched with morbid fascination as the fish launched themselves at the morsels of bread and meat, their mouths open, teeth bared. With not enough food to satisfy all who'd come for the banquet, the larger piranha quickly turned on a weaker fish, cannibalizing one of their own.

The horror of thinking what those tiny teeth might do to her flesh was enough to terrify her. She scanned the banks of the river, looking for partially submerged lumps indicating a crocodile's presence.

A shudder ran through Isabel. She sucked in a deep breath, trying to calm the nervous rhythm of her heart. "What if the boat tips and I fall in? Would I be eaten alive?"

Manuel's mustache twitched and smile lines appeared at the corners of his eyes. "If you don't tip your boat, we won't have to find out the answer to that question."

His teasing embarrassed her, and she felt her defenses rise. "You should have told me about the danger earlier."

"I thought you knew." He packed the makings of their lunch and tucked them away, seemingly calm and unconcerned about the threat lurking just inches below their boats.

"I didn't. Now that I do, I wish I could forget." She shuddered.

He laughed. "Guess we better get moving. We have a lot of water to cover."

~ * ~ * ~ * ~ * ~

Two days later, Manuel shifted on his cot, and his muscles screamed in protest. Rowing against the current left his arms and back sore and tender. He wondered how Isabel would feel when she awoke. She'd done her share of work without complaint. No doubt her muscles would feel worse than his. His body was accustomed to hard labor. Hers wasn't. If he felt sore, she would be miserable.

He decided to get up and start packing. With any luck, they'd reach their destination by evening, then no more rowing for a while. He rolled from his cot and stepped outside his tent. While stretching out his stiff muscles, he glanced around. The hammocks used by the guides no longer hung from the tree. *Maybe they rose early to prepare for the day.*

Manuel walked into the woods to take care of his morning needs. When he returned, there was still no sign of the guides, and something struck him as odd. He stared at the scene for a moment, willing his tired mind to focus. Then it dawned on him. Their guides had each carried a small pack with them. The packs were gone. Manuel rushed to the boats and found some of the food supplies missing as well.

Furious, he grabbed up a nearby stick and hurled it out into the water.

Abandoned in the Amazon. He punched the air and released a frustrated growl. *Is it asking too much to have just one thing on this trip go right?*

After a moment of grumbling and kicking the dirt, he forced himself to calm down. Feeding his anger and frustration wouldn't accomplish anything. They'd simply have to deal with the problem the best they could. Gathering supplies to make breakfast, he returned to the camp and started a meal.

Isabel wandered out a short time later, scrubbing her eyes with her fists. "Morning." She groaned when she crouched down beside him.

"Sore?"

"Very." She held the plate while he dished hot ham from the pan.

"Me too." He broke a few eggs into the pan and listened to them sizzle. He scraped a spatula around in the eggs and wondered how to deliver the news. "Isabel, we need to talk."

"Sounds serious."

"It is."

She smiled. "Are you sure you want to have a serious conversation this early in the morning? I'm only half awake."

He didn't know how to soften the news, so he just said it. "The guides are gone."

She remained quiet for a long time. "What do you mean by gone?"

"They abandoned us."

Her blue eyes widened. "Why would they do that? We paid them for several weeks of assistance."

"I know."

Isabel sighed. "Is this some kind of tourist scam?"

He shrugged. "Could be. Or it's possible someone paid them to do it. Maybe the same people who caused the other trouble we had."

"What do we do now?"

"Paddle back to the substation, I guess. We can float with the current most of the way. Shouldn't be as hard as paddling further upriver."

"Why not go on?"

"Our gear won't fit in one boat, and I don't think you can manage to row on your own."

She stood and propped her hands on her hips. "I can handle it."

"Isabel." He moved the pan off the flame and stood to face her. "I think we need to get you back to civilization and talk to the police about everything that's happened. You'll be less vulnerable on familiar territory."

"Do you think they've followed us here?"

Pearls

Manuel considered the possibility for a moment before rejecting it. "No. A person has to obtain permits from several government agencies to enter the Amazon. They don't let many people in. We received permission because this expedition is considered scientific."

"Would men like that be concerned with legalities? Wouldn't they just pay someone off like they did our guides?"

He scowled. "You have a point, but you don't know it's them for sure, Isabel."

"You seem pretty certain. That's why you're insisting we leave, isn't it?" She narrowed her sleepy eyes, and her tousled hair framed her face with wild abandon. She looked adorable, and he couldn't help but smile.

"What?"

"You look cute in the morning."

She snorted and ran her fingers through her hair. "Don't change the subject."

"Okay. I think we should go home."

Her gaze dropped to the ground. "But if we go home empty handed, you lose your career, right? You'll have to go work your mother's farm. Where does that leave us? Will I ever see you again?"

He gritted his teeth, hating the answer he had to give her. "I have obligations. Maybe in the future when she's back on her feet ... but I can't promise anything. It wouldn't be fair to you."

"Then be fair to me now, Manuel. This is our last shot at finding the pearls. Let's at least try."

The pleading look she gave him brought a knot to his throat. He wanted to offer her the world, but he had nothing to give. Maybe she was right. They had nothing to lose and everything to gain by making one last attempt. "I don't like it, but I guess we could try it for one day."

She flung herself into his arms and planted a warm kiss on his cheek. "Thank you, Manuel."

He held her tight and cherished the feel of her in his arms. He would savor the time they had left together. The whispers in the back of his mind told him there wasn't much of it left.

~ * ~ * ~ * ~ * ~

Working hard to row against the current, Isabel wasn't watching where she was paddling. She heard a loud clunk and felt her boat jolt as she collided with a sizeable piece of driftwood.

Manuel obviously heard the collision, too, because he turned around and shouted to her from his *bongo* a few lengths ahead of hers. "Watch it, Isabel. You're supposed to be steering around those things."

"I know that, Manuel, but thanks for the reminder." She couldn't help the peevish tone of her voice. While the first day on the river had seemed like an adventure, by the third, a mind-numbing boredom and foul temper settled over her. Rowing alone proved much harder than she expected, and the effort made her grouchy, changing her outlook considerably.

The foliage that had looked so exotic at the onset of their journey now aggravated her with its unvaried sameness. The hum of the rain forest had changed from harmonic to irritating, reminding her of the incessant buzzing of a swarm of gnats. Isabel chafed at the uncomfortable feel of her clothes sticking to her skin caused by the damp rain forest climate. Even her feet felt wet.

She glanced down and noticed with some concern that an inch of water swirled around the bottom of the boat. How long had that been there? She watched as the water rose an inch in just a few seconds. Panic seized her.

"Uh, Manuel, I think I might have a problem," she shouted.

He turned. "What?"

She jabbed her finger toward her feet. "Water." The cool water spilled over the tops of her shoes and gurgled around her ankles. A glance over the side showed the boat was riding dangerously low in the water and sinking fast. A few more inches and the river would spill over the edge and suck her under. Panic rose as she remembered the brutality of the hungry piranhas the first day of their trip.

"Steer toward shore!" Manuel yelled.

She dipped her paddle and rowed with fierce determination, but her efforts seemed futile at best. She stared at the rising water in wide-eyed disbelief, her pulse thundering in her ears.

"Manuel, help me!" With the scream, bile rose into her throat and tainted her mouth with its bitterness. Manuel had turned his boat and was trying to row to her, but Isabel didn't see how he could reach her in time. She stood with water halfway up her shins and watched in horror as a crocodile slid off the riverbank and disappeared into the murky depths.

"God, I don't want to die like this!"

"Isabel, can you climb into my boat?" Manuel's *bongo* slid alongside hers, creating a small wake that threatened to capsize her boat. She bent and gripped the sides to keep from falling, and momentum carried him past before she could make a move.

"No!" she screamed, reaching out with a desperate, helpless hand to grasp at her lost chance at rescue.

As he shot past the tip of her *bongo*, he snagged her boat's mooring line and wrapped it around a cleat on his boat. His muscles rippling with effort, he rowed his boat toward shore and towed hers along behind him. "Hold on, Isabel!"

Interminable seconds passed, every slow moving meter of water threatening to be her last. Too panicked to pray, all her mind could conjure was a one-word cry of desperation. *God!*

With painful persistence, the water climbed toward the edge. Two inches. One inch. Half an inch. Water poured over the back of the *bongo*, the lowest point of the boat. She screamed and stumbled over equipment and supplies, trying to reach the front to gain a few seconds' reprieve from the fate that now seemed inevitable.

The water chased at her heels, swallowing up the length of the boat with a voracious appetite.

"Jump, Isabel! Jump!"

She saw the front of Manuel's *bongo* buried in the riverbank, while he scrambled across his cargo. With the docking rope wrapped around the taught muscles of his forearm, he tried to pull her close enough to his boat to leap to safety.

The tip of her *bongo* dipped under the water.

She leaped with all her might.

Twenty-One

The distance spanned further than Isabel could hope to clear, but she managed to connect one arm and shoulder painfully against his boat. Not stopping to think about the pain of the impact, she hoisted herself up and rolled into his *bongo*, hearing the thrash of predators splashing in the water she'd just vacated.

"Isabel, can you help me?"

The edge in Manuel's voice alarmed her, and she turned to see him still straining at the rope.

"What are you doing?" Clutching her throbbing shoulder, she made an effort to rise.

"The supplies and equipment. We have to try and salvage them if we can."

Realizing the predicament they'd be in if they lost even a portion of their gear, her system flooded with adrenaline again. Forgetting her injury, she grasped the rope and pulled with all her might. They made enough progress to step off the boat and onto the mucky shore. Digging their heels into the bank, they leaned their weight into the struggle, and the tip of the *bongo* soon appeared in the shallows along the water's edge.

"That's probably far enough for now." He relaxed his grip on the rope and reached out to pull her against him. His chest heaved with the exertion as he held her tight in his arms. "Are you all right?"

She nodded. "Shaken but intact."

"I'm afraid I can't say the same for the gear stored in your boat. I bet we lost most of it."

The burning heat of embarrassment flooded her face and chest. "I'm sorry. It's all my fault. If I'd been watching where I was going, I wouldn't have hit that submerged branch."

Manuel studied her for a moment in silence. "You didn't do it

189

on purpose. Accidents happen."

His understanding attitude only increased Isabel's guilt, and she compensated by talking too much. "I don't know how you can be so calm. I've probably done irreparable damage to our trip. If we don't have the supplies we need, how will we continue? Can we even get back to civilization? And how much is the lost equipment going to cost? We rented that stuff."

Manuel silenced her with a finger to her lips. "We can't change what's done. Let's focus on salvaging the situation. Help me tie the boats to that tree. We need to move away from the waterline before some crocodile decides we're offering him lunch."

Isabel gathered the mooring lines, scurried up the slight rise to the tree, and tied off the boats. When she looked back, she caught Manuel's unguarded expression, and her heart withered. He was more disappointed than he'd let on, and she felt terrible about her blunder. In a careless moment, she had jeopardized an already crippled mission.

She slid back down the bank and laid her hand on his arm. "If it makes you feel better, yell at me or something. I'd swear this trip is cursed."

He slipped an arm around her shoulders. "You ready to give up yet?"

She thought about returning to Caracas and saying goodbye to him. Determination shot through her. "No. I'm ready to pull that boat out of the water and see if we can repair it." She grabbed the line and pulled, making little impact on the submerged boat with her attempt.

Sighing, he grabbed the line and added his strength to hers.

After twenty minutes of tug-of-war with the river, they managed to reclaim the boat and its remaining contents. Isabel stared with dismay at the paltry leftovers of her cargo. "We're not going to make it, are we?"

~ * ~ * ~ * ~ * ~

April 27, 1515
A bend in the river turned us toward the eastern
horizon. We traveled east for several hours when a grand
and glorious mountain filled the sky ahead of us. Unlike the

*jagged peaks of our last home, this mountain's top has been
sheared away, leaving a uniquely flattened summit.
Fascinated, I followed a branch off the main river until we
arrived at its base. There we discovered a small clearing
surrounded by fruit trees, and a sparkling waterfall flows
nearby. I sense that God himself has prepared this place for
us. Here in the protective shadow of this great rock tower,
we will make our dwelling.*

Manuel knelt by the bow of Isabel's *bongo*, finding it difficult to
believe what he was seeing. Isabel thought her carelessness had
caused the damage to her boat, but he could no longer blame her.

"Look at this." He beckoned her to his side and pointed at the
cleanly cut lines around the hole. "Someone used a knife or saw to
cut almost through the boat. The damage is low enough that a
person wouldn't notice it while the boat was in the water."

"You're saying this is sabotage?"

"Afraid so."

She shuddered. "Why is someone trying to kill me, Manuel?"

"I wish I knew." He took her hand in his and tried to reassure
her with his touch.

"Can you fix it?"

"Even if I could fix the boat—and I don't think I can—the trip
is hopeless. Half the equipment we need sank into the river, and
we can't retrieve it because of the crocs and piranhas. We might as
well go home."

"Please, Manuel, can't we even try?"

The muscles in his jaw tightened. "We knew the Amazon was
the least likely location of the three. That's why we put it at the end
of the list."

"But we're so close. The waterfall we're looking for couldn't be
more than a few hours upriver." She stared up at him, a desperate
look in her blue eyes.

He couldn't resist her when she turned those eyes on him. He
looked away.

Isabel persisted. "Whoever is orchestrating these accidents
wants us to give up and go home. I don't intend to give them the
satisfaction. Let's go on."

He shook his head. "You're being unreasonable. We can't haul all this gear and two people in one *bongo*. We'd have to set up camp here and paddle upriver each morning, then return by nightfall. It'd make for long, exhausting days."

Isabel moved closer to him and slid her arms around his waist. "We can do it, Manuel. We should do it. We'd never forgive ourselves if we didn't at least try."

He sighed, knowing she was using her feminine wiles against him and not caring in the least. He'd do almost anything to prolong their trip together. She'd become precious to him. Her sleepy morning smiles. Her enthusiasm. Her support and admiration of his work.

"All right. Tomorrow morning after breakfast we'll make a trip upriver and see what we can find. But I'm only committing to one day at a time. We lost half our fresh water and some of our food when the *bongo* sank. We can only stay as long as our supplies hold out."

She grinned, looking triumphant at her victory. Funny, he didn't mind falling victim to her at all. Making her happy or gaining one of those brilliant smiles left him feeling slightly intoxicated. She was addictive, and he didn't mind being under her power. Could he say goodbye to her once the trip ended?

~ * ~ * ~ * ~ * ~

"We've reached another fork in the river. Which way now?" Isabel let the paddle droop across her lap and dug her fingers into her stiff shoulder muscles. Each morning for a week, they'd risen early and paddled up river, systematically searching the waterways for a sign of the location Rodrigo had mentioned. Though they had the *corro* in their sights, finding Rodrigo's former camp had proved difficult. Because of the tremendous rainfall in the region—nearly 200 inches a year—a labyrinth of streams, creeks, and rivers criss-crossed the region. Rodrigo could have followed any one of them.

Manuel lifted the map and studied the maze of blue waterways. "I don't know. At this point I'm just glad we're not completely lost."

"You sound discouraged."

He sighed. "We hired the guides for a reason. These waterways are impossible to navigate from a map. Who's to say the map is even right? The land floods yearly, and the waterways may emerge from the wet season in completely different patterns than the year before."

Isabel refused to be discouraged. "We've narrowed the search area to a few square miles. It's just a matter of persistence."

Manuel sighed. "Your optimism is admirable, but you know that's not exactly true. We might paddle right past Rodrigo's village and never know it. The building materials they used back then would have decomposed centuries ago, and the jungle would have reclaimed the land. Unless someone is still living there, it's probably gone."

Isabel turned and studied the majestic outline of the *corro*. Blue sky outlined the russet tower of stone. The view inspired her with confidence, and she understood why Rodrigo would want to live in its shadow. "We have a few hours of daylight left. Let's search a while longer."

~ * ~ * ~ * ~ * ~

Manuel sat in a canvas chair and watched Isabel move around the camp, tidying up after their meal. Just before dinner, she'd washed her hair in a small stream nearby. Afterward, she let it hang loose around her shoulders to dry. When she knelt to return the dishes to their storage space, her hair slid across her face. Lifting a delicate hand, she smoothed the strands behind her ear in a gesture both feminine and alluring. His breath snagged in his chest. He enjoyed watching her. Her natural grace and womanly softness appealed to him.

There was *a lot* about her he found appealing.

He never thought to see a woman so at ease with his lifestyle, but she had remained content throughout the trip, as if born for the life he could offer her. She hadn't uttered a single complaint at "roughing it," foregoing creature comforts that most women deemed necessities ... like a bathroom and a kitchen. In fact, she seemed to enjoy the challenges.

God, was I wrong when I abandoned hope of ever marrying?

After two relationships failed due to the unusual demands of his career, Manuel assumed marriage was a lost cause. Giving up his desire for a wife and children seemed more practical than continuing his search for a woman who could accept his ambitions. Thinking back, he realized he'd never prayed about that decision. His wounded heart made the choice seem obvious at the time.

Now that he wanted to change his mind, his career wasn't the problem. His mother's financial situation was. He might spend years working to free her from debt. He couldn't ask a woman like Isabel to join him in that prison sentence. They would have to live in his mother's home, and any income earned would go to the farm. He couldn't imagine Isabel happy in that life. The strain of dealing with his family's problems would make her bitter toward him and destroy any hope of happiness.

No matter how much he wanted her, he wouldn't ask her to consider it. She deserved so much better. Still, everything inside him ached to have her. He'd give up anything— *anything but my promise to my mother.*

His stomach knotted. Their search for the area near a waterfall Rodrigo mentioned had proved fruitless. Maybe their failure was a good thing. He needed to put some distance between himself and Isabel before he gave in to temptation. Honoring his word would have to come first.

Twenty-Two

Two nights later, Isabel collapsed into a chair, every muscle in her body limp with exhaustion from the arduous work they'd done that day. Their efforts had proved fruitless. She tried not to let disappointment weigh her down, but she couldn't ignore the fact that they'd come to the end of their mission. Time had run out along with most of their resources, and they would have to return home in a few days.

Strong, warm hands slid onto her shoulders and began to massage away the aching tension accumulated there. She closed her eyes, a soft sigh of pleasure escaping her lips. His fingers moved up the back of her neck and down her arms, relaxing the muscles and electrifying her skin with his touch.

After several minutes, she tipped her head back and gave him a lazy smile. "That feels wonderful, Manuel. How did you know I needed it?"

He bent and brushed his lips across her forehead before taking the seat beside her. "The scrunched up way you held your shoulders half the day gave me a clue."

His playful smile relaxed her further, and she batted her lashes in his direction. "Well, thank you for being so observant."

He settled in his chair, crossing one foot over his knee and lacing his fingers behind his head. With heavy-lidded eyes, he stared into the growing darkness around their campsite.

Isabel sensed that something troubled him, but she hadn't the energy to pry it out of him. She leaned her head against her chair and absorbed the tranquility of the rain forest. Howler monkeys called to one another in the high canopy of trees while tropical birds sang their final song of the evening. The fragrance of the abundant plant life tickled her nose as she drew a deep, contented breath. During their weeks in the rain forest, she'd come to wonder if Adam and Eve had enjoyed such a paradise. She couldn't imagine a setting more beautiful or more enjoyable companionship with which to share it.

Her gaze came to rest on Manuel's profile, and the tightness surrounding his eyes interrupted her pleasant thoughts. "What is it, Manuel?"

He met her probing gaze and offered her a gentle smile. "I was just thinking maybe it's time we went home. I don't think we're going to find what we're looking for."

Though reluctant, she nodded her agreement. "We've both known for a while. I suppose it's time we admitted defeat."

"I'm sorry, Isabel. I really thought we had a chance."

Isabel sat in silence, grieving the sudden death of their shared dream. But more, she ached for Manuel. Adventure and history had fueled her interest in the project, but he had much more at stake. His future hinged on their success or failure. "What will you do when we return to Caracas?"

He reached out and grasped her hand. "I suppose I'll sell my car and most of my possessions and buy a bus ticket to my mother's farm. I can't put it off any longer. She needs me, and I'm not making any progress in the archaeology field. Part of me thinks this is God's way of telling me I wasn't meant to be an archaeologist."

She squeezed his hand. "You *are* an archaeologist, Manuel. I've been so impressed with your knowledge and professionalism."

"Does that mean you'll write me a letter of recommendation?"

His wry smile pierced her heart. She could tell he was trying to hide his feelings. To address the subject of their relationship now would seem selfish in light of all he was losing. Reluctantly, she smothered the questions she wanted to ask him.

Yawning, Manuel stood and pulled her to her feet. "I'm going to turn in now. How about you?"

"I might stay up a while and read over the journal. Maybe I'll see something we missed."

"Don't waste your time."

Even in the dim light she could see his grim expression. "The journal entries are fascinating and romantic. I'll enjoy reading them regardless of whether or not they yield a clue."

"Don't stay up too late. The journey home won't be easy."

They gazed at one another, Isabel feeling loathe to end the pleasant day together. Her eyes traveled over his face, taking in the features she had come to know so well. His mustache needed trimming, and he'd not shaved since half their supplies sank into the Orinoco River. His hair was unkempt after a day of hard labor, his clothes mussed and wrinkled, yet Isabel thought he looked more handsome than ever.

As if noticing her scrutiny, he ran a hand over his face and hair. "I know I need to visit the barber."

She lifted a hand to touch his dark, silky hair, now long from weeks without a haircut. "I think you're very handsome."

He shivered at her touch, and his expression changed to one of need. Pulling her close, he claimed her lips with a gentle hunger that made her stomach flutter wildly. When the kiss ended, he held her tight in his embrace for long moments, his chin resting atop her head. "You've become very precious to me, Isabel. When I have more to offer you—"

He released her, swallowed convulsively, and with a tortured look, retreated to the seclusion of his tent.

~ * ~ * ~ * ~ * ~

Isabel closed the flap on the larger work tent and lit the kerosene lamp they sometimes used at night. Taking the journal from its case, she held it in her lap and studied its rustic beauty. She hadn't looked at the book for over a month. The working copy was easier to understand and saved wear and tear on the original, but Isabel preferred the journal to their fancy translation. The worn leather cover and yellowed pages penned in elegant script best portrayed the beauty of the love between Rodrigo and Karwa. She heaved a deep sigh. Their love had been a rare and priceless treasure, worth more than any pearls. Rodrigo had realized that and walked away from a promising career, wealth, and a comfortable life in order to be with the woman he loved.

Isabel wondered if Manuel had ever considered making such a sacrifice for her. But their circumstances were different. He seemed to feel he had nothing to offer a woman, so he denied himself the opportunity to love Isabel in order to protect her from his financial struggles. In their situation, Manuel was slave to his finances and

Pearls

Isabel was the one who would have to give up position and security to be with him. Perhaps, Manuel had too much *machismo* to ask it of her. Or maybe he didn't love her the way Rodrigo had loved Karwa.

No. She'd seen the love in Manuel's eyes and heard it in his voice. He'd even slipped and blurted his feelings for her during the heated argument with Raúl. She suspected he cared more than he would allow himself to admit. Rodrigo and Karwa's romantic tale offered her hope. They had overcome seemingly impossible odds, so maybe she and Manuel would find a way.

Returning her focus to the journal, she opened the cover. The leather seemed stiff and refused to open fully. She heard a soft popping sound and stared with dismay at the break in the stitching.

Manuel will be upset with me.

She lifted the journal and studied the damage. The journal's cover consisted of two pieces of leather sewn together with a sinewy cord, probably catgut or other natural material. Apparently, the cord had weakened over time and her carelessness had snapped it. The release of tension caused the torn ends of the cord to pull away from one another, slipping out of several holes of stitching and leaving a gap of nearly an inch.

I can probably find someone who specializes in restoration to repair the damage. As she turned the book this way and that studying the break, she noticed the tiniest speck of white protruding from the gap.

What's that?

Grasping the edge with her fingernails, she gave a soft tug and the corner of a slip of paper emerged from the break. *There's a piece of paper in here!*

Her heart beat a heavy rhythm as she pulled out several inches of the stitching that held the pieces of leather together. After she widened the gap, she freed the hidden note. Laying it on the table next to the lamp, she studied the words written in Rodrigo's familiar handwriting. Excitement stole the breath from her lungs.

This is it!

She let herself out of the main tent and hurried to where Manuel has staked his smaller pup tent. Crouching beside the opening, she called to him in a hushed voice. "Manuel. Manuel!"

The soft, steady drone of his snoring answered her.

Remembering her own exhaustion, she decided to save the exciting news for the morning. Besides, in the light of day, she could get a better look at his face when she told him she knew where to find the pearls. Returning to the journal, she pulled out a notepad and pen and began translating the words that would lead them to the treasure.

~ * ~ * ~ * ~ * ~

Isabel stepped outside the tent and kneaded the horrible kink in her back. She had fallen asleep in the main tent, slumped over the makeshift worktable. Thankfully, the lamp had guttered out while she slept and didn't cause a fire. She wouldn't mention her carelessness to Manuel. She glanced at his tent and heard his steady snoring.

No problem. I'll just get a jump on packing. He's going to want to leave here as soon as possible once he hears my news.

She walked to her tent and unzipped the canvas flap. Reaching in, she grasped her cot and bedding and pulled them outside the tent. She started to reach for the blanket, but froze in terror.

A red- and black-banded snake lay coiled atop her bedding. Her activity had aroused its temper, and now it eyed her with malevolence, head arched back ready to strike. She stood perfectly still, not even daring to breathe. One bite from the Coral snake, and she'd be dead within minutes.

Movement stirred on the other side of the camp. From the corner of her eye, she saw Manuel step out of his tent.

"Morning," he mumbled.

She didn't respond.

"Packing up already?" He paused. "Isabel, what's wrong with you?"

When she didn't speak, he moved closer. His gasp assured her he'd spied the danger. "Don't move!"

He ducked into his tent and emerged with something in his hand.

Gunfire blasted through the quiet rain forest, and the snake exploded, sending a revolting spray of blood and tissue across her legs.

Isabel glanced from the mutilated snake at her feet to the gun in his hand, not sure which horrified her more.

Manuel came and laid a comforting hand on her arm. "It's okay, Isabel. The snake is dead."

She stared at him, her eyes wide with fear. "Where did you get the gun, Manuel?"

His attention turned to the weapon. Frowning, he stuffed it in the waistband of his pants. "I always take a gun along when I go into the field. You never know what you might encounter. With all the wild animals here, I thought it best to have the extra protection. I left it in my bag until now."

"Why didn't you tell me you were carrying a gun?"

"I didn't want to frighten you."

Her hands began to shake uncontrollably, and her knees felt as sturdy as gelatin. Stumbling to a chair, she sank down and drew deep breaths to calm her rapid heartbeat.

Manuel came and knelt beside her. "You okay?"

"Yeah. Just give me a minute alone, would you?"

He studied her for a moment then nodded. "Sure, but I'll be close by if you need me."

As he busied himself tearing down and packing up the camp, Isabel pressed her eyes closed. *Something isn't right. I zipped that tent myself. It was closed up tight. No way a snake got in there on its own.*

Very few people had an aim as accurate as the one she'd just witnessed. Law enforcers, hunters, and criminals … like men who were involved with organized crime rings. Isabel wondered if she had misplaced her trust over the last few weeks. Someone must have put the snake into her tent. The same person could have sabotaged her boat and orchestrated the incident at the well and the avalanche too.

Pressure squeezed her heart as she considered the frightening possibilities.

Manuel thought I'd be sleeping in there, and if I had, I'd be dead. Was he responsible for the other incidents?

But if Manuel was trying to kill her, why did he come to her rescue at every occasion? Was it a game to him—a ploy to scare her then win her trust when he played the hero? Alone with him in the wilderness, she had no chance of defending herself should he choose to follow through with a plan to harm her. Terrified by these shocking new revelations, she decided the sooner they returned to the safety of civilization, the better.

She slid her hand into her pocket to reassure herself that the paper was still there. Perhaps she should wait to share the news of her discovery. She might need to use it as a bargaining chip to save her life.

Pearls

Twenty-Three

Manuel couldn't help but notice Isabel's brooding silence as they navigated the last stretch of river before they reached the little airstrip. She had barely spoken two sentences to him all day. He guessed her change in mood was related to his gun. He'd seen the fear in her eyes when he'd used it that morning. Maybe she disliked firearms, but even then her reaction seemed extreme. She hadn't even thanked him for killing the snake and saving her life.

The tiny wooden pier near the airstrip came into view as the sun dipped low on the horizon. *Perfect timing.* He'd hoped to reach the little airstrip before dusk. Barely more than a rough runway and a shack monitored by a part-time attendant, it offered no amenities, but little airstrips like this one were the only way in and out of the dense rain forest. They could camp there and contact a pilot to retrieve them tomorrow.

Turning the *bongo* toward shore, Manuel steered the craft alongside the weathered posts and planks that formed the crude pier. Grabbing a rope, he quickly secured their boat to the dock.

Without a word Isabel rose and tied her end then lifted an armload of supplies and carried them to shore. Manuel gathered up the tents and followed her lead, passing her as she returned to the boat for another load.

Just as Manuel stepped ashore, Raúl appeared, agitated and smelling of liquor. "Where have you been? I've waited here for days."

Manuel dropped the tents at Raúl's feet and faced him, hands on hips. "Looks like you found ways to occupy your time."

Isabel joined them, the crate of cooking supplies propped on one hip. "How did you get here? Or even know where we were?"

Manuel lifted the load from her hands and set it down. "He has our itinerary, and I gave him an estimated date of return."

"Which came and passed two days ago." Raúl glared at them like a petulant child, his gaze accusatory. "I hired a pilot to fly me in because I need a progress report. Did you find anything?"

Manuel braced himself for the confrontation, but Isabel cut in before he could answer. "Look, Raúl, we've been on the river all day. I'm tired and stiff, and all I want is to clean up and get some rest. Can't we talk later?"

"Oh, I see. Either you're trying to hide your findings or you've found nothing. My guess is you've failed miserably. That's just what I would expect from someone like him." Raúl jerked his head in Manuel's direction, adding a look of disdain to the insult.

Manuel knotted his fists, barely resisting the urge to take a shot at the irritating man. *A broken nose might add character to Raúl's flawless features.*

Isabel intervened. "Raúl, do you ever think of anyone besides yourself?"

A look of anger flashed in his eyes, and he stalked away from the dock. The rusted-out vehicle the airstrip attendant used to transport people the short distance from their plane to the river waited nearby. Raúl climbed in it and drove away.

Manuel bristled when he saw tears of frustration form in her eyes. One drop carved a shiny path down her cheek, accentuating the dust and grime accumulated there. Compassion softened him, and he cupped her cheek in one hand, smoothing away dirt and tears with a gentle stroke of his thumb. "Don't let him get to you. We'll be home by tomorrow night, and you won't have to see him again."

Manuel felt her stiffen, and she stepped away from his touch. The distance he'd sensed between them widened into a rift. "Isabel, are you all right?"

She nodded. "Sure. Just tired. Why don't we finish unloading and find a place to make camp. The sooner I can eat and rest, the better."

~ * ~ * ~ * ~ * ~

Isabel's stomach churned as she collapsed her tent and packed her gear the next morning. Raúl had chosen to ignore them the night before. She'd considered his absence a blessing. While she needed to share the news of her discovery, she had no desire to talk with a drunken Raúl and an armed Manuel in the dark of night, separated from civilization by miles of untamed wilderness. She did not trust either man, and the men certainly held no affection for one another. The animosity between them felt like a volatile powder keg, and she was always waiting for the spark that would set off an explosion.

A deep weariness plagued her emotions, its tentacles reaching throughout her body, draining away her energy and resolve. She'd love nothing more than to go home to her grandmother's hacienda and hide away from the turbulent feelings these two men stirred in her. Raúl whose beautiful face masked an unfaithful heart, and Manuel, who presented himself as a pillar of strength and virtue, yet seemed to bring danger into her life. At times, she had wanted to believe in them both, to love them and be loved by them.

Now, she only wanted time away to nurse the sense of trust so bruised and battered by the events in her life over the last months. Despite her reluctance to interact with either man, she had to tell them today. Perhaps telling them together would work for the best. She was certain one man couldn't be trusted, only she didn't know which one.

A vehicle rumbled up to their campsite a short time later. Raúl stepped out and swaggered toward her, looking jaunty despite his drinking binge the previous night.

Manuel's hands went to his hips, a posture Isabel was beginning to recognize as a sign of impending confrontation. "Nice of you to come, Raúl. We waited for you last night, but you didn't show."

"Well, I'm here now. Let's hear your report. Tell me all about your grand and pointless adventure."

Manuel's face took on a pinched expression. "I don't know why Isabel didn't just tell you last night. We didn't find anything."

Isabel saw her opportunity and interrupted before their bickering escalated into a fight. "That isn't exactly true. I found something."

Silence.

Both men stared at her, wearing similarly puzzled looks.

"Manuel, Raúl, sit." She pointed at the chairs near the fire pit. The men complied in silence.

Taking the remaining seat, she clasped her hands tightly in her lap. "A few nights ago, I was up late reading the journal, and I found something we missed before. I found a paper sewn between the two pieces of leather that make up the cover of the journal. I translated it, and I know where the treasure is hidden."

Manuel's expression showed shock and hurt at her failure to confide in him sooner while Raúl's burned with something akin to hunger.

"Where is the page now?" Raúl asked.

"The original page and my rough translation are here." She reached into her front pocket and pulled out the folded slips of paper. "Let me read it to you."

> *September 13, 1523*
>
> *During our years together, I have explained the tenets of my faith to Karwa. She understands the beliefs which caused me to intervene on her behalf and rescue her from the Spaniards' cruelty. Karwa has accepted my God, yet she desires to receive the blessing of an official of the church. Word has reached us that white men have set up a mission on the coast. Karwa wishes to visit them and make her commitment to God known.*
>
> *But as we journey to where the priests have set up a mission, Karwa grows feverish and weak. The jungle, though beautiful and generous to mankind, carries the taint of sickness that now plagues Karwa.*
>
> *My son, now 20 years, travels with us, offering comfort and help. I pray the remainder of our journey passes quickly and the priests can help her.*
>
> *September 27, 1523*
>
> *The Franciscan Friars did all they could to save her body, but in the end they could only minister to her soul. I held her hand and stroked her fevered brow as death passed over and carried her away from me. I long to follow her from this earthly sphere, but for the sake of our son, I will press on.*

Life afforded me one truly great and priceless treasure, that love which Karwa freely bestowed upon me. Perhaps God has chosen to punish me for the sins I committed in order to love her.

As I laid her to rest, I buried the pearls beside her. Because of the evil they wrought, the pearls never seemed a treasure to me, but Karwa thought them lovely and enjoyed making baubles and trinkets from them. I left them with her, along with my heart, the best of my life buried beneath the cold hard ground.

Isabel glanced up and tried to gauge the men's reactions.

Manuel fidgeted with anticipation. "Cumaná. There was only one mission in Venezuela during the early 1500s. The ruins are still there today. We can return to Caracas to regroup and put together supplies for another trip."

"There won't be any *we*." Raúl glared at Manuel. "I funded your expedition, and you failed to find the pearls. This new development takes us outside the boundaries of our original contract, so I am under no obligation to include you. Consider yourself fired."

Manuel stared at Raúl, incredulous. "Now, wait a minute. You can't just dismiss me after all the effort I've put into this project. The new information was uncovered during the course of the expedition. So technically, my team and I did discover the location of the pearls. You aren't cutting me out of this."

Raúl jumped to his feet, his face flushed with anger. "I can and I will."

Manuel took Isabel's hand. "Maybe we'll cut you out, Raúl. Isabel and I fulfilled our part of the contract, and now we've decided to continue on our own. In fact, we'll be so generous as to offer to repay you with interest and a sizable bonus for your support, but we no longer wish to partner with you."

Raúl shook with anger. "You have no right to exclude me."

Manuel approached Raúl and jabbed a finger into his chest. "The journal and all the information inside belong to Isabel. You don't have any say over how she chooses to pursue the search after today. We're through with you and the trouble you've caused."

Raúl shoved Manuel away then bent and fumbled with the hem of his pants. When he stood and lifted his hand, the sun glinted off the smooth metal surface of a gun.

Isabel's chest clenched with fear. The situation had become more dangerous than she had imagined it could, Raúl more a wild card than she realized.

"Raúl, put that away." She tried to keep her voice calm and reassuring, but the quiver of fear was noticeable. "We'll work out a deal that is acceptable to all of us."

The muzzle of the gun jerked her direction, sending a flood of ice water through her veins and locking up her knees so she couldn't have run if she'd tried.

"That's not possible now."

"Sure it is. Just put the gun down and we'll talk," she coaxed.

Raúl laughed, a chillingly desperate sound. "You don't understand, Isabel. I can't afford a deal. If I don't get my hands on that treasure, I'm dead. A cut or percentage won't be enough. I need it all if I want to survive another week."

Isabel noticed Manuel inching toward Raúl, and she tried to distract him in the hope that Manuel could disarm him. "I don't understand, Raúl, but if we can sit down and talk about this calmly—"

"No!" Raúl whirled and the gun exploded, pummeling Manuel to the ground with the force of the bullet.

"Manuel!" Isabel rushed to his side and dropped to her knees. Tears streamed down her face as she examined the bloody wound in his shoulder. She ran to the main tent and emerged seconds later with a small medical kit. Fumbling through packages of gauze and tape, she tried to assemble a makeshift bandage from inadequate supplies.

Raúl stood over them, his gun trained on her as she desperately tried to stop the bleeding.

"He needs medical attention, Raúl. Help me get him to the airstrip."

"There's no one there but my pilot. The attendant is sick."

"Let us use your plane. I'll give you the journal and sign the treasure over to you. Just don't let him die." She looked up, pleading, but the coldness in his eyes told her she'd get no help or sympathy.

"I'm sorry, Isabel, but you've made your choice. I could have given you anything you desired, but you wouldn't have me. Now, I'm forced to leave you here with him." He raised the gun and pointed it at Manuel's head. "Give me the journal entries."

"Raúl, please!"

"Give me the journal entries, or he dies." He cocked the gun with a loud click.

With trembling hands, she pulled the papers from her pocket and handed them to Raúl.

He tucked them away, a sneer marring his handsome features. "Now find something I can use to tie you up."

"If you ever loved me, Raúl, please don't do this. Don't leave him here to die."

"I'm leaving you both, Isabel. I can't have you warning the authorities before I have a chance to get away. Get the rope."

She kept a tight hold on the panic building in her chest as she retrieved a length of cord. How would they get out of this situation alive? Manuel wouldn't last long without medical help, and she wanted to collapse under the strain of the events she'd just witnessed. Her arms felt limp as she returned to Manuel's side, carrying the rope in her listless fingers.

He snatched the rope from her hands. "Sit behind him, your backs together."

Isabel did as he ordered, tenderly helping Manuel to sit and supporting him as much as she could with her body.

Raúl tied a loop in the end of the rope, somehow managing to keep the gun pointed in their general direction while he worked. When he moved in closer to tie their hands, he tucked the gun in his waistband behind his back, out of her reach. As he slid the loop over their hands and cinched it until the fibers dug into her skin painfully, her hope of escape was rapidly fading. The bindings were so tight that her hands tingled from loss of circulation. She could only imagine the pain Manuel was in. Isabel wanted to cry and beg for mercy as she watched Raúl stalk away. Knowing she'd get none, she gritted her teeth and prayed for a miracle.

Raúl jumped into the vehicle, and the engine roared to life. Without a second look in their direction, he drove away, abandoning them to a cruel fate.

When she heard the distant whir of the plane engines fading away, Isabel succumbed to the sobs that clawed at her throat.

~ * ~ * ~ * ~ * ~

Isabel could feel the blood seeping from Manuel's shoulder and soaking into her shirt. His breathing was labored, and she wondered if the bullet had punctured his lung or damaged other vital tissues. "Manuel?" she whimpered. "Are you okay?"

"I love you, Isabel." The effort to speak brought on a fit of coughing, and he moaned with pain.

"Don't talk now. You'll make it worse." She glanced around, frantically searching for a way out of their dilemma.

"Isabel."

"Shhh."

"There's a knife...." He coughed again.

Her pulse quickened. "Where?"

"My back pocket. It's not big, but maybe...."

With their hands tied together, she could not move her arm without moving his too. She knew his injured shoulder hurt, and any movement on that side of his body would cause him pain. She opted to use the other arm to retrieve the knife.

"I'll need you to work with me. Since you're in pain, let me do most of the hard stuff. I'm going to move away from you if I can, okay? Ready?"

He grunted and she shifted her hips forward, trying to put some space between their lower backs. He sucked in a sharp breath, and she knew even that small movement had cost him dearly.

"Sorry," she muttered. "I think there's enough room between us now. I'll do the work, but I need you to slide your hand along with mine as I try to reach the knife."

Moving slowly, she flattened her hand and slid it into the gap between them. She felt him making a similar movement, and the tension on the rope binding their hands together eased just enough.

After a moment of fumbling, she managed to slide the knife from his back pocket. Moving her hands to one side, she studied the Swiss Army knife and selected a blade from the myriad attachments. Fumbling with one hand, she managed to flick the blade out with her thumb, slicing her finger in the process. She struggled for several minutes, trying to maneuver the blade to an angle that would cut through the rope, but doing it all by feel behind her back wasn't working.

She blew out a frustrated breath. "I can't see, and I can't maneuver the knife in this position."

"Keep trying," Manuel gasped.

"I'm not giving up, but I need to shift around, try to get my body at an angle to yours so I can see and move my hands a little more."

"Then do it."

She knew the position would stretch his wounded shoulder and put him in excruciating pain. "Are you sure? Maybe I can think of another way."

"No time. Do it."

The thought of inflicting pain on him made her feel physically ill. But the alternative—sitting by and doing nothing while he slipped into unconsciousness then death—was unacceptable. She found a reservoir of strength somewhere deep inside.

"Ready? Go." Her muscles shook with strain as she fought the resistance of the ropes and Manuel's limp body. He gasped in pain as she wrestled into a better position so she could see and maneuver a little better.

Shaking with strain, she sawed through one of the ropes. The pressure on her wrist eased, and she shook her hand until the rope fell free. Shifting, she quickly loosened the bindings and unwound the ropes.

Once free, Manuel rolled to the ground and curled into a fetal position, favoring his injured shoulder. "Leave me, Isabel. Go for help." His eyes rolled back in his head and his body went limp.

Pearls

Twenty-Four

Isabel searched the sky, looking for the source of the hum that filled the air. She couldn't see a plane approaching, but she was certain one was coming in for a landing. Maybe Raúl had grown a conscience and decided not to abandon them. Or maybe it was just the average delivery run or transport flying in. There was no way to be sure without walking the half-mile to the airstrip and checking. She wasn't sure that was possible.

Manuel wasn't doing well at all. She had managed to stop his bleeding and had given him some over-the-counter painkillers from the first aid kit once he woke up. Though conscious, he didn't have the strength to walk to the airstrip to find help, and she didn't intend to leave him.

He sagged against the pile of supplies Isabel had fashioned into a makeshift support. She watched his head droop and worried he might pass out again. "Manuel, are you okay?"

His eyelids opened with groggy slowness. "I'm tired."

She moved closer. "You're going into shock from losing blood."

He nodded. "Probably."

"Please, fight it, Manuel. I can't lose you. I love you."

His eyes were instantly alert. "Saving that information for a special occasion, were you?"

She smiled through her tears. "Just too stubborn to admit it before, and too foolish. I'm sorry I didn't trust you. I should have known you'd never hurt me. You've risked your life several times to save me."

"S'okay. Even I thought I looked suspicious."

"Somehow I should have known. I should have listened to my heart."

He shook his head. "You're listening now. I love you, Isabel. I

213

have for months. Since you're feeling guilty and sympathetic, I'm thinking this might be a good time to ask you to marry me."

If she hadn't been kneeling, she would have fallen over from shock. "Are you serious?"

"I've been a fool, too. I was too proud to consider marrying you because of my financial problems. Now I realize the feelings I have for you are precious, more than money or anything else. If you'll have me, Isabel, I want you for my wife."

She leaned over, gave him a long, deep kiss, and found his wounds hadn't hindered his ability to use his lips. "Swear you won't die, and my answer is yes."

His eyes twinkled. "I wouldn't dream of leaving you now."

Isabel laid a hand on his forehead. "You're cold. I know I should keep you warm, but what else? Aren't you supposed to prop your feet up or something?"

He smiled. "I don't know, but it's worth a try."

"I'll help you." She jumped up. "I'll get blankets from your bedroll."

Isabel helped him change positions then ran to his tent. As she emerged, arms full of bedding, the rumble of a vehicle's engine neared their location.

"Maybe this is someone who can help us." She tucked the blanket around him and arranged the pillow beneath his head. She rushed to the side of the dirt road and waved her arms at the fast-approaching vehicle. The rusted truck skidded to a stop, spraying dirt and gravel.

Waving away the cloud of dust, Isabel ran toward the vehicle. "Thank you for stopping. My friend is hurt and he needs—"

Her plea froze on her lips as the man stepping out of the passenger door turned to face her.

Him.

The man from the police photos. The other doors opened and rough-looking men spilled out, waving guns and shouting. Isabel backed slowly toward Manuel, the thought of protecting him taking prominence in her mind.

The man she recognized leered at her, his eyes dark and cold. "Hello, Isabel. It's good to see you again. You look healthy considering all you've been through; the swim in the well, a rockslide, that unfortunate incident with your boat, and a poisonous snake. You could have been hurt." He laughed, a cruel, heartless sound.

She knelt by Manuel and took his hand, drawing comfort and courage from the touch. "Who are you? And why have you been following me?"

"We're business associates of Raúl's. He owes us some money, and we're here to collect."

"Sorry, you missed him. His plane flew out about an hour ago."

"Yes, we figured that." He glanced at Manuel. "Pity your friend was hurt."

"Look, I don't know where Raúl went, but being the resourceful person you obviously are, I'm sure you can find him. I'd love to stay and chat, but I need to get my friend to a doctor." She grabbed up a few loose items and pretended to pack their gear, hoping they would pursue Raúl and leave her and Manuel to fend for themselves. They'd be safer that way.

A gun jabbed into her back.

"Not so fast, little lady. What I need, I can get from you."

She waved a hand toward the camp. "Take whatever you want."

"I want you. You're going to lead me to the treasure."

Isabel swallowed hard. They knew more than she suspected, but how much? She decided to force their hand. "I don't know what you're talking about."

"Of course you do. The pearls your ancestor hid—we want them. Raúl was kind enough to tip us off about your project, and we've decided to take our share—all of it." He laughed at her angry scowl.

The idea of cooperating with these men galled her, but to resist would be dangerous. Maybe she could strike a bargain with them, make a trade for Manuel's sake. "I'll give you the location of the pearls after you take my friend and I to a medical facility."

"But if I set you free, you won't have any reason to cooperate. Keeping you with me is my insurance policy."

"Take me. Let her go." Manuel's weak voice interrupted their argument.

Isabel swung around and flashed Manuel a warning look. "I appreciate your gallantry, Manuel, but you've saved my life enough times on this trip. I owe you one. Besides, you're in no condition to lead an expedition."

"Isabel …."

"Don't argue, Manuel. Save your energy."

He growled and tried to rise, but the pain stopped him. Isabel could see his agony at not being able to protect her, but she couldn't afford to hide behind his strength this time. She turned back to her captor. "I'll draw you a map, give you the best directions I can. In exchange you drop us at a hospital or clinic."

"No deal. Men, put these two in our vehicle then check the camp. Take anything of value."

Two men descended on Isabel and dragged her to the truck. She glanced over her shoulder and saw them yank Manuel from the ground. They showed no concern for his injured shoulder, jerking him around as they escorted him to his new transportation. He grimaced with pain, and Isabel wondered if his wounds would tear open and bleed again. One thing was certain. His body wouldn't endure much more abuse. He needed help—fast.

~ * ~ * ~ * ~ * ~

Isabel stayed awake as long as she could, monitoring Manuel's pulse rate and breathing. But as the adrenaline wore off, she found herself fighting heavy eyelids. The thugs had transported them to the small airstrip and boarded a waiting plane. She sat in a small cargo area with Manuel spread out beside her.

The hum of the engines lulled her, and she succumbed to sleep. Her nap brought fitful dreams, and she awakened at sunset covered in sweat. Manuel's forehead glistened with perspiration from the fever that had settled over his body. His breathing had grown labored, and she couldn't wake him.

"He needs medical attention. Antibiotics." She pleaded with the one who appeared to be the ringleader. "Please, help him."

He stared at her for a moment, his face reflecting disinterest. "We're almost there."

"Where is 'there'? Does this location have a medical facility?"

He shrugged, offering no more information.

"If you let him die, I won't help you." She heard the

desperation in her voice, and hated feeling so powerless.

He turned away and ignored her, obviously unconcerned by her threat.

Isabel wanted to throw herself at him, to dig her fingernails into his dispassionate face until he agreed to give Manuel the help he needed. But afraid she'd only make the situation worse, she distracted herself with making Manuel more comfortable. She could do little for him, but she felt better just sitting near him. She smoothed a hand across his fevered brow and ran her fingers lightly over his hair. He jerked and twitched in his sleep, as if a battle raged behind his closed eyelids.

Ten minutes later, the plane circled and descended over a crude landing strip in the middle of heavy woods. Isabel pressed her face to the window, praying help was near.

As soon as they stepped off the little plane, an SUV appeared and transported them down a long drive leading to a small complex of buildings. A stately air surrounded the largest one, a white stucco hacienda with iron-railed balconies on the second floor. The others were less elegant and seemed more suited for work. The vehicle stopped in front of a small shack, and the men piled out. Isabel's captors pulled her from the truck and shoved her toward a rickety door covered in peeling white paint.

Unable to walk, or even awaken, Manuel was dragged along behind her. Her captor shoved her through the doorway. By the dingy light of a bare light bulb, Isabel saw an iron-framed bed sitting in one corner of the shack. The only other furniture was a table and chair whose scarred surfaces showed years of mistreatment. Bars covered the windows, but the opening let in a cool breeze along with the moonlight.

The men heaved Manuel onto the bed, unconcerned with his injuries.

"Be careful. He'll start bleeding again." Isabel rushed to his side and rolled him onto his back. As she arranged his arm across his chest to alleviate pressure from his shoulder, the door slammed behind her. The click of a turning lock punctuated her panic. She scrambled to her feet and yanked at the doorknob. Though it rattled and shook, the frail-looking door proved a surprisingly effective barrier. Obviously, their captors had used the shack as a prison before.

~ * ~ * ~ * ~ * ~

She returned to the bed and sat at Manuel's side, praying help would come. Minutes dragged by. Feelings of guilt increased with each labored breath Manuel dragged into his lungs. Her bad decisions and lack of discernment had caused his suffering. If only she'd seen Raúl's true nature earlier. She could have cut off contact with him completely rather than continuing to do business with him. She'd arrogantly assumed she could control the situation. Now Manuel was paying for her bad judgment.

Noise at the door drew her from her regrets, and she stood to face the visitor. An older man let himself in and closed the door behind him. He didn't even glance at the bed as he walked to the shoddy table in the corner and plunked down a medical bag. A bottle and syringe emerged, and he drew up a dosage of the medicine.

"What is that?" Isabel moved between Manuel and the man, shielding Manuel until she had some answers.

He gave her an irritated look. "Is antibiotics. He has fever, no?"

"Are you a doctor?"

"I give medical service to people on complex."

"Where are we? Are we near a city?"

The man shook his head and pushed past her. "No more talking." He shoved Manuel's sleeve up to his shoulder and jabbed the needle into his bicep. After tossing the empty syringe into his bag, he started to leave.

"Where are you going? His bandages need to be changed." Isabel couldn't believe they would offer so little help. Manuel needed a hospital and a trained medical staff, not some quack on the payroll of an organized crime ring.

The man hesitated at the door.

"Please," she begged.

He opened his bag and removed a roll of gauze and a bottle of peroxide. "Here, you do."

She took the supplies he offered and watched him leave, despair overtaking her. *God, where are you?*

As she unwrapped Manuel's dressings, she noticed he'd

stopped sweating despite his high fever. Neither of them had drunk anything at all that day, and with Manuel's blood loss, he needed water more than ever, but a quick glance around told her there was nothing to drink in the room. The best she could do was care for his wound.

She carefully peeled away his bloody bandages and poured peroxide on the wound. He didn't move as she cleaned the bullet hole with a pad of clean gauze and applied new dressings.

When she'd done all she could for him, she paced the room, pausing at the window to study her surroundings. Occasionally, she spied other people on the grounds, but no one paid her any attention. After an hour, her legs grew weary, and she perched on a corner of the mattress near Manuel's feet.

She lost track of time as she stared at the dirty wall, considering her situation and grasping for a plausible solution. The door rattled, and a timid girl entered, shadowed by a man with a gun. She scurried to the table and set down a tray of food.

"Thank you, miss." Isabel tried to catch the girl's eye, but the young woman hurried out the door as if afraid of punishment if she lingered.

Alone again, Isabel rushed to see what the girl had delivered. The pitcher of water snagged her attention. She poured a glass and snatched up a spoon. Returning to Manuel's side, she dribbled a few drops of water onto his parted lips and was pleased to see him swallow. Encouraged, she offered him one spoonful at a time until he'd consumed half a glass. Satisfied with the small accomplishment, she quickly ate some of the food and took care of her own needs.

Night deepened, and the lights in other windows around the complex went out. Isabel's energy waned and her eyelids grew heavy. Fighting sleep, she spooned more water into Manuel's mouth until she'd emptied the cup. Exhausted emotionally and physically, fatigue pressed into her until she couldn't fight it anymore. After turning off the light, she sat on the floor beside Manuel's bed and laid her head against the mattress. When he moaned and started to toss, Isabel stretched a hand across his chest. Her touch calmed him, and he quieted. Isabel sat in her protective stance and listened to the steady rhythm of his breathing until she, too, drifted off to sleep.

~ * ~ * ~ * ~ * ~

"Isabel." Manuel rasped her name from a dry throat and parched lips. Faint light glowed in the window and birds chirped a happy song, leading him to believe dawn had arrived. He felt guilty for having slept in the bed while she reclined on the floor beside him, her hand draped across his chest. After a second look he realized the ripped and stained mattress wasn't an accommodation she would covet.

He tested his uninjured arm and found he could move it without causing too much pain. He slid his hand to his chest and folded it over her fingers. "Isabel."

She lifted her head and blinked a few times, as if trying to focus. Her gaze drifted to his face, and she summoned a sleepy smile. "You're awake."

"You sound surprised."

"I am. You were in bad shape last night." She moved her free hand to his forehead. "The fever broke."

She smoothed his hair back from his brow, and he relaxed under the comforting touch. "I still feel terrible."

"Trust me, terrible is an improvement. I thought you were going to die last night. You'd lost too much blood, and your fever spiked so high. I guess the shot of antibiotics helped."

"A doctor came here?" He'd obviously missed a lot while he slept, and his failure to help Isabel deal with the situation disturbed him.

"The man didn't show me his medical license or anything, but I got the impression he had some experience. Are you hungry?"

"I'm thirsty. Do we have water?"

"Sure." She pushed to her feet and moved away from him, taking the warmth of her soft hands with her.

She poured a glass and returned to his side. He tried to sit up but collapsed back to the pillow in pain.

"Let me do the work." She slipped a hand behind his neck and supported his head while he drank. His inability to help himself irritated him. When she tried to wipe his mouth with a napkin, he pushed her hand away, unable to hide his frustration.

Her eyes widened in surprise. "What's wrong?"

He turned his face away from her and stared at the wall. "I promised to protect you. How am I supposed to do that when I can't even hold a cup?"

Her hand slipped over his, and her eyes told him she understood.

"Maybe I'm old fashioned, but I think a guy should defend his girl. I hate being incapacitated."

"It'll work out, Manuel."

"How, Isabel? You don't believe they'll let us go, do you?" He disliked the angry tone of his voice, but he had to make her understand.

Her lips drew into a tight, thin line. "I don't know."

"You know you can't reason with these men. People like them have no conscience. They can kill someone and then go to dinner as if nothing happened."

Isabel shuddered and pulled away from him. "Why are you being so morbid? You're alive, aren't you? They sent someone to give you antibiotics and clean bandages."

"We're alive because we can lead them to the treasure. When they have what they want, we'll be a liability." Fear of seeing her harmed and frustration at being helpless to do anything to protect her made his tone harsh.

"I'm scared enough as it is, Manuel. I don't need you pointing out the danger to me."

The tremor in her voice pierced through his anger, draining him of every emotion except regret. "I'm sorry, Isabel. I can't stand the thought of them hurting you."

"I feel the same way about you. If anything happened to you, I don't know how I could go on."

"Don't say that." He drank in the smooth lines of her face and sighed. "I want you to promise me you won't do anything foolish."

She looked away. "I already did. I got us into this mess."

"You can't take all the blame for that. I didn't see this coming either." His head started to cloud, and he felt sleep descending over him like a heavy blanket. "Now, promise me you won't do anything foolish."

"I don't know what you mean."

"Promise you won't let them manipulate you with threats

against me. What happens to me doesn't matter. I want you to do whatever it takes to get out of this alive. Understand?"

Tears filled her eyes and spilled onto his arm. "If you're asking me to turn my back on you to save myself, I can't do that."

"You can, and you will. They'll try to use our relationship against us. I don't want you hurt trying to save me. Whether I die now or later, my future is in God's hands. You can't change that and I don't want you to try."

"Manuel—" Quiet sobs choked off her protests, but he refused to back down. If it were the last gift he could give her, he'd make sure she could walk away without guilt.

Certain she understood his wishes, he changed the subject. "Do you know where we are?"

She sniffed and rubbed at her eyes. "We flew north most of the trip. I fell asleep late in the afternoon, and it was dark when we arrived at this compound."

"What's the compound like?"

"A large house and several smaller outbuildings. It's obviously one of their hideouts, but I couldn't tell you where."

He nodded, fighting his heavy eyelids. "I'm getting tired again. Don't think I can stay awake much longer."

"Can you try to eat something before you sleep? You need to build your strength."

He wasn't the least bit hungry, but her pleading look convinced him to try. "Okay, what's on the menu?"

~ * ~ * ~ * ~ * ~

Isabel paced the tiny room, unable to calm the emotions raging inside her. Their conversation had left her terrified and furious. Though unable to protect her physically, he was doing what he could to prepare her emotionally for the difficult choices she'd face. Part of her was grateful for his concern, but the other part rebelled. Did he really think she could walk away and leave him to whatever cruel fate their captors would devise for him? The idea left her sick to her stomach. She didn't even want to consider that she or Manuel might not live through this ordeal. The thought was too horrible.

Just when she finally found the man she wanted to spend the rest of her life with, a man who loved both her and God with intensity, circumstances threatened to tear them apart forever. *God, how am I supposed to deal with this?* The tears she'd suppressed for Manuel's sake now streamed down her cheeks. Not wanting to wake him, she pressed a hand over her mouth to muffle the sobs she couldn't deny. Perhaps it was selfish of her to want a promise of a future with this man. At the very least, she hoped he wouldn't pay with his life for her foolish mistakes.

She dropped to her knees beside the rickety chair and let her deepest plea spill out of her heart. *I never realized how much impact one decision could have on my life. I keep thinking, if only I'd known. If only I'd taken time to pray about dating Raúl. But I didn't, and I can't change that now. So, I'm asking You for mercy. If there is a way to salvage our lives in spite of my mistake, please rescue us. If not ....*

She swallowed back the knot in her throat. "Don't punish Manuel for my stupidity."

Too upset to continue, she sat on the floor beside the bed and took his hand in hers. "I love you," she whispered. Laying her head against the mattress, she concentrated on taking deep, even breaths until exhaustion overtook her.

Pearls

Twenty-Five

The door slammed open, jarring Isabel from sleep. Men bearing guns rushed into the room in a chaotic frenzy. Two of them grabbed her arms and jerked her to her feet, while another aimed a gun at Manuel's chest. Their ringleader strolled in behind them, taking a deep drag from his cigarette.

He leaned his muscular shoulder against the doorframe and blew a plume of smoke. "Good morning."

Isabel tried to jerk her arms free from her captors, but they held firm. "What do you want?"

"I need a guide. I've chosen you."

"I won't help you until you release Manuel."

The man's eyes narrowed. "If you don't cooperate, we'll kill him."

The cold way he stated the threat left no doubt in Isabel's mind that he would follow through if she resisted. Her gaze swung to Manuel's helpless form lying on the bed. Sweat beaded across his brow, and his eyes glazed with fever. He had weakened during the night, but he was alert at the moment. He managed the strength to shake his head and mouth the word no.

She knew what he wanted her to do, but her heart wouldn't allow her to sacrifice him for her own good.

"I'll help you if you give him another shot of antibiotics and a servant girl to care for him."

The man shrugged, not promising anything. "You're wasting my time. Take her to the truck."

Isabel caught one final glance of Manuel before they dragged her from the shack. His face twisted into a grimace and one hand feebly reached for her. As the shack's door closed between them, she felt her heart rip in two.

~ * ~ * ~ * ~ * ~

Isabel rode in the back seat of the SUV, smashed between two men who desperately needed to bathe. The stench of their body odor mingled with cheap tobacco made her stomach churn. They had traveled for hours, bumping along unpaved roads in sparsely populated regions of the country. Isabel wondered where they were taking her. They didn't ask her for a location, and she didn't offer one. Yet they seemed to have a destination in mind.

She had needed to use the restroom for more than an hour but refused to mention it to any of the four men in the vehicle. Surely, one of them would need to stop before long. As she crossed her legs, the truck rolled to a stop in the middle of a deserted dirt road.

She glanced ahead of the vehicle and saw that the road intersected with another just a hundred meters ahead. "Why did we stop?"

No one acknowledged the question. They sat staring out the windows, acting as if this sort of delay was routine.

A cellular phone between the two front seats rang. The ringleader answered it. "Yes?"

Pause.

"Very good. We're in position."

Pause.

"I'll be waiting."

He hung up the phone and turned to the driver. "When the phone rings again, move to intercept." He waved toward the intersection, and the other man nodded.

Isabel didn't understand. "What are we doing?"

The ringleader turned and leered at her. "We're rendezvousing with your friend. Of course, he doesn't know we're coming."

Isabel frowned. *Who is he talking about?*

"One of my men caught up with Raúl in Caracas, and we have monitored his activity since. It would seem he's in a hurry to get to Cumaná. The two of you can show us where it's hidden."

The phone chirped just then, and the driver slammed the SUV into drive. The tires spun, then the vehicle shot forward. The momentum threw Isabel backward and pressed her against the seat.

They approached the intersection at an alarming speed, and

Isabel closed her eyes, unable to watch. As quickly as it had taken off, the truck came to a screeching halt, blocking the intersection. Three of the men spilled out of the vehicle, guns bared, while the other held his weapon to Isabel's head.

"Stay put," he hissed, his eyes focused on a point beyond her.

She turned and saw a car sweep around a bend in the road. Encountering their roadblock, the driver slammed on his brakes and spun in a half circle before coming to a halt just meters away. The door of the car flew open, and the driver jumped out. Though he couldn't see her through the tinted windows of the SUV, Isabel could see Raúl. She watched the armed men take up positions surrounding him.

His head jerked from side to side, no doubt assessing the odds and finding himself outnumbered. Despite his underdog status, Raúl stood his ground, posture stiff and angry. "What are you doing here?"

The ringleader spoke in a placid voice. "We came to collect our payment."

"I told you I'd bring you the money when I had it."

"We're changing the terms of our agreement." The man flicked his cigarette to the ground and watched it smolder for a moment before crushing it beneath his heel.

Raúl smirked, obviously thinking he had the upper hand. "I don't accept your proposal to change the deal."

"You don't have a choice."

"Why not? Are you going to kill me if I don't agree?"

"No. We'll kill her."

The man guarding Isabel jerked her from the truck and dragged her into Raúl's line of sight.

She glared at him.

Raúl's eyes widened with alarm. "Why are you here?"

Isabel wanted to spit in his face. "Don't act like you don't know!"

"Isabel, I did not involve you. I never mentioned your name or any details of this project to them. I swear!" He turned back to their captor. "She has nothing to do with this. I'll give you what you want, but first let her go."

"She has everything to do with this."

"I owe you money. I'll take care of my debt."

The ringleader laughed. "You're such a fool. A useful one but a fool regardless. This was never about you, Raúl. We only approached you because we knew you could get to her."

Raúl's brow wrinkled with confusion. "What?"

"That's right. She led us to you. We arranged for your financial hardships so you would cooperate when we approached you with the offer to ship our goods. We even stole our own shipment so you'd get desperate and careless."

Raúl shook his head. "I don't understand. Why?"

"One of her grandmother's lawyers is on our payroll. He passed along the tip about the journal. We intended to arrange an accident for the old woman and obtain the book legally through an estate sale, but she refused to add it to the list of her assets. The old woman insisted on keeping it hidden until she bequeathed it to her granddaughter. She didn't seem to trust her lawyers."

He grinned and the men around him laughed. "We've wanted that treasure for some time now." He turned to Isabel. "It was nice of you to arrange an expedition to search for the pearls. You've been very helpful."

"You took the journal from our camp. You have what you want. Let us go," Isabel pleaded.

"Releasing you is no longer an option."

He stared at her with cold, hard eyes and Isabel knew he meant to kill her. "I won't cooperate."

"You have more guts than your boyfriend here. He'll give us the information we need. He always has." He turned to his men. "You two, go with Raúl in his vehicle. We'll take the girl in ours. If he doesn't cooperate, call me. I'll see that she pays."

They shoved her back into the SUV. With each bump in the road, the knot of dread in her gut grew. She could almost see the specter of death hovering nearby, waiting to claim her.

The road carried them through a small village. Several old men sat outside a ramshackle store, smoking pipes. Without being too obvious, Isabel tried to catch their attention as the truck passed by, but they didn't notice her pleading look.

They drove on, traversing another barren stretch of road with only a few modest farms dotting the landscape at wide intervals.

Finally, the vehicle slowed and turned into a dusty drive, overgrown with weeds. The two vehicles came to a stop before a dilapidated home. Although large and probably stately in its day, broken windows, a sunken roof, and the front door hanging on one hinge testified to its abandonment.

With some prompting, she climbed from the truck and walked toward the rotting steps of the front porch.

"Where is it?" the ringleader asked.

Raúl pointed to the field behind the house. "You have to find her grave. My guess is it's back there in the family graveyard."

The ringleader turned and pointed at one of his men. "You, get the tools out of the truck." He glanced at the other. "You, take a look around. Make sure we don't have company."

"What do we do with them?" The remaining thug waved the muzzle of his gun toward Isabel and Raúl.

The ringleader paused. "Cuff them to that fence. I don't want any unexpected interruptions."

The man followed orders, pulling a pair of cuffs from his pocket and securing Isabel's wrist. Dragging her to the wrought iron fence, he wrapped the cuff around a spindle and snapped the other half on Raúl's hand. Looking satisfied with his work, he marched off and took a position under a distant tree that offered him a view of the road, his captives, and his partners' activity behind the house.

Alone, Isabel asked Raúl the question burning in her mind. "The grave is at the mission ruins. Why did you lead them here?"

"I'm buying some time. Did you tell them where the treasure is hidden?"

"No. They never asked. They were fixated on finding you. I still don't understand why you brought them to this old farmhouse."

"These old estates always have a family graveyard. I figured I could mislead them. We have to keep them busy until we find a way to escape."

Isabel shook her head. "I can't run. They have Manuel, and they promised to kill him if I don't cooperate."

He grabbed her hand and squeezed until it hurt. "Isabel, they intend to kill us as soon as they have the treasure. If you and I escape, they'll need Manuel alive to lead them to the grave."

Pressure built in her chest, and she began to shake. "I can't abandon him."

"You're not abandoning him. Once we're free, we can go to the authorities. We'll try to get help."

"I don't see how we'll get these cuffs off." She lifted her hand, and the metal cuff clinked against the iron bars holding her captive.

"Look around. Maybe we can find a sharp stick or a big rock. Something that might help us break them."

Isabel glanced around but saw nothing useful. "Wait!" She fumbled in her pocket with her free hand. "I have Manuel's Swiss Army knife. Maybe we can pick the lock."

"They let you keep that?"

Isabel shrugged. "They never bothered to search me. I guess they didn't realize I'd have something like this in my possession."

She pulled out various attachments until she found one that fit into the keyhole. After several minutes of twisting and turning, the lock clicked and the cuff dropped loose. She stared in amazement. "I did it."

"Good work." Raúl smiled and squeezed her hand. "Now here's the plan. We wait until the guard looks away or gets distracted, then we'll make a run for the vehicles."

"They left the keys in the SUV. I remember seeing them hanging in the ignition when they pulled me out."

"Good! When I say 'go,' run for the SUV."

Adrenaline shot through her veins, speeding her heart to a frantic pace. *This will work. It has to. Please, God.*

They waited in silence, anticipation building until Isabel thought she might explode.

The guard turned his back.

"Go!" Raúl leaped to his feet and took off at a full sprint.

Isabel shot up behind him. Fear propelled her forward. She reached the truck and slid into the passenger seat, knocking her shin against the frame. Just as Raúl closed the door behind her, shouts carried from the direction of the guard. Raúl glanced over his shoulder. Through her window, Isabel watched the man run toward them waving his gun, his face twisted in anger. He stopped and pointed the gun directly at her.

"No!" Raúl threw himself in front of her door.

A shot echoed across the distance.

Raúl slammed into the window, his face a gruesome mask of shock and pain. A small circle of blood appeared on his chest and smeared across the glass. He stumbled away from the door, and Isabel seized the opportunity. She shoved the door open and wrapped her arms around his waist, pulling him into the vehicle in the midst of another volley of gunshots. He sagged in the passenger seat, drawing jagged breaths while she scooted into the driver's seat and started the ignition. Gravel and dust shot out in a plume as they fled their pursuers. A few shots followed the vehicle but none inflicted significant damage.

Isabel drove hard and fast, putting distance between them and their dangerous enemy. "I'll get you to a doctor, Raúl. There's probably something around here, maybe not a fancy modern hospital but a clinic or doctor's office."

A bloody hand wrapped around her arm. "No use—" He coughed and a spray of blood spattered across the dash.

Bile rose in Isabel's throat, and she fought to control the tidal wave of panic sweeping through her. She'd lived this situation only days earlier with Manuel. She did not want to watch another man bleed and suffer.

"Don't talk that way, Raúl. I can't do this alone. I need you now."

"Pull over."

"You need a doctor."

"Pull over."

"No!"

Her refusal upset him, and he struggled to grab the wheel. The effort demanded more strength than he had to give, and he fell back against the seat, moaning and clutching his wound. "Stop, please."

Tears streaming down her face, Isabel steered the car to the side of the road and came to a stop. Leaning across him, she rummaged in the glove box for some supplies to use as first aid. "They're probably right behind us. We can't afford to stop."

"No. They can't follow."

"Why not?"

"I have the keys to my car. We have their vehicle." His voice sounded weaker than moments before, and Isabel frantically searched for a way to help him. She wadded some tissues she'd found and pressed them to the seeping wound in his chest.

He pushed her hand away. "Don't. It's too late."

She shook her head, sobbing. "I won't let you die."

"No choice. It's too late for me." He coughed and a line of blood trickled down his chin.

Isabel dabbed at the disturbing red stream, noting the glazed look stealing into his eyes. Acceptance of the inevitable crept in and settled heavily in her gut.

"Why did you do that, Raúl? Why did you jump in front of me when he shot?"

He drew a labored breath. "I love you."

She swallowed the painful knot in her throat. He'd stepped in front of a bullet for her. She repented for every angry, vengeful thought she'd had toward him during the last month.

"Isabel, I'm sorry I got you into this. I only wanted to give you the best ... needed the money ... wish I could change what I've done ... how I've lived."

His eyelids drooped and closed, and she watched the life draining from him. His breathing grew shallow. "Wish I'd been a better man."

Isabel felt the jolting change in the atmosphere and knew what she needed to do. "Raúl, listen to me. You can't change how you lived, but you have time to choose something better before—" She swallowed hard, unable to say the words aloud. "Please, ask Christ to be your Savior."

"It's too late."

"No, it's not. Life dealt you some harsh blows, Raúl, and pride and stubbornness helped you cope. But those attributes won't help you where you're going." She knotted her fists in frustration. "You said you wanted a piece of the goodness you see in me. Take it, Raúl."

He gasped and clutched his chest, muscles straining against the pain. "I want to, but I don't know how."

"Don't talk any more. I'll pray out loud, and you pray in your heart. God hears and He'll honor your request."

Knowing time was short, Isabel bowed her head and prayed with more fervency than she'd ever before felt. When every last impassioned plea had spilled from her lips, she opened her eyes and found him staring at her, a look of wonder on his face. "I felt Him. Like a wind of peace."

Isabel dropped her face into her hands and wept, overcome with relief and gratitude.

His hoarse whisper interrupted her tears. "I loved you. Never doubt that."

A hiccupping sob escaped her throat as she nodded. "I loved you, too, Raúl. Despite everything, I still care very much about you."

"Thank you for sharing your God with me."

She blinked rapidly and sniffed.

"See you ..." He coughed more blood and labored to draw another breath. "See you ... up there."

Isabel leaned toward him and placed a kiss on his cheek. "I look forward to it." As she held his hand in hers and wept, he shuddered and drew his final breath. She rested her head against his shoulder, tears falling on his chest and mixing with his blood. "Go with God, my friend."

Pearls

Twenty-Six

Isabel didn't know how long she sat staring out the window before the chirp of a cellular phone penetrated the grief-induced fog in her mind. Her hand closed around the phone sitting in the cupholder, left there by her captors. She lifted it to her ear.

"Hello?"

"You shouldn't have run away."

"I shouldn't have been a prisoner in the first place. You started this."

"And I will finish it. Do you remember my promise? I still have your friend."

The blood in Isabel's veins ran cold.

Manuel. God forgive me.

In her haste to save Raúl and escape her captors, she had abandoned Manuel. She remembered their last conversation and his instructions for her to do whatever she could to escape, even to the extent of sacrificing him to save herself.

She had done just that, and the guilt was nearly unbearable. "You won't hurt him. You need him to show you where the treasure is."

The man on the other end of the line growled. "Yes. Raúl was clever to mislead us, but we won't make the same mistake again. Manuel will lead us to the treasure, and then he'll pay for your disobedience."

The line went dead, and Isabel's heart died with it. Manuel remained in the hands of the enemy, and her choice to flee had sealed his fate. *God help me.*

Fear turned to anger and anger to determination. She wouldn't hide somewhere cowering in fear while Manuel remained in their clutches. Drawing a deep breath, she turned the key in the ignition. She needed to report her kidnapping and make arrangements for

Raúl's body. The police would know how to help her. She lifted the cellular phone and dialed information.

"I need a number for Detective Ramirez, Caracas Police Department."

~ * ~ * ~ * ~ * ~

Manuel stared at the ceiling, stronger after three days of rest and medication but no less frustrated. His failure to protect Isabel in her time of greatest need burned like acid in his gut. He had last seen her two days ago. Was she still alive? If he lost her, he'd lose his heart, too, and live the rest of his life as half the man he could have been with her at his side.

He closed his eyes and released his pain to God as he had so many times in the last few days. With lives hanging in the balance, he found it difficult to accept his helplessness and trust in God. But wasn't this the time to depend on Him the most? The same thoughts had swirled about his head for days, and he had grown weary of his lack of faith.

Maybe some food would distract him.

He pushed to a sitting position and waited while his body adjusted. Because of his blood loss, he remained weak and dizzy, but he'd been able to eat the last two days. His strength was slowly returning.

Just as he reached for a piece of fruit, the door flew open and his captors entered.

"Get your shoes on!" The ringleader tossed him a disdainful look.

"Are we leaving?"

"You're going to show us where the treasure is hidden."

"What about Isabel? Where is she?"

"Your girlfriend was not so helpful."

Fear and anger flared in Manuel's chest. "Did you hurt her?"

The man's lip pulled up in a sneer. "She chose not to cooperate. I hope you are smarter."

As Manuel pulled on his shoes and followed them to the car, he mulled over the conversation. The men's body language said they were agitated and frustrated, as if Isabel had thwarted their plans. *Did you escape, Isabel? Did you run like I told you?*

An ancient truck covered in rust sat in front of the shack.

"What happened to your fancy SUV?" he asked one of the men.

The man only growled and shoved him inside the decrepit vehicle.

If anyone could outsmart these thugs, Isabel could. She had proved she was a resourceful woman.

As they pulled away from the compound, a slow smile spread across his face.

~ * ~ * ~ * ~ * ~

Isabel drove into the small town where Detective Ramirez had asked her to meet him. He was there, waiting in the street with a team of men who took over the care of Raúl's body and began a search of the vehicle.

His face showed alarm when she slid from the truck. "Good heavens, Isabel, are you hurt?"

Isabel glanced down at her clothes and realized how startling she must look. She still wore the shirt stained with Manuel's blood, now dried to a crusty black. Raúl's blood, red and sticky, dotted her clothes and smeared over her hands. "It's not my blood," she muttered, fighting tears.

With fatherly concern he guided her into a building-turned-command-center and showed her to a restroom where she could wash. A female officer brought her a change of clothes and some basic toiletries. When she'd finished cleaning up, she joined the detective in a small waiting area. Isabel glanced around, overwhelmed by the number of people and the buzz of activity. "Are you in charge here?"

He laughed. "No. The federal government is handling this operation. They let me tag along because I've supplied key information and a star witness."

Isabel offered a faint smile. "What's being done to find Manuel?"

"Everything possible. But you could help us immensely. We would like to interview you about your captors and the locations they took you. Anything you tell us could narrow the search."

"I don't know where they took me, but I know where they're going."

"You do?"

237

"They want the pearls, and aside from me, Manuel is the only one who can lead them there."

He took her hand and pulled her to her feet. "You need to give this information to the men in charge. We may not have much time."

~ * ~ * ~ * ~ * ~

Isabel sat by the police scanner, listening to the sound of radio static. One of the lookouts had warned of an approaching vehicle, and the strike teams had gone to radio silence. It wouldn't be long now.

Isabel fidgeted. "They won't shoot him, will they?"

Detective Ramirez, also listening intently to the static, jumped at her question. "Who?"

"Manuel. They'll be careful not to shoot him if bullets start flying?"

"Don't worry, Isabel. They have pictures of him and know to protect his life at all costs."

Isabel nodded, but the knot in her stomach didn't go away. Just a few miles down the road at the ruins of the old mission, the feds had laid a careful trap for Isabel's kidnappers. The pearls were the bait, and busting a crime ring was the prize. Manuel was an unfortunate participant in the scenario.

She caught herself chewing on her nails and frowned. "How much longer?"

"Anytime now." Detective Ramirez patted her hand.

"Can't we start driving over there? By the time we arrive it'll be over."

"You know the rules, Isabel. They didn't have to let us come this close. We wait here until they radio that the operation is complete and the area is secure."

She blew out an exasperated breath.

"The strike team is well-trained, Isabel. Trust them to do their job ...."

Shouting from the radio interrupted him. "Police! We have you surrounded. Drop your weapons and put your hands—"

A gunshot answered the police commands. The next few minutes sounded like a nightmare of violence. Muscles clenched in terror, Isabel listened to the exchange of gunfire, shouts, and pain-filled screams filtering through the radio.

She couldn't breathe.

The shots slowed to an occasional pop and finally ceased.

A voice came through the system. "The hostage is down. Repeat, the hostage has been shot. Medical team, stand by. We are securing the area."

"Manuel!" Isabel jumped up, knocking her chair over in her haste for the door. "We have to go."

"The area is not secure yet." Detective Ramirez grabbed her arms and forced her to calm down.

"Please, Detective. I love him. He asked me to marry him a few days ago. If he dies ...." Sobs broke off her plea.

Detective Ramirez softened. "Okay. We'll start driving, but I'm not letting you near there until it's safe."

"Thank you." She gave him a quick hug then ran for the door, desperate to reach the man she loved.

~ * ~ * ~ * ~ * ~

The area surrounding the mission looked like a war zone. Her stomach lurched at the blood on the ground and on the uniforms of injured men. So much blood. And where was Manuel?

Several bulging body bags lay in a neat line. Isabel averted her eyes, refusing to believe the worst. On the far side of the grounds, medical personnel bent over a victim, working at a frantic pace. Isabel recognized the man's clothes and inched closer, fearing what she might see.

One of the paramedics stepped to the side, and Isabel glimpsed the fresh bloodstains on Manuel's shirt. The gunshot wound in his side looked bad. She bit her lip and tried to remain strong. "What happened?"

Detective Ramirez leaned close. "The supervising officer said as soon as he shouted the command to surrender, one of his captors turned and shot Manuel at close range."

She squeezed her eyes shut, willing away the haunting image. "They told me they'd punish him for my failure to cooperate."

He squeezed her shoulder. "Don't do that to yourself. It's not your fault."

A helicopter roared into the sky above the clearing and began its descent.

Detective Ramirez put an arm around her and guided her to a safe distance from the makeshift landing pad. "They're flying Manuel to the nearest trauma center. He'll get the best treatment there."

"Can I see him for a moment before they take him?"

The detective stared down at her, reluctance and compassion warring on his face. "Let's see what we can do."

When the paramedics lifted Manuel onto a gurney, preparing to board the helicopter, Detective Ramirez pushed her forward. She ran to the stretcher and laid her hand on Manuel's arm.

The paramedic tugged at her sleeve. "Miss, you can't do that."

"She's his fiancée," she heard Ramirez argue. "Let them have a minute."

While the men continued to argue behind her, Isabel stroked her fingers lovingly over Manuel's arms and face. "I love you," she whispered.

His eyelids fluttered and opened to a narrow slit. The barest hint of a smile softened his lips.

"Miss, we have to go." The paramedics pushed her away and loaded the gurney into the helicopter. In seconds, the craft lifted into the air and disappeared beyond the treetops.

Finally able to release the fears and anxieties from days of trauma, Isabel collapsed to the ground and cried.

~ * ~ * ~ * ~ * ~

Soft, moist earth cushioned Isabel's knees as she knelt beside the gaping hole in the corner of the cemetery.

Manuel stood at the bottom of the six-foot trench, removing the last few handfuls of dirt from the lid of a box. He looked up and gave her a smile. "I think this is it. Are you ready?"

She smiled back. After two months of rest and recuperation, he was nearly whole again. Scars on his shoulder and side were the only lingering evidence of his ordeal. He seemed self-conscious about the puckered pink flesh that remained once his injuries had healed. How could Isabel make him understand that the marks of his suffering were beautiful to her? They represented the depth of his love, the lengths he would go to to protect her.

"Isabel? I asked if you're ready."

She drew a deep breath. "Sorry. My mind wandered off for a

minute. Do you want to open it, or should I?"

"Let's do it together."

He helped her climb down into the hole, and they grasped the lid of the small metal chest. The old hinges stuck for a moment then popped loose. The lid opened to reveal hundreds of lustrous white orbs.

"Whoa!" Manuel plucked one of the larger pearls from the top and held it between his thumb and forefinger.

Isabel dipped a slender hand into the chest and lifted out a dozen or so pearls. "Amazing." She tipped her hand and watched the pearls fall back to their case then began to laugh.

"What's so funny?" Manuel asked.

"After all that's happened, everything we suffered and endured to find these pearls ...." She shook her head, giving him a wry smile. "I thought this moment would be so incredible, but it's actually anti-climactic."

"How so?"

She leaned toward him and left a kiss on his cheek. "I've already discovered Venezuela's greatest treasure. I'd trade a hundred chests of pearls for you, Manuel."

Wearing a mischievous smile, he took her hand and pressed the large pearl into her palm. "I treasure you, Isabel."

She laughed at the double meaning behind his words. Grabbing a handful of pearls, she deposited them in the front pocket of his shirt. "I treasure you too," she said in a sappy, overdramatic voice.

He trailed his fingers up her arm and rested his hand on her shoulder, his fingertips brushing against her neck. "Enough to accompany me to Istanbul?"

His question caught her by surprise. "Istanbul?"

"Seems our little adventure received international attention, and one of the sponsors I'd approached about your expedition called and would like to fund a dig in Istanbul."

She swallowed hard, worried about the implications to their relationship. "You'll be leaving?"

"I told them the job sounds terrific, but I couldn't accept unless my wife said yes." He moved closer and wrapped her in his strong, solid arms, bringing a flurry of butterflies to her stomach.

Pearls

His lips claimed hers, and she found herself helpless to resist his persuasive abilities.

"So what do you say, Isabel? Will you go to Istanbul with me ... as my wife?"

She hugged him a little tighter and smiled up into his warm chocolate eyes. "You bet your pearls I will."

Acknowledgements

A book is never written by one person alone. Many people contribute to the effort through various means. I couldn't imagine putting out a book without the help of wonderful critique partners, Karen, Pam, Diana, Faye, and other generous writers who have given of their time to help me develop my craft over the years.

My GCC Girls and Crochet Club, more than just friends ... you are sisters, cheerleaders, and sometimes therapists. What would my life be without your love and support?

And finally, to my wonderful husband, best friend, soul mate, love of my life. Because of you, I know that happy endings still exist. Thank you for your support in making my dreams come true.

Connect with Lisa Mills Online!

Website:
http://www.authorlisamills.com/

Facebook:
http://facebook.com/authorlisamills

Twitter:
http://www.twitter.com/sheloves2write

Jewels of the Quill (Dame Citrine):
http://www.jewelsofthequill.com

Join my Yahoo Group and receive a coupon for dollars off the price of one of my books along with "Friends & Fans Specials" on each book I release. Be the first to learn of new releases, enjoy special early-bird prices, and lots of freebies and giveaways! No spam, just savings! Here's how to join:

Just send a blank email to:

authorlisamills-subscribe@yahoogroups.com

Once you've confirmed your subscription, you will be emailed information on how to save on your next book purchase. I look forward to connecting with you online!

Books by Lisa Mills

Holding On ~ Women's Fiction

Pearls ~ Romantic Suspense

Coming Soon:

No Place Like Motorhome ~ Inspirational Romance

At the End of Forever ~ Women's Fiction

Pearls

Made in the USA
Charleston, SC
13 March 2012